"I came here for all. You."

She froze, her eyes going wide. "I don't understand."

"I wanted to apologize." He swallowed.

"While I do appreciate that, it could have waited." She frowned. "Or you could have said so. On the phone. Not driven through that—" she pointed at the window "—to do it in person."

"I could have." But if he'd done that, he wouldn't have seen her with his own eyes—and known that she was safe.

"Then why didn't you?" Her voice was shaking.

She was flustered and breathing fast, and for the life of him, he didn't get why. "You're awful upset. What happened?"

She pressed her eyes shut. "You...you..." She broke off. "You're making me upset."

He couldn't win. "I'm going."

"No." She grabbed his arm and tugged him close. "You're not." She slid her arms around his waist and held on tight as she buried her face in his chest. "You can't."

He stared down at the top of her head, beyond lost now. But, dammit, she was soft and warm and pressed against him. He wasn't going to resist. His arms went around her. "You're shaking."

Her fingers gripped his shirt but she stayed silent.

"Stay."

Dear Reader,

Welcome back to Granite Falls! It's that special time of year: Christmastime. And there's nothing like a small-town holiday. Dougal McCarrick tends to be more like Scrooge than Santa, but he's about to meet someone who will make his heart grow three times its original size. Emory Swanson is doing her best to move beyond the grief of her past but it'll take a surprise pup and a secret admirer for her to embrace the future. Between Emory's Dolly Parton–loving aunt and Dougal's friends and family, they have a whole lot of people rooting for them. Throw in a bunch of familiar faces and places and pets, and this might just be one of the best visits to Granite Falls yet!

Wishing you and yours the happiest holiday season!

Sasha Summers

XOXO

LOVE LETTERS
FROM HER COWBOY

SASHA SUMMERS

SPECIAL EDITION

Harlequin®
SPECIAL EDITION™

ISBN-13: 978-1-335-40214-1

Love Letters from Her Cowboy

Harlequin Enterprises ULC
22 Adelaide St. West, 41st Floor
Toronto, Ontario M5H 4E3, Canada
www.Harlequin.com

Printed in U.S.A.

USA TODAY bestselling author **Sasha Summers** writes stories that celebrate the ups and downs, loves and losses, and ordinary and extraordinary occurrences of life. Sasha pens fiction in multiple genres and hopes each and every book will draw readers in and set them on an emotional and rewarding journey. With a puppy on her lap and her favorite Thor mug full of coffee, Sasha is currently working on her next release. She adores hearing from fans and invites you to visit her online.

Visit the Author Profile page
at Harlequin.com for more titles.

To the best writing companions a writer could ask for:
Raven and Bella! Always by my side!

Chapter One

Emory opened the oven door and pulled out the pan of oversize gingerbread cranberry raisin muffins. If the smell of spiced baked goodness and fruit hadn't made her mouth water, the bacon, egg and cheese breakfast casserole should have. One of Emory's favorite parts of cooking had been the taste-testing. Now, not so much. The last year had seen her appetite wane—her jeans had gone from a size eighteen to a fourteen, but she still had shapely thighs and a well-rounded bum. Aunt Ruthie said she had the classic hourglass figure of Marilyn Monroe or Rita Hayworth. Emory's doctor, however, had used other, less-flattering terms to describe her extra weight.

"Heavens to Betsy, Emory Ann, I could smell breakfast all the way upstairs. I hope you made extra." Aunt Ruthie swept into the kitchen, her white hair piled on the top of her head and her two fluffy calico cats trailing after her. "Colonel Jimenez likes to eat—as I'm sure you've noticed."

Emory nodded. "I have. I doubled the batch."

"That's my girl." Aunt Ruthie patted her cheek, her bright pink lips and well-rouged cheeks creasing from her impish smile.

Emory attempted to smile in return. "Can't have anyone leaving hungry."

"No, ma'am. That'd be a downright crime." Aunt Ruthie nodded.

Aunt Ruthie was old school. She believed in a tidy house, a full belly and putting yourself together, every single day. It didn't matter if it was five in the morning or ten at night, Aunt Ruthie would have on a full face of makeup, piled-high and sprayed-in-place hair, and wrinkle-free clothing. Thankfully, she'd let Emory's less than put-together appearance slide the four months she'd been here in Granite Falls.

"I'd best get everyone's invoices printed up for checkout. Save me a muffin, won't you? The smell makes it seem like Christmas is tomorrow—not a full month away." She gave Emory a long, searching look. "It's going to be a good day today, Emory Ann." She gave Emory's cheek another pat. "So much to do." With that, she swept out of the kitchen, her cats trailing after her, as always.

Emory finished artfully stacking the muffins on one of her aunt's cheerful Christmas platters, carried it out into the large dining room and placed it on the sideboard, ready and waiting for the current bed-and-breakfast guests.

This weekend they had a full house. Colonel Jimenez, three women from Austin here for a girls' weekend and a large family taking a road trip from Galveston, Texas, all the way up to Wichita, Kansas. Granite Falls was an adorable town, but Emory hadn't expected it to be such a tourist destination. She'd begun to realize that the quaint boutiques and Main Street vibe plus the easy access off the state highway made it a quick getaway from the larger metroplexes of Texas. Plus the rodeo.

Rodeo was always a big draw for tourists looking for an authentic Texas experience. Which was good for Aunt Ruthie's bed-and-breakfast and the handful of Texas dude ranches in the surrounding vicinity.

Emory stepped back to assess the festive breakfast display one last time. She straightened the green carnival glass bowl of berries, checked that the chafing dish was warm enough to keep the breakfast casserole the right temp and counted the silverware and red-and-green plates to make sure there was enough for everyone. From the squeaking wood floors and muffled conversation spilling down the stairs, the guests were up and moving already.

Once she was satisfied with the dining room aesthetic, she went back into the kitchen to finish up the final prep. It was mindless work but she appreciated the routine of it. Pouring orange juice in a cut crystal pitcher, filling the coffee urn and putting on another pot to brew, loading up a tray with cream, half-and-half, milk, sugar and artificial sweeteners of all types. Aunt Ruthie was all about giving her guests exactly what they liked. It was, she said, the best way to guarantee those guests would be back.

That was one of the many things Emory admired about her aunt. Aunt Ruthie did everything at 110 percent. She was a doer. The older woman was always busy. She didn't believe in "wasting daylight."

Once upon a time, Emory had been a doer, too. Now, she was happy to get by. With every passing day, it was getting easier. But easier didn't mean bearable. Not yet. There were still mornings she woke up clutching her stomach—holding on to the baby she'd lost. Other days, she'd reach across the bed for Sam. Then she'd remember and realize they'd never be there, with her, again. Those were the really hard days.

"All done." Aunt Ruthie came back in. "What can I do to help?" She paused. "It looks to me like you've got it all under control."

"I'm trying." Emory adjusted the tie of her apron and ran a hand over the bold stitching that read, This Is My Christmas Cookie Baking Apron.

"And succeeding." Ruthie reached up, smoothing the tower of white hair on her head. "Am I all straight? No holes?" She spun slowly so Emory could check her hair.

"No holes." Emory gave her a thumbs-up. "Perfect. As always."

If there was ever a doubt as to how much her aunt Ruthie loved the one-and-only Dolly Parton, all a person had to do was check out Ruthie's hair. Emory didn't know how many hairpieces or wigs her aunt owned, but they were all an homage to the iconic country singer. The fact that each room of the bed-and-breakfast was named after one of Dolly's greatest hits, and she'd framed every bit of memorabilia she'd acquired from the many concerts and trips to Dollywood only solidified Aunt Ruthie's devotion to the icon.

"You are sweeter than sugar." Her aunt winked. "Now, I'm feeling in the mood to dazzle the good colonel this morning." She took the tray.

Emory followed her out into the dining room, smiling. It wasn't long before the chairs were full and Emory was entirely focused on working. As long as she was refilling coffee or serving food or washing dishes, she could ignore the pressure on her chest and the lead weighing down her stomach.

After breakfast was over and the kitchen was clean, she headed out to the vegetable garden with her basket. Fresh vegetables always made soup or salad taste best. Texas's mild fall and winter meant there were plentiful veggies all year round. Plus, out here, it was peaceful and quiet and just what she needed.

Except it wasn't peaceful. Or quiet. She frowned, staring around her to find what was making that pitiful, repetitive whimper-howl.

She set her basket aside and dropped to her knees, crawling across the yard to peer under the bushes that surrounded the property line's wrought-iron fence. For a Main Street property, the old house had a big, sprawling double lot for their garden and the carriage house out back—where Emory lived. It was only while crawling the length of the fence that she fully realized just how sizable the property was.

She paused when the whimpers stopped, flattening herself in the grass and holding up the lower branch of the bush.

A small dog stared back. A very unfortunate-looking dog. Its white hair was matted in tufts, its eyes were on the bulgy side and its tongue dangled out the side of its mouth. To top it off, the dog was shaking so badly the whole bush seemed to be moving, too.

"Where did you come from?" she murmured.

The dog's head pivoted one way, then the next, before starting up its mournful whine-howl again.

"Come on." She held her hand out. "It's okay. I can't see what's wrong and fix you if you won't come out."

The dog backed farther away, barely visible now.

"Emory Ann, sugar, what is making that awful racket?" Aunt Ruthie called out.

"A little dog." Emory sat up and turned to her aunt, shrugging. "It might be hurt. But I can't tell how bad. Poor thing is shaking."

Aunt Ruthie wasn't the only one standing on the large wraparound porch—most of their guests were, too. "I'll go give Buzz Lafferty, our vet here, a call. Good man." Aunt Ruthie held up her pointer finger. "You keep it there until I reach him."

"I'll try." Emory lay on her stomach in the grass and rested her head on her arms, facing the dog. Well, all she could see were two white paws, but the leaves on the bush still shimmied so it was safe to assume the dog was still there. "Hey, little thing. It's okay. I promise. It's not that bad." At least, she hoped that was the case.

The whimpering, however, suggested otherwise.

"Okay, okay. Maybe it is," she said, keeping her voice low. "And if it is, I'm sorry. I'm sure we'll be able to find your owner and get you fixed up and it'll all be okay."

The dog lowered his head, sniffed, then mimicked Emory's position. It lay, bulging little eyes glued on her, and continued to whimper.

Emory couldn't help but smile. "We can stay like this until you're ready, okay?"

The dog grunted, tried to move, then whimpered sharply.

"Are you hurt?" She frowned, wishing she had her phone or a flashlight to see what, exactly, was going on with the poor little dog. "Oh, please come out. Please, puppy. If you're hurt—"

"Um, hello?" A deep voice came from the other side of the bush, making Emory and the dog both jump. "Everything okay? Need any help?"

She sat up on her knees and craned her neck to see over the hedges. "There's a dog that might be injured, but it's wedged itself under a bush so I can't get to it."

"Well…" The man stepped forward, though the shadow of his cowboy hat made his features indistinguishable. "There's some blood out here on the sidewalk."

"Oh no." Blood? She shook her head, truly worried now. "The little thing won't come out. It's scared, probably. And hurting."

"We'll come around," the cowboy said.

A minute later, two men walked through the gate and across the grass to where she knelt. One man stood while the other, a giant of a man, folded his massive frame at her side to peer under the shrubs and assess the dog's condition. "Come on out now." This voice was deeper and gruffer than the one she'd talked to. That, with his sheer size, made him more than a little intimidating. He reached one massive hand under the shrub. "Come on."

"Is it safe to move it?" Her medical knowledge extended to the rescue show her aunt loved—and they never moved any accident victims unless they'd made sure there wasn't a head or neck injury. Whether or not that applied to canines, she wasn't sure.

"If it's bleeding bad and we leave it, things could get a lot worse." The man's arm moved one way, then the other.

There was no arguing with that alarming, but true, statement. She wasn't about to sit here and let the poor dog bleed to death. Just thinking about that happening had panic deflating her lungs.

"Emory," Aunt Ruthie called out. "Emory, Buzz said he's on his way. He said... Who's that? Trace? Trace Dawson, is that you?"

"Yes, ma'am." Trace, the man standing, tipped his hat in Aunt Ruthie's direction. "And Dougal McCarrick, too. He's got a real way with animals. He'll get the dog out."

Dougal grunted, murmuring, "It bit me."

A way with animals, huh? Emory could only imagine the poor dog's fear. Dougal McCarrick was a mountain of a man—to a small, panicked dog, he'd be a downright monster. She went back to lying in the grass. "Come on, puppy. It's safe, I promise." The dog didn't know the giant man digging around, attempting to drag it out, was trying to help. It was hurting and scared and defending itself. "Please come out. Please." Every second the dog bled was a second lost—Emory was keenly aware of that. She drew in a wavering breath. "Please."

The dog started scooching toward her, yelping and barking the whole way. When it made its way out and to her, Emory bit into her lower lip to stop herself from crying.

Trace hissed the words. "That doesn't look so good."

Dougal sat back and ran a hand along the back of his neck, his eyes fixed on the dog's left hind leg.

The sight of the dog's back leg bleeding and dangling at an awkward angle had Emory's heart in her throat. "Poor thing," she crooned.

Even wounded, the little dog wagged its tail and managed to pull itself into Emory's lap where it curled into a ball.

"Oh, sweet thing," she whispered, gently resting a hand on the dog's back. "It will be okay." It would be. It had to be. She couldn't bear to think of any other alternative. "I promise," she said more firmly. "You're going to be fine."

Something in the woman's voice grabbed ahold of Dougal. Until now, he'd only cared about the injured animal. But now... There was a force behind the woman's words that was almost a challenge. As if she could will the dog into surviving its injury. He watched her lean forward, protecting the dog.

"Miss." Dougal didn't want to get the woman's hopes up but stumbled to a stop. He shot Trace a look, uncertain.

"There's no way of knowing how badly the little guy is hurt," Trace said what he was thinking.

"Guy? It's a boy?" She didn't bother to look up. "*He* will be fine." Her tone said she wasn't going to hear anyone tell her otherwise.

Dougal sighed. "Maybe." Maybe not. He'd grown up on a ranch with all sorts of animals. Sometimes, life wasn't fair. It was a lesson he'd learned as a boy. And, Trace was right. That leg didn't look good.

"Here." Ruthie Baumgarten arrived, a fluffy pink towel in her hands. "What a sad little thing. Oh, Emory, sugar, try not to fret. Dr. Lafferty will be here any minute, now." She handed Dougal the towel. "Thank you, Trace and Dougal, for helping Emory out."

"I didn't do a thing." Trace shrugged. "Neither did Dougal. He came straight out to Emory."

It wasn't for lack of trying. Instead of scowling up at Trace, Dougal held the towel out for Emory. The little dog growled and cowered back into her lap, whimpering from the effort. "Hey, hey, now." He kept his voice low and soft. "No one's going to hurt you."

"I don't think he believes you." Trace shook his head.

"Thanks for the towel, Aunt Ruthie." Emory draped the towel over the dog. "I don't see a collar."

"I'd say he hasn't had a good meal in some time," Ruthie said, clicking her tongue.

Dougal agreed. The little dog was skin and bones. He shook his head. One thing about living in the country that bothered him the most was people driving out to dump their animals.

"How far do you think it walked like this?" Emory gently rubbed one of the dog's ears.

"No telling." Dougal studied the bug-eyed canine. White hair stood out in every which direction, and it had an underbite that rivaled his brother's dog, Gertie. "But I'd say the dog is tougher than it looks."

"You hang in there," Emory whispered.

He loved animals, but there was something about Emory's determination that bordered on desperation. He glanced at Ruthie Baumgarten. The older woman was frowning, her eyes pinned on her niece with genuine concern. He didn't know Ruthie Baumgarten all that well, she'd only been here a couple of years now and, since he'd no reason to stay at a bed-and-breakfast, their paths rarely crossed. Still, he'd heard only good things about the woman and her efforts to become an active member of the close-knit community he called home.

He hadn't known Ruthie's niece, Emory, had existed until now. But, from the way she was cradling that dog against her chest, he suspected she had a tender heart.

Trace caught his eye and shook his head.

Dougal's nod was slight. He had the feeling Emory's tender heart was going to be broken before the day was through. Still, the minute Dougal saw Buzz coming through the front gate, he hoped he was wrong. Buzz was one hell of a good veterinarian—and he didn't just think so because they were friends.

"Ruthie?" Buzz hurried across the yard. "Dougal. Trace." He nodded and crouched in the grass. "What do we have here?"

"Hit by a car, I'm thinking." Dougal winced when Buzz lifted the towel and revealed the dog's back leg again.

Buzz nodded. "Stray?" He looked back and forth between Ruthie and Emory.

"I think so." Ruthie hugged herself. "I've never seen it around here."

"But it's mine, now," Emory murmured. "I mean, I want to be responsible for it. I'll take care of it now."

Ruthie's tone was soothing. "Emory Ann, sugar, after everything you've been through, are you sure that's what you need—"

"Yes, Aunt Ruthie. It is." Emory ran a hand over the top of the dog's head. "Whatever you need to do to save this dog, Dr. Lafferty, please do it."

Buzz's assessing gaze swept over Emory before returning to the dog. "Okay. First, we need to get to the clinic so I can take a good look at what's going on." He reached forward, sliding his arms under the towel and the dog. "And we'll make sure there's no chip—in case there is an owner out there looking for him." He scooped the dog up in the towel.

The dog didn't approve of this maneuver and made sure they all knew about it, too.

Buzz nodded, holding the dog tightly. "I'd be mighty unhappy, too." He glanced at Dougal. "We should probably get that taken care of, as well"

Dougal looked down at his hand. He hadn't realized he was bleeding. "I'm fine. Got a tetanus shot last year."

"Good." Buzz nodded, meeting his gaze. "I don't think Skylar's in yet. I might need extra hands."

Dougal nodded, so did Trace, and they headed back to the gate.

"I'm coming, too." Emory trailed after them.

There wasn't much talking as they rushed down the six blocks and across Main Street to Buzz's veterinary clinic. The dog's whimpers had gotten softer by the time they were inside—and Emory seemed more distraught by the second.

"Hey, Buzz. Everyone..." Buzz's vet tech, Skylar, was inside—just setting her purse down on the front desk. "What do we have here?" She headed around the desk, her expression guarded as she assessed the little dog.

"Glad you're here." Buzz nodded to the back as he spoke to Skylar. "We can handle this, but it'll be a while. I can call the B and B when we know more."

"I'll wait." Emory stared after Skylar as she carried the dog into the back. "If that's okay?"

Buzz nodded, shot Dougal a meaningful look, then disappeared behind the swinging doors.

His brother and friends liked to give him grief for being on the "reserved" side—they used the term emotionally constipated to describe him—but he wasn't completely clueless. As awkward as this whole situation was, he wasn't going to up and leave Emory alone in the waiting room—especially when he feared the outcome was so bleak.

Trace tapped his watch. "I've got to get to work. Hope it turns out…okay." His gaze bounced between Dougal and Emory before he offered an apologetic shrug.

Dougal worked on the family ranch—as long as he got the job done, his hours were up to him. Trace, on the other hand, had a nine-to-five job so he couldn't just roll in to work whenever he wanted. Meaning he'd be staying here, alone, with Emory. He waved his friend off, then stood, awkwardly as seconds turned into minutes. Emory stood still as a statue, hugging herself, with her pale blue eyes glued on the door Skylar and Buzz had taken the dog through. "Want to sit?" he asked, indicating the chairs along the wall.

She sat, tucking her hands under her thighs.

He sat beside her, took off his cowboy hat and spun it slowly in his hands. He normally preferred silence but this was different. This silence was loaded with tension—so much so, he could feel a trickle of sweat slide down his back. He rubbed his palms on his thighs and wracked his brain for something appropriate to say. "I'm Dougal. Dougal McCarrick."

She barely glanced his way. "Emory. Swanson." She stared down at the floor.

He'd thought the dog had been shaking but maybe it had been Emory the whole time. She perched on the edge of the seat, her entire body shuddering.

"You okay?" he asked, knowing it was a stupid thing to ask. Clearly, she wasn't okay. But he didn't know how to make small talk, and this seemed like the sort of a thing a person would ask—under the circumstances.

She nodded, then shook her head. "I'm trying to be."

The wobble in her voice had him sitting forward. He lifted up his hand, hesitating. It went against his nature to invade the personal space of a stranger. Normally, it took him quite a bit of time to feel comfortable enough to engage in any sort of physical exchange. But Emory was on the verge of tears, he could tell. And, distant or not, his heart wasn't made of stone.

"Hey, now," he murmured, giving her back a pat. "Buzz is one hell of a veterinarian." He kept on patting her. "I know he will do everything he can for that little dog." He gave her another awkward pat before resting his hand on her shoulder.

She sniffed, turning big, tear-filled eyes his way. "He will? Good," she whispered. "That's good to know."

All he could do was nod. The hurt in her eyes slammed into him. Raw and too much… Too big. Her gaze was haunted—clouded with the sort of torment he'd rather shy away from. There was no way this little dog was the sole reason for Emory's bone-deep grief, but that didn't stop him from hoping like hell that Buzz could save the little dog. Not just for the dog, but for Emory. Something told him she was close to breaking in a way there was no recovering from. Maybe that's why some new instinct took over and he slipped his arm around her shoulders. And when she turned into him, buried her face against his chest and proceeded to soak his shirt with her tears, he pulled her closer. Awkward or not, he'd give her whatever comfort he could while they waited for word on the little dog's fate.

Chapter Two

"I think he's adorable." Emory sat on the floor of the veterinary clinic with the little dog in her arms. "You are, aren't you, Frosty?" She smiled. "Adorable and strong. You'll be up and around in no time."

Frosty's white plume of a tail wagged rapidly. In the four days since his arrival at the vet hospital, the dog had gone through quite the transformation. He'd had surgery, been treated for a flea infestation so bad he'd been anemic and been washed and groomed. While he had some healing to do from his surgery, he looked like an entirely different dog. He was still awkward with his bulgy eyes and his too-long pink tongue always hanging out of the side of his mouth, but that hadn't stopped Emory from becoming 100 percent smitten with the canine.

"And smart, too. You already know your name, don't you, Frosty?" She leaned forward—earning her a doggie kiss down the side of her face. "Thank you."

"Whatever you say, Emory." Aunt Ruthie chuckled. "I think he looks like a drowned rat." But then she shook her head and said, "But I guess he is a very cute, three-legged drowned rat."

Buzz had done all he could, but there was no saving

Frosty's leg. The hip socket had been injured too significantly to attempt to pin the femur in place—and that was if the femur had been intact. It hadn't. Buzz had said the dog's leg was like a jigsaw puzzle with missing and jagged pieces. His assurance that Frosty would bounce back and adjust to life with three stable legs made the decision easy.

"But we'll get along just fine." Aunt Ruthie sat forward in her chair to speak to the dog. "As long as you don't go chasing after the girls. Tammy and Loretta are sweet, sensitive souls. I don't want them thinking they're not mommy's favorites anymore."

If Aunt Ruthie's warning had any effect on the dog, there was no sign of it. His tail kept right on wagging.

"I'll keep a close eye on him, Aunt Ruthie." Emory was quick to reassure her aunt. Even after numerous husbands, those cats were Aunt Ruthie's only children. They were pampered and adored and were going to have a hard time sharing their home with another four-legged creature. *Er, three-legged.*

"I don't think Frosty will be much of a threat." Skylar offered the dog a small treat. "He's fifteen pounds soaking wet." She waited, holding her hand out. "Plus he only seems to care for Emory so he might not have any interest in your girls."

Frosty carefully took the treat but kept a wary eye on Skylar. After everything he'd been through, Emory thought it was perfectly normal for the dog to be suspicious about the vet technician's intentions.

"Don't worry, Frosty. I'm not going to take you away from your mommy." Skylar smiled at her. "He sure lights up when you're here. I'm sure he'll be tickled pink to go home with you."

Emory assessed the shaved patch and bandage along Frosty's left side. "It's amazing how quickly he's healing."

"In about a month, you'll barely know it's happened." Skylar nodded. "He was one lucky pup."

Frosty grunted as he buried his face in the front of Emory's shirt. His little sigh, plus the way he relaxed into her, flooded her with pleasure.

Emory wasn't sure who was luckier—her or the dog. It had only been days, but Frosty had given her back her smile. It wasn't as if the dark moments and grief over losing her baby or Sam had magically disappeared. They hadn't. And, likely, never would. Not entirely, anyway. But with Frosty, there was newfound reason to get up and do and be—a sense of hope and love.

"I should get back." Aunt Ruthie stood. "I'm expecting some new visitors this afternoon. You take your time." She gave Frosty another long look. "Only a mother could love that face."

"Or an aunt." Emory smiled up at her.

Aunt Ruthie chuckled all the way to the door.

"Tammy and Loretta are going to have a rude awakening when Frosty goes home." Skylar started restocking the cabinets. "Those two cats think the world revolves around them."

"It took them a while to get used to me." Emory nodded, running her hand along Frosty's back. "I'm still not sure they like me, but they tolerate me."

Skylar smiled at her. "You haven't been here that long, have you? How are you liking Granite Falls?"

"Almost four months now." Was that all? Time had

gone wonky since losing the baby—that had been almost two years ago now. "It's a lovely little town. I haven't explored much... Honestly, I've been a bit of a hermit since I got here." She glanced at the woman, hurrying on to prevent any further questions. "Taking this one on walks will help with that. When he's ready, of course."

"I'm happy to show you around." Skylar sat in the chair Aunt Ruthie had vacated. "I moved here almost three years ago and, since then, I've found where I'm meant to be. Granite Falls is home." She shrugged. "Of course, that might also have something to do with my husband. Nothing like falling in love with a local, and his family, to make you feel at home."

Emory swallowed against the lump in her throat. "How lovely."

"What about you? Ruthie is your aunt. Any other family in these parts?" Skylar pushed her long blond braid from her shoulder.

"No. My parents are snowbirds. They have a place in Montana for the summers and a place in Florida for the winters. I was a very late-in-life surprise—they'd never planned on having children." As a result, she'd been the apple of both her parents' eyes. It's the way she imagined she and Sam would have been if she hadn't lost the baby. She shook off the thought and shoved aside the pain it caused.

Her parents called and texted regularly—even more so the last two years. She loved that they wanted her to come stay with them, but she couldn't do it. All their hovering and worrying over her would only make it harder for her to move on. And she was trying, desperately, to feel something other than sadness and anger.

"Do you get to visit them? In Montana and Florida?"

"Sometimes. It's been a while." They'd stayed with her for a month after the accident. It was one long blur now but their presence had been a buffer. "They'd mentioned something about coming for the holidays." She hoped they'd change their minds and take the cruise they'd been invited on instead. A quiet, low-key holiday with her aunt and, now, Frosty, was what she really needed.

"That'll be nice. The holidays are always better with loved ones." Skylar stood when the doorbell sounded. "I'll go check and see who that is." She headed out front, the door separating the reception area and exam room swinging shut behind her.

Emory kept running her hand along Frosty's back. She closed her eyes, the dog's slight weight and steady breathing remarkably calming. She knew she had a laundry list of things to do at the B and B, but she could afford to stay a few minutes longer.

If Frosty hadn't started growling, Emory wouldn't have known they were no longer alone. But the growl had her opening her eyes to find Dougal McCarrick before her, his cowboy hat in his hands. "Do you have a stealth mode?" She was more than a little rattled by his sudden appearance. "How did I not hear you?" Her gaze fell to his feet. Cowboy boots. She should have heard him. "Did you tiptoe?"

"I don't tiptoe." His grin was crooked. "How's the patient?"

She stared down at the dog in her lap. He was no longer growling, but he was definitely unhappy that the giant of a man was looming nearby. "Frosty." She rubbed one silky ear between her fingers. "Frosty is doing amazingly well."

"I didn't think he was going to make it." Dougal's voice was low.

She glanced up at the man. "I hope this doesn't offend you but...I'm glad you were wrong."

He was smiling as he sat. "No offense taken."

She scratched the dog's side and Frosty grunted and wriggled until he'd turned onto his back. His three legs stuck straight up and his head was upside down on her lap with his tongue flopping out. As long as she kept scratching him, he didn't seem to care.

"Looks like he's going to have some trust issues." Dougal chuckled.

Her answering laugh was a surprise. "I'm sensing that." It felt good to laugh—for a minute. Ever since Sam's accident, it had felt wrong to laugh.

Because it is *wrong to laugh.*

She was here, talking and laughing and petting Frosty. Losing her baby had opened the door to a pain she'd never understood before. Then... Sam and his accident. She'd never be able to take back her hurtful words or make amends for their last argument. He'd never know how sorry she was or hear her apology in return. It wasn't right. It wasn't fair.

She managed to stop herself from spiraling. There was no point in replaying that fateful night again—it filled her dreams enough as it was.

She cleared her throat and stared down at Frosty.

"Dougal." Skylar poked her head in. "Willow really wants to come back here with you."

Emory saw the way the man's brown eyes shifted from Frosty, to her, to the door. Who was Willow?

"You know she'll be good." Skylar almost sounded impatient.

"I'm not worried about her." Dougal stood, then nodded. "Fine."

Emory watched as Skylar held the swinging door wide and a large black Labrador appeared. The dog headed straight for Dougal and sat at his side, staring up at him.

"This is Willow?" Emory asked.

He nodded, giving the large dog a quick scratch behind the ear. Considering how big Dougal was, his dog seemed proportionate—Willow was one of the largest dogs Emory had ever seen.

"Don't let her size fool you, Emory. She is the sweetest dog. Considering how many dogs I work with, that says a lot." Skylar smiled. "Who knows, maybe she and Frosty will make friends."

Emory glanced down at the dozing pup in her lap, a reluctant smile forming. Willow had to be at least four times the size of Frosty. Considering how he responded to Dougal's size, she thought it was unlikely the little dog would want to make friends with this canine behemoth.

Skylar frowned at the sound of a phone ringing. "Duty calls." The door swung shut behind her.

Until Willow's tawny eyes landed on her, all Emory had really noticed was the dog's size. The dog's blue-black coat was thick and shiny and her rudder-like tail rhythmically tapped against the linoleum floor in greeting, but it was the eyes that drew Emory in. Was a dog supposed to have such...soulful eyes? Because that's the only way to describe Willow's intent gaze. Soulful.

Not that Emory had much experience with dogs. Her father was allergic to almost everything, so she'd only ever had a pet turtle growing up.

The Labrador stood, sniffing the air, her ears perking up as she continued searching. As big as Willow was, there was nothing threatening or intimidating about her. When the dog discovered Frosty, her big black head cocked to one side. She didn't move closer to Emory or show any sign of distress or agitation, more like curiosity.

Emory studied the dog that was studying her dog. "She's beautiful."

"And gentle." Dougal gave the dog's back a pat.

Frosty chose that moment to stretch—which resulted in him jolting awake with a whimper.

"Poor thing." Emory stroked Frosty's head. "I'm sure you're sore."

But Frosty had forgotten whatever discomfort he was feeling now that he'd spied Willow. He sat up, his ears alert and his bug-eyes glued to the massive dog. He was frozen. No wriggling or sniffing or growling, just staring.

"Is this bad?" Emory whispered, resisting the urge to lift Frosty to her chest. After everything she and Frosty had been through the last few days, she wasn't going to sit by and let Dougal's big "gentle" dog hurt her new little friend. Soulful eyes or not, Emory wasn't so sure about what was happening. The longer the dogs stared at each other, the more agitated she became. Until she said, "I think you and Willow should leave. Now."

Dougal knew there was nothing to worry about. The two dogs were sizing each other up, but there was no posturing or baring of teeth or hint of aggression. Not that he expected anything like that from Willow. Frosty, however, was the wild card. He might be little but his bite still hurt—he knew this from personal experience. Not that Dougal was holding any grudges. He glanced at the healing wound on the edge of his hand. If he'd been hurting and scared and had strangers pawing at him, he might have gone on and bitten someone, too.

All of a sudden, Frosty barked, his tail waving so quickly it was a blur of white fluff and fur.

Willow stretched, going from a downward dog pose to flopping and sprawling on her side on the linoleum floor.

Good girl. Showing him you're no threat. Dougal smiled. "All is well."

Emory's posture eased somewhat, but she didn't look fully convinced. When Frosty started to climb out of her lap, he could tell how hard it was for her to let the dog go.

Frosty walked awkwardly around Willow, sniffing every inch of her, before coming back to her face.

"We'll need to have a conversation about personal space, Frosty." Emory's brows were elevated.

Dougal couldn't help but chuckle then.

Willow stood, touched noses with Frosty and circled the little dog—taking extra care to inspect the bandage and shaved spot from Frosty's surgery. She whimpered, looked at Dougal, then Emory, then touched noses with Frosty again.

"That's the sweetest thing I think I've ever seen." There was a wobble to Emory's voice.

Dougal stared at the woman he'd spent a whole hell of a lot of time thinking about the last couple of days. Emory Swanson. Ruthie Baumgarten's niece. Chef. Been here four months and rarely ventured off the Baumgarten Bed-and-Breakfast property. Meaning, his efforts to learn more about her had come up empty. She was, for the most part, a mystery.

A beautiful, sad-eyed, tenderhearted mystery.

The unshed tears shining in her pale blue eyes unleashed the same protective instinct he'd felt the last time he saw her. She sniffed once, then again, so he offered her his handkerchief.

She stared at the handkerchief, then him.

There it was. Pain so raw he could feel it. He didn't know what the hell he was supposed to do about it—but that didn't stop him from wanting to try. Somehow. Some way. With a handkerchief, to start.

"Thank you," she whispered, taking his handkerchief. "I'm a mess." She dabbed at her eyes. "I don't have to tell *you*." She sniffed again. "You've been lucky enough to see it for yourself. I've cried every time I've seen you."

He wasn't sure *mess* was the right word but, since he'd never been very good with words, he didn't say a thing. Luckily, the dogs caught and held Emory's attention so he could shake off the odd pressure building in his chest.

Willow flopped onto her back, all four legs in the air, and wriggled.

Frosty tried to lean forward into a pounce pose but realized too late the lack of his leg threw his balance off. He tipped to one side but caught himself. He spun in a circle, hopped toward Willow, then lay down at her side and yawned.

"You're tuckered out, aren't you?" Emory shook her head. "I wonder if it's good for him to have so much…

activity so soon." She wrinkled up her nose, her blue eyes searching out his again.

He couldn't look away. He should, but he couldn't—especially since the tug in his chest seemed to intensify. It was unsettling, to say the least.

"But I guess Skylar wouldn't have let Willow back here if there was a concern?" She paused, waiting for an answer.

He was no vet but he *was* a dog person and she had a point. Frosty did look tuckered out. *And* since he was so confounded by his reaction to her, it was probably best that they go. "We'll head out."

"Now?" Emory frowned.

He stood and glanced at the two dogs, both peering up at him from where they lay on the floor. "Willow and I have work to do." And he needed space. The sooner the better.

Emory held out his handkerchief.

"Keep it." He waved aside her offer.

"Thank you." She drew in a deep breath. "I'll be ready if this happens again next time I see you." But her attempt at a joke fell flat. With her empty hand, she patted her lap and Frosty happily returned, curling up and yawning. "You should rest, baby boy."

Willow stood at his side, waiting for his next move. Did he have a next move? It's not like he'd made a first move—he didn't have *any* moves. The only thing he was certain of was that he *wasn't* going to stand there like a fool. He really did have to get back to the ranch or his brother, Angus, would get suspicious and start asking questions. That was something he wanted to avoid at all costs. "Have a good day, ma'am."

"You too, Dougal," she murmured.

He was relieved he made it out of the exam room without pausing or turning back or tripping over his own words or feet.

"Nice of you to stop in, Dougal. I get the feeling she could use a friend. How'd it go?" Skylar asked, glancing up from the computer screen.

He nodded, then shrugged, heading toward the door. How did it go? Willow had made a good impression, but he had no idea what Emory thought of him. Or why it mattered. Maybe some fresh air would clear his head.

"Dougal?" Buzz called from his office, the sound of his boots announcing his approach. "What's up? Willow okay?"

Willow's tail wagged at the sight of Buzz, who meant treats and Willow loved treats.

Dammit. He was maybe five feet from the door. "She's fine." He crossed his arms over his chest, wishing he'd come up with a reason for being here that made sense.

"He's checking in on Frosty. Emory's dog." Skylar started clicking away on the keyboard.

Buzz's brow furrowed but he nodded. "Right. You were one of his rescuers that day. Frosty's going to be okay."

Dougal nodded, stepping closer to the door. "So I saw." And he was grateful, for Emory's sake. Something in his bones told him she'd have been devastated if it'd turned out any other way.

"Pretty proud of my surgical skills, if I do say so myself." Buzz pretended to straighten the cuffs of his white doctor's coat.

"As modest as ever." Skylar laughed.

"You did good." Dougal reached for the front door.

"Wait, a compliment? From Dougal McCarrick?" Buzz scratched his temple, a mix of surprise and confusion on his face. "Well, thanks." He was studying Dougal a little too intently. "Skylar, do we have a gas leak or something?"

With a sigh, Dougal slipped out the front door and down the sidewalk to his waiting truck. He opened the passenger door for Willow, giving the dog a scratch behind the ear, before closing the door and heading around to the driver's door.

Dougal climbed into the truck and started the engine. "It's not like I never give a compliment." He glanced at Willow, put the truck into reverse and backed onto Main Street.

Willow cocked her head to one side and rested a paw on his forearm.

Still…he couldn't remember when that might have been. "Coming here was a mistake." He sighed, shifted the truck into drive and headed out of town to McCarrick Ranch.

When he'd got the delivery email for some tack and equipment they'd been waiting on, he'd headed straight into town. Stopping in at the vet clinic after he'd picked everything up hadn't seemed too out of the ordinary— at the time. He'd wanted to see how the dog was doing, that was all. If Emory happened to be there then…well, that was okay, too.

"But I didn't go there to see her," he murmured, glancing at Willow again.

The dog blinked.

"I didn't." He ran a hand along the back of his neck.

Willow snorted and rested her head on the armrest between them.

"Enough of that." He turned onto the drive leading to McCarrick Ranch, home of McCarrick Cutting Horses. Once he drove through the wood-and-stone arched gate, he put thoughts of Emory and Frosty and his visit to the vet clinic behind him. He had work to do—work that required his concentration.

He glanced at the clock and parked in front of the main house. He didn't have much time to spare, but he would never pass up a chance to spend time with his three favorite people in the world. His nieces and nephew might not be a year old yet, but they appreciated the simple things in life—a philosophy Dougal wholeheartedly agreed with.

A chorus of "Doo" greeted him when he walked through the front door, making him grin from ear to ear. The triplets were just starting to walk, and every day they had new words. He'd gone from "Doo" to "Unca Doo." Angus thought it was hilarious but he didn't mind a bit.

"Good morning, little critters." Dougal headed straight for the quilt spread out on the floor of the great room. "Learn anything new since I saw you last night?" He squatted on the edge of the blanket.

Willow took up her spot along the far side of the blanket. She'd become the triplets' dog nanny—at least, she thought she was.

"Wee." Little Henry barreled straight for Willow—the boy didn't walk, he ran full tilt at all times. "Wee." He threw his arms around the dog.

"Wee." Emilia, with her tiny red ringlet cap of curls, toddled after her brother on less steady legs to the dog.

"Unca Doo." Tabitha reached for him, squealing with glee when he swung her up and into his arms.

"Why aren't they that happy to see me?" Angus leaned against the kitchen counter.

"You're just their dad. I'm their favorite." Dougal gave Tabitha a great big bear hug. "Isn't that right, Tabby-cat?"

Savannah, Angus's wife, laughed. "They do love their uncle Doo."

"Of course, they do." Dougal rested Tabitha on his hip.

"I hate to break it to you, brother of mine, but I was talking about the way they're falling all over Willow." Angus pointed at the dog. "I guess they like you all right, too."

Dougal made a face at Tabitha. "Your daddy thinks he's so funny."

Tabitha giggled. "Da Da."

"I always laugh when I think about him, too." Dougal nodded, shooting his brother a look. "Picked up the tack this morning. Figured we could try it out on the Castillo horse? He's awful head shy."

Angus's expression was perplexed.

"What?" Dougal asked, swinging Tabitha up before setting her down on the ground.

"Wee!" Tabitha squealed, toddling to Willow.

Willow lay on the blanket, content for the three of them to pat and scratch and kiss her nose and head.

"I'm surprised you didn't mention it last night, is all. Savannah, Ma and Aunt Nola are about to go into town for story time at the library this morning—they could have picked it up and saved the gas." Angus took a sip from his coffee mug. "Since you're always on me about spending money."

Dougal shrugged, determined not to share anything unnecessary. "I was up." He glanced at the kids. "Story time, huh?" He smiled when Henry planted a wide open-mouthed kiss on the top of Willow's head. "Need help loading the critters into the Suburban?"

"I'll never say no to help." Savannah nodded.

"I've refilled the diaper bags." Their mother came into the room, a stuffed backpack over one shoulder.

"Land sakes, these three go through diapers." Aunt Nola followed. "Wouldn't be a bad idea to stop and pick some up on the way home."

"Morning, Dougal." Ma gave him a quick hug.

"You lose your razor?" Aunt Nola frowned, reaching up to tug on his black beard.

Dougal sighed. He'd trimmed it up in the hopes his aunt would cut him some slack on his facial hair. It hadn't worked.

"You're too pretty to hide yourself away behind all that…" Aunt Nola pointed at him, her expression disapproving.

"Pretty?" Angus laughed like this was the funniest thing he'd ever heard.

"Hush." Ma gave Angus's shoulder a smack. "You be nice to your brother. Your aunt is right. Dougal is a handsome man. As are you."

Angus was still struggling not to laugh. "Aunt Nola said *pretty*." He snorted, then laughed.

"All I meant was that, if he'd scrape all that off his face, he might catch the eye of some sweet young thing for him to settle down with—and make *critters* of his own." Aunt Nola glared at Angus.

"Since when has Dougal wanted to catch the eye of

anyone?" Angus glanced at his brother. "Dougal is a lifelong bachelor."

Hours later, Angus's comment was still lingering at the edge of Dougal's mind. What the hell had Angus meant by that? He didn't want to remain a bachelor. He wanted a family. He wanted a wife and partner—like his brother had. He didn't have his brother's smooth-talking charm and confidence, but he had a few talents his brother didn't have—or know about. Well, one talent, anyway. His poetry. No one knew about it. But, when he did find the right woman, he'd use the written word to say all the things he was too awkward or tongue-tied to say.

He ran his hand over what remained of his bushy beard and sighed.

Until then, he'd take his aunt's advice and shave. Maybe, just maybe, he'd catch the attention of the sad blue-eyed woman he'd offered his handkerchief to and the real reason he'd driven into town this morning— not that he was going to fess up to it. The last thing he needed was his brother, mother or aunt deciding he needed help courting Emory Swanson.

Chapter Three

Emory wiped her hands on the kitchen towel, a smile on her face. "What does this one say?" She glanced over her shoulder at her aunt, who held a letter in her hand.

"I'm opening it." Aunt Ruthie was aglow. "More sweet nothings… I hope."

Emory stooped to scoop Frosty up and into her arms. He'd been curled up between Emory's feet on the thick mat while she was washing dishes. Since he'd come home, he seemed keen on keeping her within his line of sight. Emory didn't mind one bit—even if she did have to take extra care not to step on him.

"Isn't it sweet that Aunt Ruthie has an admirer, Frosty?" she asked, dropping a kiss on top of his head. Since Frosty's arrival, Emory had developed a new tone. Aunt Ruthie called it her "baby voice" as it was higher pitched and more singsong than anything. She'd never, ever talked to anyone or anything this way before. But, with Frosty, there was no helping it. He was her baby. It was that simple. "Any ideas who it could be?"

Frosty stared up at her with his bulgy brown eyes, the floof-topped white tail wagging frantically.

"Oh, we have plenty of ideas." Aunt Ruthie opened the plain business envelope.

Which was true. After the arrival of the first letter, Aunt Ruthie had pulled out her yellow legal tablet and pen and made a long list of all the single men she knew of here in the Granite Falls area.

Colonel Anthony Jimenez was on the top of Aunt Ruthie's list. In a way, it made sense. He did spend one weekend a month at their bed-and-breakfast instead of staying with his sister and her family. He said it was because he liked having his privacy, but Emory had spied the older gentleman shooting her aunt openly appreciative looks.

Then there was Benny Myers. Emory had only met the man once—at the grocery store. He seemed nice enough, but she hadn't picked up on anything that would warrant the swoon-worthy poems and notes that had started appearing a little over a week ago.

Simon Wurz was another candidate. He was a retired professor who liked to come to breakfast on Sunday if their bed-and-breakfast wasn't full. Emory liked him. He was soft-spoken and quiet, and generous with his praise for her cooking. But he'd always seemed more interested in her food than anything or anyone else— Aunt Ruthie included.

Even though Aunt Ruthie had listed *all* the bachelors in Granite Falls, she'd immediately dismissed several of them for being closer to Emory's age. The Dawson brothers, Trace and Jesse, for example. Even if they were into *older* women, Aunt Ruthie felt confident her age was above their limit. Dean Hodges, a good man, was also too young. And since Dean's mother, Penny, was Aunt Ruthie's friend, it would be sort of weird. Dougal McCarrick was immediately dismissed because he was too young, plus neither she nor Ruthie could imagine the man writing such prose.

Ruthie was going to save the list for Emory—for when she was ready to think about dating again. Emory hadn't said a word. Her aunt meant well, but she couldn't imagine ever being interested in dating again.

"Oh, my. Are you ready? It's a poem this time." Aunt Ruthie sat back in the kitchen chair, pressing one hand to her chest.

Emory sat in an opposite chair, Frosty in her lap. "I can't wait." It was true. Whoever her aunt's secret admirer was, the notes and poems had certainly added a sense of excitement to their relatively quiet days.

Aunt Ruthie cleared her throat and began to read. "'I saw a shooting star last night. It raced across the sky, so bright. And when I laid my head to rest, my wish for you was to have the best. If darkness weighs upon your heart, I'll wish you light and a bright new start. If sadness pulls forth your tears, I'll wish you peace to ease your fears.'" Aunt Ruthie sighed. "'And if life brings you to the ground, I'll wish you my strength until yours can be found.'"

Emory pressed another kiss to the top of Frosty's head, her heart pounding in response to the words. "That's lovely."

Ruthie nodded, reading over the page again. "I think this is my favorite."

"I'm pretty sure you said that about the other two." Her aunt's eyes remained on the page as she spoke.

But Emory did like this one the best. It was deeper than the other two, more soulful. Even though the note wasn't meant for her, it was oddly encouraging.

Aunt Ruthie stood, folding the letter and tucking it back into the envelope. "Goodness." She shook her head. "I need to see if I can catch the mailman, Buford. See if he's seen anyone poking around in our mailbox…" She froze, eyeing the envelope. "Oh dear."

"What?" Emory saw the surprise on her aunt's face.

"Well, Buford's single." Ruthie frowned. "I never stopped to consider… That is to say, he's such a curmudgeon." She shook her head. "No, no, it wouldn't be Buford." Another head shake. "It *can't* be Buford."

She smiled. "It can't be? Or you don't want it to be?"

"Both." Ruthie smiled. "That man has been a thorn in my side since… Well, since I moved here." She patted her too-tall hair.

"I can ask him," Emory offered. "We were going to take a walk around the block. Weren't we, Frosty?"

Frosty was all wiggles then.

"Fine." Aunt Ruthie nodded. "You can handle the old codger."

Ten minutes later, Emory and Frosty were taking a leisurely stroll around their block. So far, no sign of Buford. She might have to wait to grill the elderly mailman when they took their walk tomorrow. Buzz had told her getting regular exercise would help Frosty grow steadier on his three paws. So far, Emory had seen little to indicate her brave pup was struggling. Or maybe his overall happy disposition led her to believe he was faring better than he was.

"Is that it?" she asked, stopping so Frosty could give a patch of grass a thorough sniffing. "Are you being brave for me?"

Frosty was too enraptured with whatever scent he'd unearthed to answer.

She was frowning down at the dog when she heard someone coming. She glanced up, looking for Buford Heinz and finding Dougal McCarrick, Willow and a small black dog that could have been Frosty's sibling.

Frosty's frenzied yip-bark was all excitement.

Willow's long tail wagged in greeting while the little black dog yapped back with such force, all four paws seemed to bounce off the sidewalk with each raspy bark.

"Gertie." Dougal was smiling at the little dog. "You be nice."

Gertie's tail wag was hesitant.

"Hi," Emory said, lifting a hand in greeting as the three dogs circled and sniffed and circled some more.

"Emory." Dougal tipped his cowboy hat at her. It was an old-fashioned gesture but, from Dougal, it didn't seem out of place. "Nice day."

"It is." She nodded, then asked, "I don't suppose you saw Buford? The mailman?"

He shook his head. "Need something?"

"Not really. My aunt had a question for him." She watched as Frosty and Gertie went around each other at least six more times. "You keep that up and you two are going to get dizzy."

Dougal's chuckle was warm and soft.

She glanced at the hulking cowboy, studying him. There was something different about him. But what? "Is Gertie your dog, too?"

"She was my brother's." He shrugged, his words slow and measured. "But he's a first-time father now. Triplets."

"Wow." Emory blinked. "That... I can't imagine... Wow." Three babies. So much to love and cherish. The familiar grip of pain felt tighter than normal. Miscarrying at twenty-two weeks was unusual—and devastating. "I don't blame you, Gertie."

"Don't like kids?" Dougal asked, his brown eyes sweeping over her face.

"I do." She swallowed around the lump in her throat. "I meant that Gertie probably misses getting special treatment—and quiet. And you and Willow are very... quiet." She paused. "I mean... Compared to triplets."

He nodded.

She couldn't read his expression. Dougal McCarrick was one cool character. Which was the exact opposite of how she'd been every time she'd run into the man. At least this time, she wasn't on the verge of tears. Which reminded her. "I need to get your handkerchief back to you."

Those brown eyes held hers. "No rush."

"Well... Still, it was kind of you." She took a slow breath, shifting her gaze to the dogs. "I need to wash it but, maybe, you and the girls can stop by the bed-and-breakfast tomorrow? To pick it up?" Was she making too big a deal out of this? When it came to handkerchief etiquette, she was at a loss. "If it's convenient, that is? Aunt Ruthie told me McCarrick Ranch is a bit out of town." She glanced his way.

He nodded, his gaze still heavy on her.

She really wished she had some inkling as to what the man was thinking. It was possible he was waiting for her to burst into tears again. "Yes, tomorrow is convenient? Or, yes, you live outside of town?"

"Both." That crooked grin was back.

"Oh. Okay." She turned her attention back to the dogs. "Bring the girls, too. I know Frosty would be happy to have a doggie playdate." Frosty's tail said as much. "If you have time, that is. I imagine he's bored with just me and Aunt Ruthie."

After a pause, Dougal surprised her by asking, "The cats taking to him?"

He remembered Aunt Ruthie had cats? "They mostly ignore him. Which is better than chasing him or being mean to him, I suppose. But I can't help but worry he's lonely." Seeing him excited and playful now, she hoped she was doing right by the little dog. After all, she had no idea what being a good dog owner entailed. The only thing she did know was that she loved the little dog, and she wanted him to be happy.

"Don't worry about that, Emory." The gentleness of Dougal's voice had her looking back up at him.

"I'm a worrier." Her throat went tight. "I worry about everything. Overthink everything." Why had she said that out loud—and to him? She was not going to get emotional again. She wasn't. He was going to think there was something seriously wrong with her. Not that his opinion of her should matter all that much.

Still, he'd been nothing but kind and patient with her—and she appreciated it. She liked that his dogs liked her dog. He'd helped her with Frosty and visited the vet hospital and offered up his handkerchief while sitting on the cold floor of the vet clinic next to her. Aunt Ruthie said his reputation was that of a gentleman. Emory tended to agree.

He was big, with the potential to be intimidating. But

his brown eyes held nothing but…warmth. *A lot like Willow.* The comparison made her smile. Her gaze traveled over his face long enough for her to realize what was different about him. "You shaved off your beard." And… Dougal McCarrick was handsome.

"I did," he murmured, the words thick. And, damn, but he liked that she noticed. Too much. Not that her noticing meant a thing… It didn't.

But the frown on her face suggested she might not like the new look.

Aunt Nola doesn't know what she's talking about and I'm a damn fool. He ran his hand along his bare jaw again feeling exposed.

Still, it was a surprise that she'd noticed he was clean-shaven. He'd begun to think he was invisible to her. About five days ago, he'd seen her at the grocery store with Ruth, but she'd stared right through him. A couple of days after that, he'd passed her leaving the vet clinic with Frosty—and she'd walked past him. And today? If he hadn't walked up to her or Frosty hadn't alerted her to their arrival, chances are he wouldn't have been a blip on her radar.

He didn't know what made Emory Swanson stick in his mind, but she was. Stuck. Popping up in his dreams and throughout the day—oftentimes at the worst opportune moment. That was why he had walked up to her today. He'd seen her. By the time he'd reached her side, his skin was clammy, his pulse was all over the place and he was wondering what the hell he'd been thinking.

This was why he'd started writing her notes and poems. This, right here. Locking up. Losing his words.

Staring at her. The chances of him verbalizing anything remotely resembling what he could say on the page was zero. An impossibility.

The whole thing was ridiculous and he knew it. He was a grown man, not some teenager passing notes in class. But, through his letters and notes, he'd hoped to offer her what he couldn't vocalize: encouragement and support.

He wasn't expecting anything in return. That's not what those notes were about. All he wanted was for her to know she wasn't alone. He hoped knowing someone saw and respected her struggles to overcome whatever internal demons she was wrestling was a comfort. And she was struggling—he knew it—saw it every time he looked into her big blue eyes. Hell, even in memory, he saw it—felt it. And every damn time that need to defend her rose up, words came spilling out onto the page. Maybe his notes would help?

Or maybe I'm delusional?

He was still wracking his brain for something to say when Buford Heinz walked around the corner, distracted by the mail in his hands, and almost plowed into Emory. Dougal reached for her and pulled her out of the man's way. "Buford, watch where you're going."

Buford's head popped up. "Dougal. Ma'am." He stared down at the web of dog leashes. "Well, lookie there. Might have tripped on them."

Dougal shook his head. "Or run into the lady."

"Did I?" Buford frowned.

"No. It's fine." Emory smiled up at Dougal. "Thank you." For a split second, that smile overshadowed the lingering grief in her eyes.

Dougal managed a nod, then tore his gaze from her. He took a steadying breath, watching as Gertie continued to inspect an unbothered Frosty while Willow sat, calm as ever. He could take a lesson from his dog. Calm. That's what he needed to be. He took another deep breath.

"No harm was done." Emory tucked a strand of her blond hair behind her ear. "My aunt asked me to come looking for you."

"Why's that?" Buford Heinz's expression grew pinched. "Something get mixed up? Package missing or something?"

"No. Nothing like that." Emory hesitated before asking, "Have you happened to see anyone around the mailbox at the bed-and-breakfast? Aunt Ruthie has received a couple of letters, but there's no names or addresses anywhere on them."

Wait, what? Her *aunt* had received a couple of letters? Until now, he'd just assumed they'd know the letters he'd left were for Emory. Miss Baumgarten was a fine-looking woman, he supposed, but wasn't she a little old to be getting love letters? *Apparently not.*

"Ruth Baumgarten?" Buford scratched the back of his head. "What sort of letters? Threatening ones? That's against the law, you know. We can call the sheriff—"

"No." Emory held up her hand. "Not threatening. Very nice, actually. Encouraging."

Dougal smiled down at Willow. That was nice to hear. It'd be nicer if she knew those words were meant for her—not her aunt.

"Is that so?" Buford adjusted his cap. "I've not seen anyone loitering, but I'll keep my eyes peeled. Only the homeowner and an official employee of the US Postal Service should be putting hands on your mailbox." He frowned. "Chaps my hide the way people go around breaking all the rules."

"I don't think any harm was meant—" Whatever Emory was going to say was cut off as Buford Heinz kept on railing.

"This is why folk are using those new-fangled mailboxes with the locks. So no one can tamper with their mail." Buford shifted the strap of his mailbag on his shoulder. "Or get in their business. It's a violation of privacy, that's what this is."

Dougal was having a hard time not laughing at the whole exchange.

"You tell me if this keeps up, you hear?" Buford shot Emory a look.

"Yes. You're not... That's to say... Those letters aren't from you?" She seemed to be bracing herself.

Buford? Dougal was stunned. Buford Heinz didn't have a creative word in his head. Granted, Ruth and Emory were new to the area but still. Buford? Dougal was trying not to be offended. He was no poet laureate, but he'd attended a handful of cowboy poet retreats to know he had some talent—and he had a few poems published that proved it.

"From me?" The man looked offended. "No, ma'am. What would I have to say to your aunt besides, 'Here's your mail' or 'Can you sign for this?'" Buford frowned. "Now if there's nothing else, I've got a route to finish."

"No, that's all. Thank you." Emory's smile wavered.

Dougal couldn't stop the chuckle that slipped out as

soon as the older man had rounded the corner at the other end of the block.

"You know, I believe him. He is *not* the letter writer." Emory smiled up at him. She let the little dog lead her, trotting, back toward the bed-and-breakfast. "I'll have to tell Aunt Ruthie to take Buford off the list."

Which brought Dougal up short. "List?" But Gertie pulled on until Dougal caught up, the little dog determined to stay alongside Frosty.

"My aunt wants to figure out who her secret admirer is. She's made a list of all the single men in the area— men that might be writing her notes." She paused and glanced his way. "You were on it but, don't worry, she's decided you're too young to be her secret admirer."

Her announcement was such a surprise, Dougal was laughing all over again. If only they knew... "Glad to hear it."

"It's very sweet." Emory sighed, pausing for Frosty to investigate a pile of leaves. "Someone out there thinks enough of my aunt to want to put a smile on her face. She's shared them with me and they make me smile, too. It's like the writer knows what I need to hear... Even if they're for my aunt." The look she shot him was almost embarrassed.

As nice as it was to hear his notes were having the desired effect, this was not the way he'd wanted things to play out. For some reason, it mattered that Emory know those words were for her. He walked along beside her, the dogs taking their time nosing around in every patch of grass or bush as they went. Finally, he asked, "Earlier you said there were no names on the letters? But your aunt's name is?"

"I'm not sure..." Emory shot him a confused look. "They're coming to her house, who else would they be for?"

He paused and looked at her. "Well...you live there, too, don't you?"

She blinked, then laughed. "Yes, but... No." She shook her head. "No way."

He blew out a long, slow breath. Why was she so quick to dismiss the idea?

"Aunt Ruthie is so full of life. She's funny and pretty, smart and witty. It makes sense." She paused outside the wrought-iron front gate of the bed-and-breakfast. "She deserves a secret admirer." Her blue eyes bounced from him to the gate. There was that look again. Wounded and sorrowful.

What made her think she didn't deserve a secret admirer?

"This little guy could probably use a nap now." She opened the gate, the squeak loud and grating enough to make them both wince. All three dogs tucked their tails and their ears drooped.

He nodded at the gate. "I'll bring some grease tomorrow."

Emory led Frosty through the gate and closed it behind them. "Tomorrow?"

He shook his head. She'd forgotten already?

"Oh, tomorrow. Your handkerchief. And the doggy playdate." She smiled at the dogs sniffing one another through the wrought-iron pickets. "If you come around ten, there will be fresh-baked scones. I make delicious scones."

"Will do." He didn't have the foggiest of ideas how

he was going to get away from the ranch at ten in the morning, but he'd figure something out.

She stooped to unleash Frosty's collar, then stood and waved. "Bye, Willow. Bye, Gertie. I'll have a treat for you two, as well." With another wave, she walked up to the bright green door of the bed-and-breakfast where she and Frosty disappeared inside.

Gertie barked, her nose wedged between two of the wrought-iron pickets. Willow only stood, staring at the front door, her tail wagging.

"We'll be back soon." Dougal whistled softly, the two dogs instantly at his side, before heading down several blocks and onto Main Street.

He had a lot to ponder but, for now, it'd be smart to put all thoughts of Emory aside. He was meeting Trace Dawson for lunch. Trace was a good friend but that didn't mean he'd pass up an opportunity to give Dougal grief over...whatever this was that he'd gotten himself into. Grief he deserved. He'd been the fool trying to play secret admirer. Since Ruth Baumgarten thought those notes were for her, he couldn't even get that right. If it wasn't so embarrassing, it'd be hilarious. Eventually, maybe. For now, there was no way—no way—he was telling anyone anything about this. If he was smart, he'd cut his losses and stop with the letters. But he couldn't shake the feeling that Emory needed them. *Dammit. That means I get to keep on playing the fool.*

Chapter Four

Emory lay staring up at the reclaimed barnwood ceiling of her little carriage house. Aunt Ruthie had renovated the place after her last husband's passing—the man she'd moved to Granite Falls for six years ago. The Baumgarten Bed-and-Breakfast had been in the Baumgarten family for years, and Ruthie was determined to honor the family legacy. As such, she'd renovated the carriage house so that when "she was no longer able to run the place herself," she'd have a home ready and waiting for the innkeeper she'd have to hire.

For now, Emory called the lovingly renovated and artfully restored two-bedroom, two-bath carriage house her home. After losing so much, she'd struggled to find her footing in the place she and Sam had shared a life. Being here, someplace far removed, helped. Her grief didn't care that she and Sam had only been married for a year; its vise grip was only just beginning to ease. Aunt Ruthie said it wasn't the quantity of time together that mattered but the quality. Like she and Sam, Aunt Ruthie had only had her Lawrence Baumgarten for a handful of years. Lawrence had been a delightful man. He'd made Aunt Ruthie laugh all the time, considered her his partner in all things and loved her without reservation. Which was what she'd hoped for with Sam.

Not that it had turned out that way.

Frosty, sleeping deeply against her side, wriggled and snorted, his front two paws digging at whatever he was chasing in his dream.

Emory smiled and rested a hand against the little dog's belly.

Frosty stilled, the blankets moving as his tail began to wag, before he opened his eyes and stared up at her.

"Good morning, baby boy," she murmured.

Frosty scooched up the blanket until he could rest his chin on her chest.

"How are you?" She scratched him behind the ear.

Frosty grunted, his eyes closing as he leaned into her hand.

She smiled. In the week since Frosty had come to live with her, life had seemed easier—less hollow. "You did that, don't you know? You and those eyes and that tail of yours." Emory hadn't realized it was possible to love an animal this much. "But I'm so glad you came along for me to love."

The alarm went off, the trilling sound of wind chimes flooding the bedroom.

Frosty stood, stretched and waited.

"I can't snooze you, can I?" She sat up and smothered a yawn with one hand. That was the one thing about being a pet owner—no more sleeping in. Not that she minded. After all, a new letter might be waiting in the mailbox. "I guess we'll have to go see, won't we?"

After she'd let Frosty out to do his morning business, she put food in his bowl, then took a shower. Every morning she was grateful for her aunt's attention to detail. Heated towel racks and floors, an oversize glass shower with waterfall showerhead or, if Emory was inclined, she could soak in the massive claw-foot tub. The bathroom was a much-needed mini oasis that she took advantage of as often as possible.

She dried her hair, pulled on a black sweater and red-and-green pants, put on her red tennis shoes and opened the door for Frosty. "Time for work." After a quick trip to the mailbox.

As soon as they stepped outside, Frosty sounded the alarm.

"What is it?" Emory asked, peering into the early morning darkness.

Beneath the bright LED front porch light, she saw the fur between Frosty's shoulders stood straight up. Plus his growl, a growl she'd never heard him make before, had his whole little body vibrating.

"Frosty?" She soothed. "It's okay. It's probably just a raccoon or a possum." Hopefully it was a possum or raccoon. Neither were cause for alarm but, she supposed, a dog wouldn't know that. To be safe, she scooped Frosty up.

"I've been called a few things but never a raccoon or possum." A man stepped forward. He stopped beneath one of the old-fashioned streetlamps that lined the path from the carriage house to the bed-and-breakfast. She couldn't make out his face, but he wore jeans and boots and a thick khaki-colored coat to stave off the chill in the air. "I didn't mean to startle you."

Emory paused. After living so long in Dallas, her immediate impulse was to panic. But, she reminded herself, this wasn't Dallas and this man was probably a local she didn't know. After all, she hadn't exactly made an effort to get to know the good people of Granite Falls.

"Let's start again. Good morning." He leaned against the lamp post. "My name is Lucas. Lucas Baumgarten."

That caught her full attention. "Baumgarten?" Emory repeated.

"Yes, ma'am." He shook his head, sighing. "I'm Lawrence's son."

What? Lawrence had a son? As far as she knew, Lawrence didn't have any family. Why had she never heard of him?

"But you...you can't be Ruth." He walked closer, stopping beneath the light just outside the white picket fence that lined the carriage house's small yard.

"No. Ruth is my aunt." She adjusted a still growling Frosty. "It's okay," she murmured. Was it? This whole meeting felt...off.

"I'm guessing you didn't know about me?" He sighed again. "I can't blame him. The last words I ever said to him were spiteful and mean." His tone was gruff and low, edged with something Emory recognized. "It's a regret I have to live with... But I do, regret it, so much. And now that he's..."

Emory's heart twisted. She knew that feeling—the crushing weight of regret and frustration of things left unsaid and wounds left to fester.

"I don't know why I'm here, really." His laugh was forced and brittle. "Homesick, I guess." He stared at the large house. "It being the holidays and all. I grew up here and there's so many memories—good and bad—tucked in each and every corner of that place. But you know what they say, you can't go home again."

She was torn. She didn't know this man or the extent of what had transpired between him and Lawrence so inviting him in didn't feel right. Whatever happened next was her aunt's decision, not hers. "Why don't you give me your phone number and I'll have my aunt call you?"

"I'd appreciate that, Miss…"

"Emory. Emory Swanson." She shushed Frosty. The dog's growl lowered, but it didn't stop.

"Seems to me you've got a capable protector, there." He nodded at Frosty as he dug around in his coat pocket. "My number's on there." He pulled out a business card and handed it to her.

She walked to the gate, Frosty's growl rising once more. "I'll make sure she gets it." She took the card, angling her body so the dog didn't decide to go all heroic and take a nip at the man.

"Like I said, I appreciate it. More than you know." He smiled.

Up close, Emory could make out the man's features. Oh, goodness, was he ever handsome. Ridiculously so. The kind of face that made a person look twice. "No problem." She tucked the card into her pocket.

"I'll let you get on with your day, then." He turned and walked down the stone path that led to the gate at the back of the property.

Frosty barked twice, no less outraged than he'd been when they stepped foot outside.

"Yep, you did it." She hugged the dog close. "You were so ferocious, you scared him off."

Frosty snorted and gave her two slobbery doggy kisses.

"My hero." She dropped a kiss on the dog's nose and set him down, hurrying to the back door that led into the bed-and-breakfast kitchen. "What do you think Aunt Ruthie is going to say about him?" She opened the door, closed it behind Frosty, turned on the light and pulled the business card from her pocket.

"Lucas Baumgarten. Finance and Investments Analyst." She scanned the number and email address.

Considering how close she and her aunt were, it was odd she'd never heard about Lawrence's son. Then again, it was odd that Lawrence's son hadn't come to the funeral. Regrets or no, wouldn't he have come to pay his respects to his father? It was hard to imagine something horrible enough to prevent that. Did Ruthie know he existed? Was it a good thing that Lucas had shown up or bad? Why had she volunteered to be the one to tell Ruthie her stepson was here? And how, exactly, was she going to tell her aunt? Scenarios played through her mind as she prepped and cooked the morning's breakfast. She'd pulled the gingerbread coffee cake from the oven and arranged the sugar plum cheese Danish on a green glass tray when her aunt walked finally into the kitchen.

"Good morning." Ruthie was a morning person. When she walked into a room, she brought the sunshine with her. "And how is my favorite niece and chef?"

Frosty barked.

Aunt Ruthie giggled. "Right. And her baby pup?"

Frosty's tail wagged and he spun in a circle.

"Such a good boy. Did you get the mail?" Aunt Ruthie offered Frosty his good morning treat.

With all the commotion, she'd completely forgotten. "I haven't."

"I'll get it in a while." Her aunt took a deep breath. "Goodness, everything smells delicious. I don't think Mrs. Claus could rival your holiday treats."

Emory shook her head. "Don't say such things. I don't want to wind up on Santa's naughty list."

Aunt Ruthie laughed. "Not a chance, darlin'."

Emory then blurted out, "I had a visitor this morning. Outside the carriage house."

Aunt Ruthie frowned. "From the look on your face, I'm assuming you're not telling me about a romantic tryst?"

"No." Her cheeks went hot. "That's funny." She took a deep breath and went on. "He said his name is Lucas Baumgarten. And that he's Lawrence's son." She handed her aunt the business card.

Aunt Ruthie's face went absolutely blank as she read over the card. "Gracious me."

Emory waited, watching her aunt. "Did…did you know about him?"

"Of course. Lawrence and I had no secrets but… Well, to hear him talk about his son, there was no fixing the hurt between them." Aunt Ruthie perched on one of the two bar stools around the oversize kitchen island. "And now, he's here." Her brows knitted together, her pink lips pressing into a flat line. "What did he want?"

Emory shrugged. "He said he was homesick. He said he had a lot of regrets."

Aunt Ruthie sighed. "I'm sure he does." She tapped the card on the marble top, then tucked it into her pocket. "I'll worry about that after all the guests have checked out. I suppose it's a good thing he arrived today." Since today was Monday, the bed-and-breakfast would be closed the next two days—meaning there would be time to deal with this new development. "Right." With a pat of her towering hair, Ruthie slipped off the bar stool and left the kitchen.

Emory glanced at Frosty, then back at the door. "She's upset."

But Frosty did a little dance by the back door, his three sets of claws clacking against the tile as he spun and whimpered.

"Okay, okay." She opened the back door. "Let's go." She followed him down the three steps and into the back garden. Amid the cobblestone paths and now dormant rosebushes, Aunt Ruthie had placed benches for cuddles and kisses while enjoying the great outdoors. Emory found one of those and sat while Frosty nosed around for the perfect spot to tinkle. Even with the sun rising, she couldn't shake off the unease in her stomach and the chill in the air.

At 10:00 a.m. sharp, Dougal parked along the street in front of the bed-and-breakfast. He grabbed the can of grease and stepped aside so Willow and Gertie could jump down from the truck.

He eyed Gertie—who was bouncing around excitedly. "Behave."

Gertie sat, both ears cocked up, the picture of innocence.

"Uh-huh." But he grinned.

Gertie was on the small side and the triplets were, unintentionally, rough from time to time. He didn't fault the little dog for hiding from them as it was a matter of self-preservation. And since he didn't want the dog to feel neglected, he'd taken to toting her along with Willow when they were out and about. If Angus noticed, he didn't say a thing. But, then, his brother was corralling three toddlers and doting on his wife so, as far as excuses went, Dougal didn't fault him, either.

"And no barking," he said, hands on his hips.

Gertie cocked her head to one side but stayed seated.

"All right, then." He opened the squeaky front gate, let the dogs through and pulled it closed behind him. "Definitely got to fix that."

He'd barely stepped foot on the wide wraparound porch, when the front door opened.

"Right on time." Emory stepped out, her light blue eyes bright and a smile on her full lips. "Good morning."

The sudden tightness of his throat caught him by surprise. "Morning." He sort of growled the word at her. Which caused Emory and both dogs to regard him with odd expressions. He cleared his throat, warmth sneaking up his neck and into his cheeks.

"It's such a pretty day, I thought we could sit outside." She pointed at one grouping of wicker rockers, a porch swing and a table. "You get to be the guinea pig for a new scone recipe. While you're sampling it, the dogs can play."

He nodded, not trusting himself to speak yet.

She hesitated, those blue eyes of hers lingering on his face before she said, "Then I'll go get the scones. Be right back." And she disappeared inside the house.

Well, that was awkward. He took off his cowboy hat and ran his fingers through his hair. *Breathe. Attempt conversation. I can do this.* He walked to one of the rocking chairs but couldn't sit. The dogs followed, standing, staring at him, their tales wagging. "What?" He rubbed his clammy palms against his denim-clad thighs and took a deep breath. *Act normal.* He shifted from foot to foot, then walked across the wooden porch to lean against the white painted railing.

She was right about the weather. The sun had taken the sting out of the morning's chill, leaving a mild breeze and a bright, clear sky. Light blue. Like Emory's eyes. He sighed, spinning his hat in his hands.

Willow stood in a sunbeam, sat, then slid down to her stomach on the wooden porch. Gertie turned in numerous circles, reverse direction, then flopped down beside Willow—but her little grunt said she was anything but happy about it.

He was on the verge of sitting when the front door opened and Emory backed out, carrying a large tray. A tray that seemed awfully laden down and weighty for someone as petite as Emory. He hurried forward. "Allow me."

"I've got it." Emory maneuvered around him. "As long as Frosty doesn't get underfoot, that is."

Frosty, however, was a blurred white streak heading down the porch toward the two dogs sunbathing. He let out a bark-yip when he reached them, prancing around on his three little legs.

Gertie popped up, yipped back and ran around Frosty in circles.

Emory was laughing when she slid the tray onto the table. "Looks like they're already fast friends." She wrapped her arms around her waist, entirely transfixed by the little dogs' joyful reunion.

Dougal was far more interested in the play of emotions on her face. Emory Swanson was a beautiful woman. Every time he'd seen her, he found something new to admire. At the moment, it was…her figure. He couldn't help it. The jean skirt she wore hugged her curves— curves he was mighty appreciative of. He wasn't one to get distracted by a woman's looks, so Emory had been— was—a sort of shock to his system. Whether this was a good thing or a bad thing, he'd yet to determine.

Gertie stooped, her tail wagging a million-times-a-second, then pounced.

Frosty swatted at her with one paw, then scampered down the length of the porch.

Gertie took off after him, the click-clack of their frantic paws the only sound as they rounded the corner and disappeared from sight.

"I'm with you." Emory spoke to Willow. "There's something soothing about the warm sun on your face." She sat in one of the well-padded rocking chairs. "Especially when there's a chill in the air."

Dougal took the opposite chair, wracking his brain for something *normal* to say.

Gertie tore past them, headed the opposite direction, with Frosty in hot pursuit. Willow lifted her head long enough to see the dogs' progress, yawned and return to dozing.

What qualifies as normal talk, anyway? The weather? They'd covered that, hadn't they?

Emory laughed. "Frosty will sleep well tonight." She turned, putting the two different types of scones on a plate and holding it his way. "Okay, I hope you're hungry." She pointed as she explained, "These are spiced eggnog scones and those are gingerbread scones. When I had my catering company, the gingerbread scones were a holiday must-have. Oh, right, the gingerbread scone has a maple glaze and the eggnog has an eggnog glaze."

He nodded and took the plate.

She lifted the stainless-steel coffeepot. "Do you take cream or sugar in your coffee?"

"No." He shook his head at the gruffness of his tone. "No, ma'am." He tried again. "Thank you."

She smiled at him.

Her smile had Dougal's grip tightening on the delicate plate and set his stomach on some sort of spin cycle.

She glanced between the plate and his face, still smiling.

He swallowed, hoping like hell she'd stop smiling or it was likely he'd choke on a scone—no matter how delicious they were. For fear of breaking the delicate Christmas plate, he set it on the table and took the coffee cup she offered.

"My aunt will be out shortly. She was the one that found the eggnog scone recipe." Emory nibbled on the end of an eggnog scone. "Hmm." She took a bite, chewed and swallowed. "Might be better to make these mini scones." She glanced at his untouched plate. "They are awfully sweet."

He cleared his throat and asked what, he hoped, was a relevant question. "You had a catering business?"

She nodded but her smile wavered. "Before..." Her gaze darted from him to the coffeepot to the plate of scones. "Not here, obviously." A deep breath. "In my..."

old life." She set the scone on the plate, brushed her hands together and clasped them in her lap.

His question had upset her. Instead of saying anything else and making things worse, he took a massive bite of eggnog scone. It was sweet, yes, and oh so delicious. He nodded. "Mmm." He kept chewing, dropping his gaze when a smile lit up her face. Choking was a very real possibility.

"Sorry I took so long." Ruth Baumgarten came onto the porch.

Gertie and Frosty came zooming around the far corner—having made two full circles around the house. At this point, they were going a little slower this time.

"Goodness me." Ruth pressed a hand to her chest. "They're like tiny canine tornadoes." She sat in the porch swing and sighed. "What's the verdict?"

"I think they're on the sweet side." Emory shrugged. "But Dougal seems to approve."

Dougal took a sip of coffee before sounding off. "Sweet, yes. But they taste like Christmas."

Ruth smiled. "Perfect." She served herself one and sat back against one of the red gingham print cushions lining the porch swing. "We have a Christmas menu, and the inside of the bed-and-breakfast is almost decorated. Now all we need is to break out the garland and lights for the fence. When they visit, I want our guests to feel like they're staying in one of those TV small-town holiday movies."

"I'm pretty sure you've succeeded, Aunt Ruthie," Emory said, smiling.

With a thundering of paws and all sorts of clicking,

Gertie and Frosty came skittering to a stop. They were both panting.

"Poor things." Emory stood. "I'll go get them some water." She was in the front door before either he or Ruth could respond.

"She's quite the little baker, isn't she?" Ruth savored her bite of scone. "Quite a chef, actually. I worry she'll feel stifled being here, cooking for just me and my guests. But I think, for now, it's just what she needs."

Dougal had no response for that, so he shoved the rest of his scone into his mouth.

"Dougal." Ruth poured herself a cup of coffee. "I have a question for you."

Dougal swallowed and drained his coffee cup. "Yes, ma'am?"

"We had a…surprise visitor. Emory did, actually. He was outside the carriage house this morning." She refilled his cup. "Did you know my Lawrence's son? Lucas?"

"Um…" The name was a jolt to the system. Dougal stared into the full cup of coffee, doing everything he could to rein in the anger rushing in on him. Did he know Lucas Baumgarten? Did he know the good-looking, smooth-talking asshat who had lived to stir things up, then sit back and watch as others were left to sort through the mess and try to recover? Even as a teen, Lucas Baumgarten had left a wake of destruction behind him. And no matter what he'd done, he always seemed to get away with it. Well, almost always…

"Yes, ma'am." He ground his jaws together, the muscle drawn so tight it hurt.

In fact, he knew Lucas Baumgarten a little too well.

And he knew he'd like to knock Lucas on his no-good ass. But Dougal's cousin Rory, the one Lucas had wronged the most, wouldn't want that. She wouldn't want him dragging up her past to near-strangers, either. Rory had moved on and left the pain and anger behind her to live a good life. She'd raised her smart and funny ten-year-old daughter, Allana, alone. Which was good because the girl's father—Lucas Baumgarten—denied Allana was his.

And it still ate at Dougal. Sure, it had been ten years, but he'd never forget. Rory had been sixteen years old: brokenhearted, terrified and humiliated. And Lucas? He'd had no problem tearing down Rory's reputation and turning his back on his child…

Some things are unforgivable.

Yes, he knew Lucas and he had nothing good to say about the man. But wasn't it his duty to warn Ruth? Should he tell her Lucas's charm was a cover? That his insides were rotten to the core? Ten years had passed but no amount of time would change that. After all, a leopard could not change his spots.

"Here you go." Emory came back onto the porch carrying a large bowl of water.

Dougal hopped up, then, grateful for the interruption. "I should go tend to that gate." He slammed his hat on his head, was down the porch stairs and across the yard before either woman could stop him.

Ruth's announcement had him reeling. Lucas had gone to live with his mother after the scandal with Rory. As far as Dougal had been concerned, good riddance. Rumor had it, Lawrence had been so gutted by his son's behavior that he'd sent him away hoping the boy would see the error of his ways, tell the truth and make amends. That hadn't happened. In all that time since, Lucas had never reached out to Rory—or come back to visit his father. He hadn't even shown up for his own father's funeral. Now, all of a sudden, the man shows up and was nosing around the place? Dougal didn't like it, not one bit. He sure as hell didn't want the man worming his way into Ruth or Emory's life. But he needed to clear his head and calm down before he decided what, exactly, to do about it.

Chapter Five

"There was something about the way he bolted out of here..." Aunt Ruthie sat in one of the kitchen chairs with her knee drawn up and into her chest, carefully painting her toenails a shade of bubblegum pink. "You might have noticed that Dougal McCarrick is on the stoic side so his reaction was...telling."

Stoic was the exact right word for Dougal. Except for when it came to his dogs. He adored those dogs—almost as much as the dogs adored him. It had been while she was watching him playing fetch with the dogs that her thoughts had taken an unwelcome turn. If he was that sweet with dogs he loved, she could only imagine how tender he'd be with a woman he loved. And that thought had stayed in her brain all night and into the morning—along with how handsome he was. The strong jaw. The thick, black hair and searing gaze. He might not be a talker, but there was a lot going on in those dark eyes of his...

What is wrong with me? Emory went back to rolling out cookie dough—with vigor. No more thoughts about anything other than her aunt's predicament. Her aunt needed her. "You're worried?"

Ruthie finished her pinkie toe and looked up at her. "I suppose I am. Lawrence rarely mentioned his son. All the stories that made him smile were from Lucas's childhood years—and those good memories ended with his high school years."

Emory stopped rolling the dough. "Did they have a falling out?"

"Not exactly." She shrugged. "Something happened, I don't know what, and Lawrence thought it'd be better if the boy went to live with his mother. He went and Lawrence never heard from his son again. No phone calls or letters—though Lawrence kept trying. He never failed to send Lucas a birthday card or a Christmas gift."

Emory had seen the hurt and regret on Lucas Baumgarten's face. It wasn't the sort of thing a normal person could fake. A professional con man or sociopath, maybe, but was that who Lucas was? At this point, there was no way of knowing. "Why do you think he's here?" That was the question. Why was he here and what did he want?

Ruth put the nail polish brush back in the bottle and screwed the lid shut. "I don't know, Emory. I honestly can't account for it. But, he's Lawrence's blood and it doesn't seem right to turn him away. This was his home before it was mine. He wants to visit and relive special memories, I can understand that." She sighed. "Regret is hard to live with. I'm sure he's got plenty of it where his father is concerned." She blew on her toenails, then said, "At least, I'd like to think so. I'd like to think he's eaten up with it—lost many a night's sleep, too." She giggled. "I know, I know, that's not nice."

"Aunt Ruthie." But she chuckled along with her aunt.

One of the things she'd always loved about her aunt was the fierceness of her love and protective nature.

"That sounded mean, but Lawrence was the sweetest soul that ever did live. I could tell how much he missed his son—how much he hurt. And anyone who hurt my Lawrence? Well, it's unconscionable." She sighed. "However... I'm old enough to realize there are two sides to every story *and* that people can grow and change." She stared at one of the framed photos of her late husband and smiled. "If I can somehow help this boy find peace over his father, I think Lawrence would be proud of me—I think he'd want that."

Emory came around the kitchen island and hugged her aunt.

"What was that for?" Her aunt hugged her back.

"I love you." She shrugged, her arms still wrapped around Ruth. "You're amazing. You've got the biggest heart."

"I have my moments." Ruth giggled. "Believe me, I've had my vengeful moments along the way. But all that's mellowed out over the years." She stopped, then shrugged. "Most of the time. You can ask your mother all about it."

Ruth was Emory's mother's younger sister—and, yes, Emory had heard a few tales about her aunt's "wild and reckless" youthful antics from her mother. But, even when she was using Aunt Ruthie's teen years as a cautionary tale, there'd been nothing but adoration in her mother's tones. Now that she'd come to live with her aunt, Emory felt the same. Ruth Baumgarten was an eccentric, no doubt about it. She'd been married five—no, six times, had no children, knew more about Dolly Parton and her music than any single person should and she loved everyone. It didn't matter where they came from or what sort of checkered past they might have, Ruth would give them a chance.

If her aunt hadn't invited Emory to visit, she didn't know where she'd be now. She'd struggled when she lost the baby but after Sam's death... She'd gotten out of bed every morning, walked, talked and gone through the motions, but she'd been more of a ghost than a person. After her parents' concern and hovering, Ruth's arrival had been the wake-up call she needed. Ruthie had acted like nothing was amiss. She didn't treat Emory like she was a fragile piece of glass—she treated Emory like a person with responsibilities to her company and employees. And to herself. It was Ruth who had given her a place to go when Emory knew she needed to start over again. "I appreciate all you've done for me."

"I love you, too, sweet girl." Ruthie leaned back to cup her cheek. "That's why I'm not too heartsick over the fact that my secret admirer is really your secret admirer."

Emory blinked. "What?"

Ruth pointed at the stack of mail. "See for yourself."

She stared at the mail but didn't move.

"It won't bite you, Emory. If anything, I think it'll put a smile on your face." She waved her toward the mail. "If my nails were dry, I'd get it and read it to you. Go on, now."

Emory did as she was told, sifting through the envelopes until she found the plain white business envelope that had become so familiar. A quick glance at her aunt and she pulled the paper from the opened envelope.

The sun rose high in the bright skies
It heated the earth and chased off the gloom
Like the warmth reflected in your blue eyes
Tempting the roses to give in to an early bloom
Smile on and share that comfort with all
You are not as alone as you may think
No matter what, we won't let you fall
Don't give up hope or let your spirits sink

Emory couldn't read the words out loud. This one seemed more personal than the others. Uplifting, as always, but there was also a plea here. As if the writer somehow knew that each day was a struggle.

"Blue eyes," Ruthie said, nodding at her. "You have blue eyes. I have brown eyes."

Emory scanned the note again. "That could have been a mistake."

"Maybe. Except I went back and read the others and there's not a single thing that indicates these are for me." Ruth was smiling. "I'm not disappointed, Emory. If anything, I'm more excited than ever. I've had more than my fair share of beaus and romance and love. You, sweet girl, have only experienced the tip of the iceberg."

Emory folded up the paper and slid it back into the envelope. "Who's to say it's not a woman writing this? A friend? It's not necessarily romantic."

"Emory Ann, how many women have you met since you've come to Granite Falls?" Ruth sat back in her chair, crossed her arms over her chest and cocked an eyebrow.

Emory sighed, thinking. "Skylar, at the vet hospital.

And… The cashier at the grocery store. What is her name?"

"Velma Smith?" Ruthie snorted.

"And all the guests." As soon as the words were out of her mouth, she realized that wasn't right. The guests came and went, and there was no postage on the envelope so… "Maybe you're writing them, Aunt Ruthie?" She arched her brows in return.

"Darlin', you've seen how busy I am. I love you but when I have a minute to myself, I'm asleep. I've learned a fifteen-minute nap can recharge the battery better than a cup of coffee."

Considering Ruth had thought the letters and poems were for her, that made no more sense than suggesting the guests.

"Well…" Ruthie slipped off the stool and hobbled, toes flexed upward, across the floor to the counter. She picked up her yellow legal tablet. "Now that we know this, we need to revise the list."

Which was the last thing she wanted to do. She didn't want to know who was writing them. If she knew, she'd have to do something about it. Right now, reading them, letting the words buoy and inspire her, was enough. More than enough. "Or we can embrace the mystery of it all. It's pretty obvious whoever is writing these wants to remain unknown."

Ruth frowned. "You can't be serious? You're not curious? You don't want to know who's sending you such lovely notes? I have to admit, these poems aren't your run of the mill poetry. I believe we're dealing with a real-life cowboy poet here."

"I'm sorry, what?" She glanced at the pet bed in the

corner. Frosty lay wedged between Loretta and Tammy. From this angle, it looked like he was covered in a fluffy calico-print throw. That the three of them had taken to one another warmed her heart.

"A cowboy poet. Oh, hon, it's a whole thing." Ruthie fanned herself. "Nothing like a strong, silent type pouring his heart out with such eloquence and emotion."

Cowboy poet, huh? She had something to research online tonight if her insomnia kicked in.

Ruthie was scanning her list. "Hmm… I guess we can put all these young men back on the list." She smiled at her niece. "But we have narrowed it down some."

"We have?" Emory went back to her cookie dough.

"Yes, ma'am. Buford Heinz." Ruthie winked, then burst into laughter.

"That's true. I guess that is something." She wasn't going to stop her aunt from sleuthing, but she wasn't going to get on board with it, either. Even if she found out who this secret admirer was, it wouldn't matter. Emory's heart was bogged down with guilt and regret and pain. That wasn't just going to go away. Not anytime soon. Moving on didn't seem right.

Dougal waited, watching his brother's face. The sun was high, the winter wind was crisp but bearable, and the birdcall was as soothing as ever. But there was nothing soothing about Lucas Baumgarten's return to the area. He'd had to tell Angus the man was here. Who knew what would have happened if his brother had run into the man on the street, unawares?

Angus tipped his cowboy hat back on his head, the muscle in his jaw working. He opened his mouth, then closed it, shifting in the saddle to get a better look at Dougal. "You tell Rory?"

Dougal shook his head. "No point dragging her into it if it can be avoided."

Angus nodded. "Makes sense he was snooping around the bed-and-breakfast in the dark—no telling what folks would do or say if they saw him back in town."

"I doubt he'll stick around too long." Dougal rested his hands on the pommel of his saddle, his gaze sweeping over the field of cattle below them. Riding the property always took the edge off. This place never changed—this land was in his blood. A few hours on horseback and he could solve most problems. Most. But not all.

"We can hope." Angus scratched at the red stubble along his jaw. "What do you think he wants? There's no doubt he wants something."

No doubt. And that's what ate at Dougal even more. "I didn't ask Ruth much of anything." He'd been too riled up to attempt any sort of information exchange. Whether it had been any further attempt at normal conversation or delving into the whys and the wherefores surrounding Lucas Baumgarten's sudden appearance. "We need to be on guard."

"He's not stupid enough to come sniffing around here." Angus's voice was sharp. "Trespassing in Texas is a shooting offense."

Dougal sighed, scowling at his brother. "Yeah, Rory would love that."

"I wouldn't do it. But I'd be mighty tempted."

It was a tempting idea—not that either of them would ever do such a thing. "I was thinking about watching out for Ruth and Emory. Lawrence isn't here to explain things. I'm betting they have no idea what's trying to slither into their home."

"I see where you're coming from but… We're basically strangers to them. Why would they give our word credence and not Lucas's?" Angus spat out the man's name.

"We can't do nothing. We can't let him come in and do who knows what?" Dougal didn't like it, not one bit. Thinking about that man charming Ruth—charming Emory—had him seeing red. "I won't do that. Ruth strikes me as a sentimental sort. She'll be easy prey for that son of a bitch." He swallowed against the tightness in his throat, his tone gruff as he went on. "Emory?" He cleared his throat. "She's too pretty for Lucas to ignore. Pretty and vulnerable. That woman's got more pain in her eyes…" He broke off, silently cursing himself. He'd done it now. The urge to protect the woman that filled up every free second of his time had overruled his sense of self-preservation. He'd shot off his mouth and now Angus knew that Emory was…different.

A look at his brother only confirmed his fears. Angus's shock was plain, right there, lining his face. His brows were high. His mouth was parted. Was he holding his breath?

Damn. It. All. Dougal growled. "Forget it." He applied gentle pressure to Finn and steered the horse down the steep rocky slope into the field below. The clop of Bram's hooves followed, his brother not far behind them.

The two brothers rode on in silence, but Dougal had no illusions. Angus wouldn't let this go. For a year, he and Savannah had tried to set him up with Savannah's twin, Chelsea. He liked Chelsea, he did, but she was all around too much for him. He enjoyed their friendship. But that was all they'd ever be. And since Chelsea outright laughed at the idea of settling down with any man, the only people remotely disappointed had been his family and Savannah.

If and when he decided he wanted a relationship, he didn't want his family involved. And he sure as hell didn't want some high drama affair. He wanted a friend first—someone he shared common interests with. Someone comfortable with long silences, enjoyed nature, dogs and, ideally, lit up when she saw him. How likely was it that he'd find that someone? He figured the odds were against him.

"We should talk to them." Angus cut into his thoughts. "Warn Ruth and Emory, I mean." Angus glanced his way. "But I don't want to think about the ass kicking Rory'll give us if she finds out we shared her tale of woe with folks outside of the family."

Back then, there'd been plenty of speculation about what happened, but once Lucas had gone to his mother and Rory had gone to her grandparents, talk had died down and the scandal swept aside.

Dougal chose his words with care. "Maybe she wouldn't get too worked up if she knew her story would prevent two women from being taken in by that bastard." Rory had a temper, but he'd never known his cousin to be unreasonable. "I could call her?" He sighed, tipping his hat forward into the wind. "Ask her permission?" It seemed the decent thing to do.

"I'll let you." Angus nodded. "And if she says no?"

"She won't." At least, he hoped not.

They rode on, getting a measurement on the length

of barbed wire that needed replacing and checking the water levels at two stock tanks before heading back to the barn. By the time the horses were turned out to pasture and the tack had been stored, Dougal started to relax. Maybe his brother would give him a pass on Emory.

"I gotta know." Angus stopped in his tracks and turned to face him.

Maybe not. Dougal crossed his arms over his chest and scowled. "You don't."

"Come on, Dougal, I can't just let this go." He was smiling.

"I'm betting you can."

"Nope." Angus chuckled. "You seem to have a vested interest in this Emory person."

"You seem to have an interest in getting punched." Dougal kept right on scowling.

Angus was laughing then.

"Keep it up." Dougal cracked his knuckles.

"Go ahead." Angus blew out a long breath, still grinning like a fool. "And you'll get to explain my black eye to Momma, Aunt Nola and Savannah."

Dammit. Angus had him there—and he knew it, too. It was like salt in a paper cut. Insult to injury.

"You like this woman? Emory? What's her last name?"

Dougal pressed his lips flat. He'd said too much as it was.

"I've heard she's working at the Baumgarten Bed-and-Breakfast as the cook—that she keeps to herself." Angus gave him a long look. "So the two of you have that in common."

Dougal took a deep breath.

"If she's a cook, that means she likes food. You like

food." He reached forward to slap Dougal's stomach. "Some might say a little too much." He grinned when Dougal's eyes narrowed. "So you two have that in common, too."

Dougal shook his head.

"It was bound to happen sooner or later, Dougal. Granite Falls is running out of bachelors. There's not much competition, so you might stand a chance." Angus was enjoying himself far too much.

"You're an ass, you know that?" As Dougal walked past his brother, he slammed his shoulder, hard, into Angus's, knocking his brother back a few feet. It was juvenile but gratifying all the same.

"I'm your brother. Pretty sure it's my duty to give you grief now and then." Angus jogged to catch up to him. "Sooo...you ask her out yet?"

Dougal ground his teeth together so hard, his back right molar hurt.

"That's normally the first step. You do something nice like give her flowers..." Angus came to a stop. "You... Well, damn... You grease the hinges on her front gate."

Dougal kept on walking, picking up the pace, but Angus still caught up to him. "Stop talking."

Angus burst out laughing again. "Come on, if roles were reversed, you'd be ripping into me."

Dougal stopped then. "I never teased you about Savannah..." Well, hell. That was the worst possible thing he could have said.

Angus was staring at him, open-mouthed and stockstill.

Dougal took the opportunity to escape. He headed back to the barn, hurried upstairs to his barn-dominium and locked the door behind him. He'd eat a peanut butter and jelly sandwich if it gave him a few seconds peace. But he heard a scratching sound that had him opening the front door. "Come on." He stepped back so Willow and Gertie could come inside. "Poor Gertie." He stooped and gave the little dog a scratch behind the ear. "You need an escape, too?"

He ate his sandwich on the couch, a dog snoozing on either side of him, and wished like hell he could rewind the last ten minutes. Why had he let his brother get to him? Still. After all these years, he should know better. Not only had he compared Emory to Savannah—his brother's *wife*, for crying out loud—he'd revealed just how important Emory was to him. And she was. More than he wanted to admit. If his brother knew about all the midnight deliveries he'd made to the Baumgarten Bed-and-Breakfast mailbox, he'd never hear the end of it. "Small mercies, I guess." He patted Willow.

Emory mattered. That was why he had a phone call to make. With any luck, Rory wouldn't drive down from Austin to kick his rear, she'd support him warning Emory. Something told him, deep down, that Emory had been hurt enough. If he could spare her more pain, he would.

Chapter Six

"This is Emory." She spoke into the old-fashioned phone mounted to the kitchen wall of the bed-and-breakfast. Her aunt stood close by, leaning in to hear.

"Emory, hello." The voice was cheerful. "My name is Savannah McCarrick. You don't know me, but I believe you know my brother-in-law, Dougal?"

"Yes." Why on earth was Dougal's sister-in-law calling?

"Dougal came home raving about the scones you made and mentioned that you used to run a catering company."

"Dougal raved about my scones?" It was hard to imagine Dougal raving about anything.

Aunt Ruthie grinned.

Savannah's laugh was light and breathy. "Well, Dougal said they were delicious. From Dougal, that's high praise."

Emory smiled. "That's nice to hear." But it didn't clear up why Savannah McCarrick was calling.

"I was wondering if you still catered?" She hurried on before Emory could stop her. "I have triplets. They're toddlers. They get into everything—I mean, everything. I'm lucky to wash my hair let alone cook a decent meal.

My mother-in-law and aunt-in-law are wonderful but—" her voice dipped low "—they're getting on in years and I'd love for them not to stress over anything."

Emory was getting more confused by the moment.

"Oops, let me back up. I'm throwing a Christmas party. A big one. My family is coming and, well, I want it to be a big, impressive thing that most of Granite Falls can attend. I found your old catering business online, Elegant Everyday Eats, and the reviews were amazing. So, I was hoping you'd consider catering this party for me?"

Emory sat. "Catering a party for your family?"

Aunt Ruthie clapped her hands.

"And most of Granite Falls, too." Savannah laughed. "I know there's not a lot of time and it's the holiday season, but I'm hoping you'll consider it. Otherwise, I'll have to deal with someone trendy and overpriced from Fort Worth that my parents pick."

"You should do it," Ruth whispered. "You'll do a better job than some down-the-nose catering snob."

It was the first time in a long time that Emory felt a spurt of enthusiasm. It was wonderful. "Well… Sure." Her mind opened an imaginary spreadsheet, collecting the information she would have needed when she'd been running her company. "Would you be interested in coming to the bed-and-breakfast? If you want to give me an idea of what you were thinking menu-wise, I can prepare a sampling here and we can discuss all the details."

The conversation lasted another ten minutes. Before it was all said and done, they'd exchanged contact information and agreed on a Wednesday evening sampling. Which meant she had two days to shop and cook up a storm.

"Well, that was something." Ruth scanned over Emory's notes. "We might have to make a trip into Flower Knoll or go to New Braunfels—it's likely to have everything you'd need. I'm not sure Granite Falls Family Grocery carries all this."

"I hadn't thought about that." Emory nodded. "Are you up for a drive?"

Ruth nibbled on her lower lip. "Well…actually… I invited Lucas over."

Emory forgot all about the shopping trip. "You did? When?"

Ruth glanced at the clock on the wall. "In about ten minutes. Just tea or coffee and some treats." Her gaze darted to Emory. "Would you mind if we went after his visit? We can use it as an excuse to keep it short."

"Of course." She nodded. There was no way she'd leave her aunt alone for this meeting—not that she'd say as much out loud. "What can I do?"

Emory put together a collection of her baked holiday cookies, breads, scones and mini cakes while Ruth made a pot of coffee. They were just setting the kitchen table when there was a knock at the door.

Ruth patted at her hair, looking more uncertain than Emory had ever seen her.

"I'll get it." Emory took her aunt's hands. "It'll be fine." She hoped so, for her aunt's sake. After a quick squeeze, she let go of Ruth and hurried to open the front door. "Hello, again."

"Miss Swanson." Lucas Baumgarten smiled.

Goodness gracious. The man was film star handsome. No, he was almost pretty. Gorgeous. Whatever. He was something to look at. "Mr. Baumgarten." She stepped back. "Come on in." She watched the man. Handsome or not, she wasn't about to let that put her at ease. Not yet. If her aunt needed protecting, that's just what she'd do.

Lucas stepped inside and paused. He stared around him, his face unreadable as he turned slowly—his gaze sweeping over every picture, rug, piece of furniture and lamp fixture. "It's changed some." He took a deep breath. "But, time does that." He shot her a quick smile.

Emory nodded.

"Lucas? I'm Ruth. Ruth Baumgarten." Her aunt stood just outside the kitchen at the end of the hallway. "Welcome home."

For a split second, the man's chin crumpled and his lips pulled down. The struggle was real. He was doing his best to keep it together, Emory could see it—feel it. The response was visceral and real and heart-wrenching. "It was. Once." He nodded.

"Come on in, won't you?" Ruth waved him forward. "There's an array of Emory's holiday baked treats and fresh coffee or tea." Her tone was warm.

Lucas smiled. "Thank you. That's kind of you. I hope I didn't cause too much trouble." He headed down the hall and followed Ruth into the kitchen.

Emory trailed after them. Her aunt wanted her to stay, so she would. But she had every intention of fading into the background so Ruth and Lucas could do and say whatever it was that needed doing and saying.

"Wow." Lucas stopped inside the kitchen. "This... well this is all new."

Maybe she was being a tad overprotective by watching every move or expression Lucas made, but she couldn't help it. She did her best to be discreet about it. Instead of sitting at the table, she gathered the tablet and pen with her notes from earlier. It was doubtful she'd be able to focus on making the long to-do list she needed to make, but it gave her something to look at besides Lucas Baumgarten's gorgeousness.

"Lawrence had the place updated a year or so before we met. He liked to say he picked out every knob, nail and piece of marble in the place. I think he did a good job." Ruth ran a hand along the marble countertop. "Because of that, it's like he's still here with me."

Lucas nodded but stayed silent. He sat in the chair Ruth indicated, took the cup of coffee she poured for him and let her pile up his plate with baked goods—but he remained quiet.

Once Aunt Ruthie had sat and taken a sip of her coffee, she asked, "What brings you to Granite Falls?"

It took effort, but Emory stopped herself from smiling. Leave it to Aunt Ruthie to lay it all out there—without much preamble.

To give the man credit, Lucas only sputtered a little on the coffee he was drinking. "Oh, well…" He patted his mouth with the green-and-red cloth napkin. "This year has been…tough. But sometimes it takes something tough to put things into perspective—make you take a step back and really look at your life."

Like before, Emory understood. It was Aunt Ruth's steady presence that had enabled Emory to step back and take a long look at the way she'd been living. Not living. More like existing. It had been eye-opening—and made her realize she'd needed to make a change.

"So far, my legacy isn't something to be proud of."

He paused, his gaze inspecting the kitchen. Finally, he said, "You can't wind back and fix the past. And you can't slow time down to savor what little you have left."

"The older you get, the faster time goes." Ruth cradled her cup between her hands, the steam rising up to coil and disappear.

Emory was still sifting through his words. What, exactly, did he mean when he said "what little you have left"? It was a rather odd thing to say... Almost ominous. She shook her head, mentally chastising herself. She'd been watching too many police procedural shows and crime dramas with her aunt. A normal person didn't sit down to coffee and then openly threaten someone. And, as awkward as all this was, it was a leap to assume that was what Lucas was saying.

She drew a snowflake doodle in the corner of the paper, reining in her thoughts.

So, what *did* he mean by that? Because it did mean something; she could tell.

Was he trying to hint that Ruth was aging? What would he gain by that? If he was hoping to get on her good side, that was one way to go about it. But that didn't make sense at all.

Or... She glanced at the man at the table. Could something be wrong with Lucas? He didn't look ill, but looks were oftentimes deceiving. Was he sick? Really sick? Was that why he was here, visiting his childhood home? Facing one's own mortality would be enough to want to set things right—where he could.

"When I left here, I was young and stupid and I lashed out at my father. I hate myself for it. My father was a good man. Honest and loyal."

Ruth nodded.

"Like you, I'd like to think he's left pieces of himself here. That's why I came." He sat back. "I spent a lot of time with him in his old workshop out back. He loved working on his cars—called them his babies. He taught me to love it, too." He shook his head. "I'm asking a lot but I guess… I was hoping I could spend a little time here. Ask you to tell me about his later years so I know he was happy. I need to come to terms with the past. Make peace with it." He looked at Ruth. "You have every right to say no. If you do—"

"Lucas…" Ruth reached out and lay her hand on his arm. "Son, this is your home. I know your father would welcome you home with open arms. How can I not do the same thing? We'll make a room up for you—"

"You don't have to do that." Lucas cut her off, covering her hand with his. "I don't mean to cause trouble or be an inconvenience."

"Well, I wouldn't have offered if it was either." She smiled. "I'll get the keys to the workshop for you. I'm sure he'd be tickled pink to know you wanted to make use of it."

Lucas shook his head, staring into his coffee cup. "I'm glad he had someone like you to love him, Mrs. Baumgarten. I'm glad he wasn't alone."

"He was the best part of every day. I'll tell you whatever you want to know about your father, bless him." She smiled at him. "And you can call me Ruth."

If this was what her aunt wanted, she'd support it. But she needed to know a whole lot more about him before she'd feel comfortable having the man around. Lawrence Baumgarten had been a good and loyal man. And since he wasn't here to protect Ruth, Emory would have to. She only hoped it wouldn't be necessary.

"I'm glad you called me. And I'm glad you and Angus didn't go off half-cocked and do something stupid." Rory laughed. "I didn't need the two of you defending my honor then and I don't now, okay?"

"Mmm-hmm." He'd no plans to do a thing to Lucas. With any luck, he wouldn't see or speak to the man before he left town.

"I appreciate you asking my permission."

Dougal rested one foot on the lower rung of the corral fence, watching the horses exploring their new home. "Angus was scared you'd find out and give us both an ass kicking."

Rory's answer was a laugh. "I'm flattered, but I'm not sure I could—now that you're both a foot taller than me and outweigh me by a good fifty pounds."

"What you lack in size, you make up for in spirit."

"When are you coming to visit me and Allana? It's been a while, you know. I figure you might need a break from the babies and Angus and Savannah still in their honeymoon period. I mean, I'm assuming they are. I guess it's hard when you've got three toddlers underfoot."

"They manage." Dougal snorted. The barn-dominium had come together in record time because of it. Now he had his own place, with all the bells and whistles and privacy he could want. "But I appreciate the offer. The door swings both ways—you're welcome here, too."

"It's hard to find time, isn't it?" She chuckled. "All right, I know we've both got work to do. I hope your little talk helps these women. As much as I'd like to think he's changed, I'd feel terrible if he somehow got the best of them because we stayed silent."

Dougal nodded. "I was hoping you'd feel that way." They said their goodbyes and Dougal slid his phone into his back pocket. He'd managed to avoid his brother since their morning ride, but there was no hope for it. His fridge was empty and his stomach was growling so it was off to the main house. "Come on, girls," he said to Willow and Gertie.

He opened the back door, let the dogs in and heard, "Unca Doo, pay."

Tabitha waved her stuffed sheep toy at him. "Pay, peez."

"Yes, ma'am, Tabby-cat." He hung his cowboy hat on one of the hooks by the back door and crossed the great room to his niece.

Henry lay flat on his back, sound asleep, with a building block in one hand and plastic dinosaur in the other. Aunt Nola sat in the recliner, her head back and her snores on par with a growling bear. Emilia didn't seem to mind, though. She was flipping through one of their many board books, completely absorbed.

"Playing on your own, Tabby-cat?" he asked.

Tabitha grinned. "Pay?" She held out another stuffed animal. A fluffy hedgehog.

"Isn't this a dog toy?" he asked, pressing the sides.

The toy squeaked and both Gertie and Willow headed straight for the toy. Luckily Tabitha thought it was hilarious and burst into laughter.

"Silly dogs." He loved to hear his nieces and nephew laugh.

"Siwwy dawgz," Tabitha repeated.

"Dougal?" Aunt Nola sat upright, as if she hadn't been sound asleep in the recliner. "You hungry?" Food was Aunt Nola's love language.

"I could eat." He smiled. "Thank you, Aunt Nola."

"I'll feed you—now that you've shaved off that shaggy mess." She pushed out of the recliner. "There's some beef stew I could warm up. And some corn bread?"

His stomach grumbled.

"I'll take that as a yes." Aunt Nola chuckled.

Gertie had the hedgehog in her mouth, causing a squeak every time she chewed. Every time it squeaked, Tabitha laughed some more. Emilia tossed aside her book and started laughing, too.

"What did you do?" Savannah came down the hall, all smiles. "Goodness. That's a whole lot of laughing." She joined him on the floor. "Guess what, girls? Mommy finally got all the laundry folded and put away." She rolled her eyes. "We'll see how long that lasts." But there was no resentment in her voice.

Dougal often wondered how his sister-in-law felt about her new life. Less than two years ago, she lived in a big fancy house with cooks and maids *and* an overbearing father who'd tried to pick and choose his daughters' paths. Now she was the mother of triplets, shared the housework with her mother-in-law and aunt-in-law, and was working on building healthy boundaries with her father.

"How about you? Anything as eventful as vanquishing all the laundry?" Savannah asked, taking the ragdoll Tabitha handed her. "Thank you."

He didn't know how much Angus had shared with her so he said, "Nothing new."

"Oh." Savannah made the doll dance as she said, "I spoke with Emory Swanson this morning."

He froze. What had Angus told her? And why? It was one thing to tease him, brother to brother, but did he have to go and immediately fill his wife in on the exchange? *Oh hell*. Had Angus said anything to his mother, or worse, Aunt Nola?

"She seems very sweet. I'm so glad you mentioned her the other day. I'd much rather be in charge of the food myself—and use someone local—than have my parents cart in someone from out of town."

"I...mentioned her?" he asked, wary.

"Well, not her, exactly. You said her scones were delicious." She glanced at him. "I hope you were being honest because she's putting together a menu and invited us over for a tasting tomorrow night." She must have picked up on his confusion because she said, "For the party. Remember, we're throwing a Christmas party?"

"Right." And Savannah's parents were coming. The Barretts were Texas royalty, which meant they had big expectations. Though Savannah had initially insisted on a small, intimate family Christmas, she'd agreed to host a big Christmas party. A party that, apparently, Emory was catering. "I didn't recommend her."

"You liked her food. And... I found her old business online and the reviews were amazing so I thought I'd reach out and see." She studied him for a moment. "I told her you and Angus, me and Chelsea would all come. Your mom and Aunt Nola said they'd stay here with the kids so it should be...nice." Savannah shrugged. "Grown-ups only. No diapers or dolls." She held up the doll.

"Food!" Aunt Nola hollered.

"You missed lunch." Savannah lifted her arms so Emilia could sit in her lap. "You're probably starving."

He shrugged. "Something came up."

"Angus was in a mood at lunchtime." Savannah shook her head. "He kept looking at me and laughing. Over nothing. It was unusual." She glanced his way. "Any ideas?"

Laughing, huh? Dougal frowned. "No." The only upside? It didn't sound like Angus has ratted him out to Savannah.

"I don't think I believe you." Savannah rolled her eyes. "I think there's something going on, and you know exactly what it is."

Dougal shrugged.

"Is it a Christmas present?" Savannah leaned forward. "Did he get me something nice? He did, didn't he? He always does this. Finds the perfect thing while I get him funny socks or a new saddle or something impersonal." She tucked a strand of her long hair behind her ear. "I feel terrible, Dougal. I haven't had time to get him anything. I don't want to disappoint him."

Dougal sighed. He'd come to like Savannah quite a bit, to appreciate her calming presence on his brother and how loving and gentle she was with the triplets. He didn't want her worrying over nothing. And that's all this was. Nothing.

"Can you please, please help me out? I just… I know how hard he works and he still makes time for me and the kids and I—"

"It's not a present." Dougal cut in, running a hand over his face. "Trust me."

Savannah looked at him. "You're sure?"

He nodded, hoping that was the end of it.

But she didn't look convinced.

He stared up at the vaulted ceiling overhead, defeated. "It's about a woman he thinks I like," he whispered. When Savannah didn't respond, he risked looking her way.

Her eyes had narrowed and a furrow creased her brow. She looked…concerned.

"It's true." Why was he so offended by her reaction?

"You like someone?" She paused. "You…like someone?"

Was it so hard to believe? He sighed. "Angus *thinks* I do."

"As in like-like?" The disbelief in her voice was impossible to miss.

He pushed off the floor, eager to end this whole, awkward conversation. "If you'll excuse me, I'm hungry."

"Yums?" Tabitha asked, standing and taking his hand. "Peez."

"You're ready for a snack?" Savannah asked.

Henry sat upright, yawned and said, "Nack peez."

While Dougal worked on devouring a huge bowl of stew and four corn bread muffins, his nieces and nephew sat in their high chairs eating cut up apples and carrots. As far as company went, he had no complaints. *At least they're not giving me grief about anything.* Sure their table manners weren't the best, and Henry seemed determined to mash as much chewed carrots into the hair on his head as possible, but it was still preferable to his brother's teasing.

Hours later, when he was loading a roll of barbed wire into the back of his truck, he was working through a whole slew of excuses to get him out of going to this tasting. Even if Angus hadn't found out about his developing feelings for Emory, he'd be looking for a way out. Food. Conversation. Pleasantries. Now, add his brother watching him like a hawk and listening to his every word to the mix.

"No, thank you," he said to Willow.

She wagged her tail.

Gertie yipped.

"What now?" He looked down at the little dog, his hands on his hips.

Gertie sat.

"Yeah, well, I'm not Angus. I don't carry treats around in my pocket." He walked around to the passenger door, opened the glove box and pulled out a bag of treats. "But, this time, you're in luck."

Once they'd had their treats, he let them climb into the cab of the ranch truck, and waved over their newest ranch hand, Jesse Dawson. Jesse was Trace's younger brother and a good kid—most of the time. He'd gotten into some trouble with the law as a teen but seemed to have pulled himself together.

"Up for replacing some wire?" Dougal waited for Jesse's nod. "Get some gloves. This stuff can slice you up."

"Be back." Jesse nodded, jogging to his old beat-up truck.

While he waited, Dougal made sure they had everything needed loaded into the bed of the ranch truck. Fencing pliers, wire cutters, a roll of barbed wire, a pipe and a come-along. He closed the tool bench that sat behind the cab of the truck and climbed in. "You two are going to have to sit in the back."

Willow jumped over the seat to lay on the bench seat.

Gertie peered over, then looked at him, her head cocking one way, then the next.

"I guess it's a big jump for a little girl." He gave Gertie a few pats on the head, then lifted her up and over the seat so she could lay mostly on top of Willow. "You've got no respect for personal space, have you?"

Gertie yawned and buried her nose between Willow's back and the bench seat.

"Ready." Jesse climbed into the passenger seat, gloves in one hand and an insulated water bottle in the other. "South pasture?"

They drove on a while. If it wasn't for Jesse tapping his fingers along the door handle, it would have been a quiet drive. But Jesse wasn't quiet by nature—or still. It was only a matter of time before he tried to strike up a conversation.

"You get all your Christmas shopping done?" Jesse asked. "Two weeks left."

Dougal wasn't one for shopping. In the past, he'd bought his brother bags of corn, salt blocks, livestock feed or socks. They were all needed items, and Angus hadn't complained.

His mother and Aunt Nola weren't always around, but now that they'd moved back to help out with the triplets, he'd have to figure out gifts for both of them.

And Savannah.

And the triplets.

And Chelsea—because he was pretty sure Savannah said she'd be here for Christmas.

Damn. He had no ideas and not a lot of time.

"Guess I need to get started," Dougal grumbled, then paused. This could be the perfect excuse for getting out of going to that tasting. No one could argue with him needing time to shop for Christmas presents—especially if he said he was shopping for the triplets. It was true, too. He did need to get the critters presents. As much as he'd hate to miss out on time with Emory, he knew it was the right thing to do.

Chapter Seven

Emory placed a menu on each of the place settings around the table. Savannah said there would be four of them—plus Aunt Ruthie. Her nerves would prevent her from sampling, but she'd done plenty of that while she'd prepared everything. There was no way to make sure the flavors were perfectly balanced without tasting everything herself.

She heard a knock on the door and froze. They weren't supposed to be here for another thirty minutes. The mini apple and brie tarts were still in the oven and needed the full cooking time for the pastry to be crisp, flaky and buttery deliciousness.

"Come on in." Aunt Ruthie's voice carried down the hall.

That was the thing about the bed-and-breakfast—when it was empty, sound carried. And now that Lucas was coming to stay for the holidays, she and her aunt would need to be more aware of their conversations.

"Something smells delicious." It was Lucas's voice.

Emory could breathe a little easier. Lucas had already paid for another night in his hotel so he'd chosen to stay there last night and move in today. She counted the plates around the table. Was she supposed to have made enough for Lucas, too?

"Emory's a chef." Aunt Ruthie's voice was getting louder—meaning they were getting closer. "She's going to be catering a big ole fancy party, so she's put together some samples for them to taste. You know, pick which they like best." Aunt Ruthie stepped inside. "Oh, Emory Ann, it smells downright scandalous in here."

"Scandalous?" Emory laughed. "Is that a good thing? Or a bad thing?"

"I guess decadent is more fitting?" Aunt Ruthie picked up one of the menus.

"Hi." Lucas smiled her way. It was quite a sight. Like the sun, splitting through the clouds, to illuminate the world in an unearthly glow.

Way to get carried away. Emory laughed. "Hi." But, really, it was hard to see someone that…gorgeous in person. Did he wake up like that or did it take hours of moisturizing and styling gel and posing in front of the mirror. She could picture Lucas posing—he was fully aware of his own charm. How could he not be? "The Sweet Magnolia Tree suite is all made up for you."

"The Sweet Magnolia Tree suite?" Lucas glanced between the two of them.

"I'll let you in on a little secret, Lucas, I'm a big Dolly Parton fan." Aunt Ruthie grinned as she reached up to pat her hair. "Her music. Her aesthetic. Her big ole heart. Everything about her. Thanks to be, Lawrence got to be a real fan, too. We met her a couple of times. She was as sweet as you'd imagine."

"All the rooms are named after her songs or albums," Emory said.

Lucas's brows rose. "Okay, then."

"Don't tell me you don't love a little Dolly?" Of all the things Aunt Ruthie could forgive, not liking Dolly Parton wasn't one of them.

"Who doesn't like Dolly Parton? She's an icon." He ran his fingers through his just-so tousled sandy hair. "I'm sure I'll leave here appreciating the woman on a whole new level."

Aunt Ruthie beamed at that. "All right, then. I'll show you to your room." She paused. "Emory, honey, we will stay out of your hair while you work. I just know they'll love what you've put together for them."

"If it tastes half as delicious as it smells, I'm going to agree with Ruth." He pressed a hand to his stomach. "I didn't think I was hungry but now…"

"There should be enough for me to put together a plate for the two of you." She had planned on her aunt sitting in. "You might have to share, though."

"Now, don't you short the clientele." Aunt Ruthie shook her head.

The moment they'd left the kitchen, Emory finished up the last minute prep. She was big on presentation so, while deliciousness was required, so was a certain level of flair. And since this was a Christmas event, she went all in with the greens and reds and golds—while still keeping it elegant.

She washed up, put on a clean Santa's Helper apron, and was carefully pulling the cheese puffs from the oven when the doorbell rang.

"I'll get it," Aunt Ruthie called out.

Emory gave the room a last look, hurried to straighten one of the menus on the table and took a sip of water.

She'd done this dozens of times; she should be able to do this in her sleep. There was no reason for nerves.

"Hello, hello," Aunt Ruthie was saying. "She's got everything ready for you in the kitchen." There were some mumbles, but Emory couldn't make out what was being said. "Right this way." Her aunt stepped aside to allow four people into the kitchen. "Y'all have fun." And she left.

At least there was one familiar face: Dougal. He didn't exactly look thrilled to be here, though.

"Hello. I'm Emory." She waved. "Emory Swanson."

"Emory. I'm Savannah. We spoke on the phone." The woman stepped forward to shake her hand. "This is my twin sister, Chelsea. You know Dougal, my brother-in-law. And this is my wonderful husband, Angus."

"Why does he get an extra adjective?" Chelsea asked. "Dougal's just your brother-in-law and I'm your twin sister but Angus is your *wonderful* husband? I guess we know who the favorite is." Chelsea rolled her eyes and nudged Dougal in the side.

While it was obvious Savannah and Chelsea were twins, they had their own style. Chelsea's blond hair barely brushed her shoulders, she wore makeup and bold colors while Savannah's long auburn hair hung down the middle of her back, her face was natural and her color palette was more earth tones.

Dougal stood, avoiding all eye contact, looking acutely uncomfortable while Angus McCarrick did the opposite— staring directly at her with an oddly assessing intensity.

"Feel free to have a seat and we'll get started." Emory gestured to the table and the four of them sat. "After we talked, I pulled up some of my favorite and most requested menus. You said this will be an appetizer-only menu, so I've made eight savory options and six sweet." She held up a copy of the menu. "You can mark these up or make notes. What you like or dislike, that sort of thing."

"Oh, yum." Chelsea's eyes widened.

"I hope you're hungry." Emory reached for the first tray. "Cheese puffs topped with crème fraîche. Half with salmon and half with prosciutto." She put the tray on one of the red cast-iron trivets. "These are apple and brie mini tarts." She added this tray to the table.

By the time she had all the savory options served, there was a lot of chewing—followed by what she hoped were sounds of enjoyment. The only person who stayed rigid and silent was Dougal.

"Not a fan?" she whispered.

He glanced at her, looking more pained than ever. "No." He frowned. "Yes. It's all good." He shoved another cheese puff into his mouth and went back to staring at his plate.

"Oh." Emory knew Dougal wasn't the warm and cuddly type, but she'd thought they were becoming friends.

"Dougal, stop being such a bear." Chelsea leaned closer to him, giving his arm a shove. "I know you're going for the hot aloof broody guy thing, but you really don't have to work at it. You've got it down."

Emory paused, more than a little surprised by the woman's comment. Hot aloof broody guy? She glanced at Dougal. He was handsome, she swallowed. Okay, with that stubble on his jaw, hot fit. He was definitely aloof and broody, too. So, in theory, Chelsea's description wasn't wrong. But, for some reason, Emory didn't especially like that Chelsea had said so. If Chelsea said it, that's what she must think of Dougal. *That* was what Emory didn't like.

"What are these again?" Angus asked, pointing at his plate. "I think these are my favorite."

Right. Now was the not the time to be getting jealous… Hold on. *What?*

"That's the chicken vol-au-vent," Savannah answered.

"Yes, right." Emory nodded at the remains of the puff pastry full of a delectable creamy chicken filling. "I'm glad you like it."

"I do." He smiled. "It's clear you love what you do. You can taste it."

"Thank you." It was Emory's turn to smile. "That's one of the nicest compliments I've ever received."

"Oh, Emory, I'm not sure I can pick." Savannah stared around the table at the remaining samples. "They were all so good."

"We don't have to decide now. You four can talk about it and let me know tomorrow." Emory started clearing off the table. "Now, for the sweets. Gingerbread petits fours, eggnog cheesecake, peppermint bonbons, rum balls, cranberry-orange tarts and macarons. I've made a couple of different flavored macarons for you to choose from."

Instead of hovering, she tried to make herself invisible by tidying up the plates and serving trays. She tried extra hard not to look at Dougal or Chelsea or overanalyze their interactions. While Chelsea talked and tried to feed Dougal, he kept it to one-word responses and declining her food. Not that that meant anything—Dougal wasn't exactly a conversationalist.

Were Dougal and Chelsea together? Her gaze bounced

between the two. It was hard to tell. Why did it matter? It didn't. Not in the least. She didn't want to get involved with anyone. She shook her head and turned—to find Angus McCarrick watching her.

"Did you need something?" She came around the kitchen island.

"No, thank you." He smiled. "So, Dougal, out of all the food Emory's made, what's your favorite?"

Dougal sighed and scowled down the table at his brother. "I'd say you can't go wrong, no matter what you pick."

"Thank you, Dougal." Emory smiled at him.

His gaze was warm upon her face, and there was the merest hint of a smile on his handsome—okay, fine— hot face as he nodded.

"I agree." Savannah sighed, tapping her menu on the table. "I don't know how we're going to narrow this down."

"Then don't." Chelsea sat back in her chair.

Emory wasn't thrilled at the idea of that much food prep but, if they agreed to her costs, she'd do it. One of the things she'd loved about catering was the ability to make a special event that much more memorable. By involving taste, the event could become wholly immersive. "Like I said, you don't have to decide today."

Aunt Ruthie poked her head around the corner. "Sorry to interrupt."

"Not at all. I think we're about done here, anyway." Savannah patted her stomach. "I'm full."

"Emory is pure magic in the kitchen. Everything she makes tastes so good, my willpower goes straight out the window." Aunt Ruthie shot her a sweet smile.

"Lucas and I are stepping out for a bit, sugar. We'll be back before long. And thank you for getting that room ready for him."

"Have fun." Emory might still have mixed emotions about Lucas's arrival but, again, this was her aunt's choice—and she'd support her aunt, no matter what.

"Will do." Aunt Ruthie waved. "It was nice to see you all." Seconds later, the closing front door signaled their departure.

"Your aunt is precious." Chelsea stood, giving the wall of photos a once-over. "I love that she loves Dolly Parton. She even looks like her."

"I'll be sure to tell her you said so. She'll love hearing that." Emory happened to look Dougal's way and paused.

He looked like he was going to explode. Or on the verge of a heart attack. His face was deep red. His jaw was clenched tight, and the vein running across his forehead was protruding. If that wasn't enough, his breathing was rough and he had a white-knuckled grip on the table.

"Dougal?" She headed to where he still sat, concern mounting. "Is everything okay?"

Dougal hadn't expected to react this way. Knowing Lucas was in town was different than knowing he had been right down the hall. But he had. The bastard had been right here—in this house. Just now. He took a deep breath. He'd been hoping to tell Ruth and Emory before Lucas had wormed his way in the front door, but it sounded like it was too late... Lucas was staying here?

He glanced at Angus. His brother's jaw was locked and he didn't look happy, but he shook his head.

As much as he wanted to tell Emory everything, this

wasn't the right time. He'd come back later, when he was calm and alone, and tell Emory and Ruth. This wasn't the sort of thing he wanted to dump on Emory and ask her to relay it—it wasn't fair to her. Besides, he'd rather tell the story once and let that be the end of it. Rory had told him to share with Emory and Ruth, no one else. If he opened his mouth now, Chelsea would take it on herself to get involved. She loved drama—a whole hell of a lot. Which was exactly the sort of thing Rory didn't want.

"Dougal?" Savannah asked now.

"Fine. I'm good." But he was acting like an idiot, which needed to stop now. He cleared his throat, determined not to make eye contact with anyone. Especially not Emory. He couldn't or he'd get worked up all over again, but he didn't like leaving her here knowing Lucas was around. He stood suddenly, looked at his watch, then his brother.

Angus sighed, covering Savannah's hand with his own. "Guess we should be heading out."

"Oh." Seconds after meeting her husband's gaze, the confusion on Savannah's face gave way to a smile. "You're right. I'm sure the kids are wondering where we are."

Dougal would never say it, but he admired the way Angus and Savannah had developed this unspoken communication. Angus wanted to go; Savannah got on board without putting up a fuss. If the roles were reversed, he knew his brother would do the same.

"It's barely been, what, two hours? It's not like they're going to forget you." Chelsea shook her head. "I love my nieces and nephew, you know I adore them, but it is nice to do kid-free things every once in a while. You are no fun anymore." She smiled up at Dougal. "Not you, Dougal, you were never a lot of fun but my sister was." She batted her eyes at him, then winked.

Chelsea got a kick out of flirting with him. It used to fluster him, but now he wasn't remotely fazed by her behavior or her teasing. "Never claimed I was," he murmured.

"The food was amazing, Emory. Better than I could have expected." Savannah gushed, taking Emory's hand in hers. "I'm even more excited about the party now."

As goodbyes and details were being wrapped up, Dougal slipped out the front door—Frosty following him onto the front porch. He glanced down at the scruffy white dog. "You stay here with your momma," he murmured gently.

Frosty spun slowly in a circle and wagged his tail.

He was pretty sure the tail wagging wasn't for him. "Willow and Gertie aren't here this time." And both the girls had hung their heads and their tails and flopped onto the sofa when they'd realized he was leaving them behind.

"Next time," Emory said, stepping onto the porch. "Dougal, if you're in town tomorrow, maybe you could test some of my holiday punch recipes? And bring the girls over for another playdate?"

If his brother, Savannah and Chelsea hadn't been standing there, he'd have readily agreed. As it was, the three of them were watching with wide-eyed interest and, possibly, a little shock, too.

"Another play—" Chelsea broke off when Savannah elbowed her.

"We should go… We need to…to pick up some diapers on the way home, Chelsea." Savannah took her sister's hand and tugged her down the steps and along the front path to the gate. "Thanks again, Emory." She paused long enough to wave, then dragged Chelsea to the parked SUV.

Angus trailed after his wife, wearing a smile full of mischief, but he didn't get in the car with Savannah and Chelsea. No, he climbed into the passenger seat of Dougal's truck.

Dammit. He'd planned on heading straight home—in silence. Not having to endure his brother's jokes and digs for the next twenty minutes. His mood was only getting worse.

"Dougal?" Emory looked up at him, her brow furrowed deeply. "Are you okay?"

Every time he looked at her he thought she couldn't be any prettier. Every time, he was wrong. Looking at her now…well, his throat felt so tight all he could do was nod.

"Are you…upset about something?" She crossed her arms over her chest. "Was the food bad? Or…something? I don't know."

"No." He shook his head, tearing his gaze from hers. "No… I'll come tomorrow."

"Oh." Her brows smoothed. "Okay. Great. I appreciate it. I know Frosty would, too. Would four work?"

He nodded again, trying not to get lost in those blue eyes. He blinked and tipped his hat.

Her answering smile had his throat tighter than ever. Better to leave without another word than to say something and make an even bigger mess. With a nod, he was down the steps and almost to the front gate when she called out, "See you, Willow and Gertie tomorrow."

Don't look back. Don't do it. He did, caught the toe of his boot on an uneven cobblestone and almost fell. Almost. That would have been the cherry on top of this whole visit.

"Whew." Emory had one hand resting on her chest. "I've gone down twice from that flagstone. And I have the bruises to prove it. I'm just glad Aunt Ruthie hasn't fallen."

He glared down at the offending flagstone. She'd fallen? Ruth was no spring chicken—that damn stone was a danger. He'd remember to bring a shovel tomorrow and fix it.

"Be safe, Dougal." She waved.

With a frustrated sigh, he pushed through the gate, closed it behind him and yanked open his truck door. "Not a word," he snapped.

Angus only barely managed to muffle his laughter.

Once he'd started the truck, he asked, "Why are you in my truck?"

"We can go have a beer or two." Angus draped his arm along the back of the bench seat. "I texted Trace and Buzz—they're meeting us at The Watering Hole."

Dougal eyed his brother, not bothering to hide his irritation. "Why the hell would I want to go drinking?"

Angus gave him a once-over. "Because you need it."

Dougal put the truck in gear and headed to downtown. "Whatever." Need wasn't the right word but, if he was being honest, he could use a beer. Or two. He was out of sorts and he didn't like it. Not one bit. Lucas. Emory. Embarrassing himself—in front of an audience.

The Watering Hole was relatively quiet. It was a Wednesday night, so only the locals and a handful of tourists sat around the round, polished wood tables. There were pool tables and dartboards on the far side of the room. The other wall was lined with three different big screen TVs playing a selection of sport and rodeo events. He ignored most of the conversation and settled in to watch *The Greatest Bull Rides of Rodeo*—it was interesting enough to distract him from his thoughts. They were halfway through their second pitcher of beer before Dougal felt his posture ease, somewhat.

"We gonna talk about whatever is eating him?" Trace asked, nodding his way.

Dougal pretended not to hear the question.

"You don't want to know." Angus sighed.

"I do." Buzz grinned. "I really do. He's not listening anyway, Angus. Might as well tell us."

Dougal slammed his glass down on the table with more force than necessary. "We're not talking about me." He leveled a long, hard look at his brother.

Angus held up both his hands in mock defeat. "Did I say anything?"

"Fine." Trace refilled Dougal's glass and offered it to him. "So, Dougal, you have a good day today?"

Angus and Buzz burst out laughing.

Dougal didn't say a word.

"Good to know." Trace shook his head. "How about you, Buzz?" He sat back in his chair. "How's married life treating you?"

"I'm about as domesticated as they come." Buzz grinned. "And I'm not complaining."

"From the way Angus keeps checking his phone, I'm

guessing you'd rather be at home than out with us?"
Trace shook his head and turned to Dougal. "Next time,
we'll leave these homebodies with their families and
drive into Austin, hit some bars?"

Which sounded worse than his current situation.

Angus snorted. "You'd have to drag Dougal to Austin.
Too many people and talking and…women."

Dougal glared at his brother. Was it too much to ask
to drink in silence? Or for them to talk about *anything*
other than him?

"You don't like women?" Buzz asked Dougal. "I
mean, there's nothing wrong with that—"

"Knock it off." Dougal ran a hand over his face. "It's
a miracle you two found women that will tolerate you."
He pointed at Buzz, then Angus. "I don't know how either one of you managed it."

"No denying it, it is a miracle." Angus nodded. "But,
both Buzz and I do have…a certain way with the ladies."

Buzz crossed his arms over his chest, nodding. "That
we do. Er, did. Past tense."

"Very past tense." Angus refilled his glass. "It does
beg the question, though, how did we wind up with such
damn fine women?"

"It helps that Angus got Savannah pregnant," Trace
murmured.

Dougal choked on his beer, coughing hard.

"Ooh." Buzz slapped Dougal on the back several times.
"That was harsh."

But Angus was laughing. "Harsh, but true. Lucky for
me."

Buzz rested one elbow on the table and leaned forward. "You're both still single. Why is that? Needing some tips? Angus and I could probably help with that."

"You think? I don't know, Buzz, that's a steep order. These two? Dating?" Angus sipped his beer.

"Like I'd take dating advice from you two?" Trace tipped his hat back, grinning. "Not saying it wouldn't be good for a laugh so...fire away."

Dougal slumped back in his chair, content to sit this one out. It'd be one thing if they were serious. He was no fool, he knew he had no...game. He'd damn near fallen face-first walking not two hours ago—because Emory had been smiling and so damn pretty and that stone was sticking up. He sighed, staring into his empty glass.

"The standard pickup lines aren't enough anymore," Buzz was saying. "Things like, 'I hope you know CPR because you're taking my breath away' or 'Do you believe in love at first sight, or should I walk past you again?' are getting kinda old."

"I don't know. The classics are called classic for a reason." Angus chuckled. "A cheesy line can break the ice. Smiling is always a good first impression. Try, 'I bet you play soccer because you're a keeper.' Oh, how about, 'Did you just come out of the oven? Because you are hot.' Those are good."

The flood gates were open, then, and Buzz and Angus seemed to be on some sort of mission to out pickup line the other.

Dougal glanced between the two of them. Were they serious? Before Savannah, Angus had been good with the ladies. But, after listening to them, he wasn't sure how that was possible. The more he heard, the worse the pickup lines got.

Trace was outright laughing.

"You're joking, right?" Dougal interrupted, beyond done. They were, surely. No self-respecting woman would warm to this sort of foolishness. Hell, no self-respecting man could get that sort of crap out of their mouth and keep a straight face.

Angus and Buzz looked at each other, grinning from ear to ear. Trace started laughing again—or rather more like wheezing.

"I'm getting another pitcher." Dougal grabbed the pitcher and carried it to the bar. If he was going to endure who knew how many more hours of them talking non-sense, more beer was required. While he waited, he tried to imagine saying one of those pickup lines to Emory. What would she do if he told her, "Will you send me a selfie so I can show Santa what I want for Christmas this year?" Would she laugh? Look at him like he was off his rocker? Or would she think it was cute? Because, cheesy line or not, it was true. It was. He was beginning to accept that he'd like having Emory's attention—heck, even better, her affection. Because, no matter how hard he tried to deny it, she'd kicked something open inside of him. Some ache, some yearning. And he was pretty sure she was the only one who could ease it.

Chapter Eight

"Let's go check the mail." Emory smiled down at Frosty and waited for the little dog to trot outside. On Tuesdays and Wednesdays, there was no rush to make guests breakfast, so she tended to poke around with Frosty and enjoy a leisurely cup of coffee before heading up to the main house. By now, the sun was on its way up and the birds were already happily greeting the morning.

Frosty's ears perked up, turning this way and that, before snorting and leading the way.

"All clear?" She smiled, watching the white fluffy tail swish this way and that as the little dog moved. If he was struggling with his new gait, there was no trace of it. Buzz had been right—Frosty was adjusting so well to being a three-legged pup, and it made Emory's heart happy.

"I'm telling you, I'll get it," the voice was low. "I know I don't have a lot of time."

Lucas? It sounded like him. Emory slowed, searching the garden.

"No, no…there's no need… I told you, I'll get it… Yes, I know it's a lot of money… No, I don't need your *help*." His voice sharpened. "I've got two weeks. Stop calling me."

Frosty chose that moment to erupt into ferocious barking and charge into the bushes—with Emory running after her. The dog led her straight to Lucas.

"Hi." Lucas shoved his phone into his pocket.

"I'm so sorry if we interrupted something." Emory scooped Frosty. "He likes to play guard dog."

Lucas's smile was tight. "He's good at it." He stood. "Nice to know you've got protection."

She was still getting to know Lucas Baumgarten, but it was obvious he was upset. "Is everything okay?"

He hesitated.

"Sorry. It's none of my business." Except, it was sort of her business. She was her aunt's guard dog—albeit without the fur or tail.

"Well…" His gaze darted her way. "I'm… I'm ill. Pancreatic cancer." He shrugged. "Turns out, medical debt collectors aren't exactly the most understanding people."

Cancer? "That's awful." To have cancer bad enough. Worrying about how to pay for his care was just unfair. "I'm so sorry, Lucas. Truly."

"It is what it is." His smile was bright. "My problem. I'll figure it out."

"Are you…" She broke off. "Are you on the road to recovery?"

He shrugged. "Stage four. Docs aren't all that optimistic about how much time I've got left. But, what do they know?" He chuckled. "I'm determined to enjoy every day I've got left."

Emory's insides went cold and brittle. "Oh, Lucas." She shook her head. "I'm so sorry…" What else could she say? Was there a right thing to say when someone tells you something like this?

"Hey, it's all good. I've got time to sort things out and do what I want to do, hopefully." He took a deep breath. "But don't tell Ruth, please. She doesn't need to concern herself with this. I don't want her worrying about my health or the bills. I don't want her thinking I came here for help or money. I didn't. Even if she offered it, I won't take it."

For the first time since he'd appeared, Emory felt more at ease. She didn't like keeping things from her aunt, but she understood and respected Lucas's choice. He was right. Not only would Ruth insist on paying his bills, she'd want him to stay here and let her take care of him until the…end. She swallowed against the jagged lump now clogging her throat. Looking at him, there was no sign of illness. That he was…dying was unfathomable. "It's your choice. I won't say anything. But, if she asks me, I can't lie to her. I hope you understand."

He nodded. "Of course. Lying only leads to disappointment and pain. I don't want that for anyone." He stared down at her for a long, slow moment. "I'm glad she's got you in her corner."

"I'm the lucky one. She's in my corner. You've probably picked up on how kind she is—her heart is twice the size of the average person's, I'm certain of it. She's been nothing but good to me." She smiled at him. "She's easy to love."

"We all need a little of that, don't we?" Lucas's smile faltered. "This life isn't meant to be lived alone."

The familiar ache in her heart felt sharper. "No. It's not."

"I'm sorry you lost your husband. Ruth told me. I hope that's okay?"

She was surprised but she only nodded.

"I'm sure you two have bonded over that, too. Losing the man you loved." Lucas's gaze swept over her face and he rested one hand on her shoulder. "I'm sorry for your pain, Emory."

She swallowed against the tears. "Thank you."

They stood that way for a bit before Lucas said, "I'm sure you get this all the time, Emory, but I think you're one hell of a pretty woman."

Which was the last thing she'd expected him to say. "I'm sorry?" She blinked. Where had that come from?

"I'm sorry. It sorta came out." His hand fell from her shoulder. "It's just, in the morning light…you've got the bluest eyes I have ever seen."

Her cheeks grew warm. "Oh, well…" She spun on her heel, carrying Frosty under one arm as she hurried to the back door. "I'll make breakfast."

Lucas followed her inside. When she started pulling out things to make pancakes, he put on an apron and dug out the electric griddle.

"Well, look at you two, working as a team." Aunt Ruthie came in, the mail in hand. "What are we having?"

"Pancakes." Emory glanced at Lucas. Was it her imagination or was his gaze more lingering than it had been before? *It's my imagination.*

"Blueberry?" Blueberry pancakes were Aunt Ruthie's favorite.

"Of course." She pulled a pint of fresh blueberries from the refrigerator.

"Those are my favorite." Lucas popped one of the berries into his mouth.

Aunt Ruthie was beaming now. "Another reason to

love you. They're my favorite, too." She sat on one of the bar stools at the island. "No letter this morning, Emory."

Emory didn't like how severe her disappointment was. It's not like there was a letter every morning, more like two or three times a week. But, when there were, the days seemed a little brighter—a little more hopeful.

"Were you expecting something?" Lucas asked, coming around to sit on a bar stool next to Aunt Ruthie.

"Oh, no." Emory whisked all the dry ingredients together.

"Emory has a secret admirer," Aunt Ruthie announced. "Whoever it is, he has a way with words."

Lucas chuckled. "Really?"

"Yes, really." Aunt Ruthie swatted his arm. "I don't know when handwritten love notes became a thing of the past, but it's a shame really. It's so much more personal than just a store-bought card or phone call."

"Not everyone has a way with words, Ruth." Lucas pointed at himself. "I don't." His gaze shifted to her. "They're love notes? So there's someone in Granite Falls that's after your heart?"

Emory shook her head. "No. I mean, they're more encouraging than anything. Sweet, uplifting, supportive sort of things." The longer he looked at her, the more flustered she became.

"And poems." Aunt Ruthie nudged him. "I think someone in Granite Falls *is* after her heart." She bobbed her eyebrows. "Among other things."

"Aunt Ruthie." Emory's cheeks were on fire now. It was one thing when they teased, just the two of them. But it wasn't just the two of them. And Lucas, watching her the way he was, didn't seem as amused as Aunt Ruthie was.

"Good for him." Lucas was…staring at her mouth now.

Emory didn't like it. As handsome as the man was, there was no spark of attraction on her side. Even if he was ridiculously good-looking. Until now, she hadn't realized just how appealing she found the strong, mostly silent, gruff-around-the-edges but sweet to dogs, socially awkward type. And since she only knew of one man who fit that description, she needed a minute to process this revelation.

It wasn't totally out of the blue.

Watching Chelsea bat her eyes and make jokes with Dougal had stirred up something that felt an awful lot like jealousy. Emory wasn't the jealous type. But every one of Chelsea's nudges or accidental hand brushes or too-close lean ins had Emory biting into her lower lip.

It made no sense. None at all. Dougal had shown no interest in her. If anything, he seemed more uncomfortable around her than everyone else. Or was that it? Was his disinterest what made him so appealing to her? She wasn't ready for a relationship, and Dougal was unattainable so he was the only man who sparked awareness. In an odd self-defeating way, it made sense.

Even so, the jealousy was out of character for her.

"Emory?" Aunt Ruthie waved a hand in front of her face. "Sugar?"

Emory blinked.

"Phone." Aunt Ruthie held out the house phone. "I can flip pancakes while you take the call."

"Thanks, Aunt Ruthie." She handed her aunt the spatula and took the phone. "This is Emory."

"Emory? It's Savannah. I just wanted to thank you again for yesterday. It was all so so good." She went on. "We would love to hire you. I responded to the email quote you sent me so it should be in your inbox. I was hoping you'd be free to come out and look at the space? I'm not sure of the setup and, since we've just finished the barn renovation, I might need some help making it all come together."

Savannah had convinced her husband to renovate one of the old barns on the property for event space usage. The pictures she'd shown Emory were impressive.

"I'd love to." Emory was a visual person, so walking the space would help her come up with presentation ideas that fit the overall aesthetic.

"Are you free this afternoon? Around three o'clock? The triplets have nap time then." There was a muffled crash. "Angus? You've got it? Thanks."

Emory smiled, then remembered. "Dougal was going to come by here at four."

"Dougal was coming today? At four." There was a pause. "What?" More muffled sound. "Oh, Angus just said Dougal's not feeling well today." Another pause. "He's sick in bed. That's a first."

"Oh. I'm sorry he's feeling bad." Hopefully, it was nothing too serious. He didn't need to be driving into town so the dogs could have a playdate, that's for sure. "Would you mind asking Angus to relay a message for me?"

"Not at all."

"Please tell Dougal we can reschedule another time.

I hope he feels better." She should be worrying about his well-being, not disappointed she wasn't going to see him. What was wrong with her?

"Angus will make sure he gets the message. So I'll see you at three?"

"Yes, I'll see you at three." They said their goodbyes and she hung up the phone.

"What was that all about? Who's sick?" Aunt Ruthie was stacking pancakes onto a plate.

"Dougal." Hopefully, she'd get an update on him when she visited the ranch later. "I'm going out to the McCarrick place this afternoon to look at the party space."

"That should be fun." Aunt Ruthie offered her the spatula back. "I think I let them get a little overdone."

Emory eyed the slightly darker pancakes. "They're good. I'll eat them if no one else wants them."

"Well, if you see him, please give Dougal my best." Aunt Ruthie started setting the table. "He was awfully sweet to fix the gate for me."

Out of the corner of her eye, she saw Lucas stiffen, and paused. There was something about the man's posture, about his...everything. It seemed as if he was holding himself back or something. No charming smile or easy manner or air of confidence. His face was angry and hard, his lips thinned and paled, and his jaw muscle was clenched tight. He was tense. Hostile and *menacing.*

And then he caught her watching him. In seconds, he was smiling and relaxed and back to normal. The rapidness of his complete transformation was deeply unsettling. What was more unsettling was the possibility that Dougal was the cause of Lucas's reaction. She thought back to yesterday, to Dougal, and the connection clicked into place.

Something had happened between these two men. Something bad—and she needed to find out what exactly it was so that if needed, she could protect her aunt.

Dougal had never been hungover. But, then, he rarely drank anything other than beer. Last night, Trace had suggested shots and pretty much everything after that was a blur. This morning, he was suffering the consequences. His stomach churned like a washing machine, his head banged like the full percussion unit of a marching band and his tongue was so thick and dry he could have sanded off the rough edges on the table he was building.

He was grateful he'd installed a dog door because getting out of bed had taken him a solid thirty minutes. After that, he'd taken a shower and leaned against the wall, hoping the urge to throw up would pass.

"You look like hell." Angus was standing in his kitchen. "Here." He offered him a cup of coffee. "It's strong."

Dougal was too grateful for the coffee to complain about his brother barging into his place. He grunted and took a sip. It burned all the way down. "Thanks."

"If you feel half as bad as you look, you could go back to bed. Nothing needs doing right now." Angus sat in one of the two chairs around his small kitchen table, doing his damnedest not to smile.

"There's always something that needs doing." Dougal took another sip, determined to shake off the aches and nausea. "How come you're so damn chipper this morning?"

"One, I didn't drink half a bottle of whiskey like you did. Two, I can hold my liquor." Angus stretched his legs out in front of him. "I don't know how to say this, so I'm just going to say it." He shook his head. "You get kinda chatty when you drink."

Dougal's stomach stopped churning and turned to lead. "What?" He set the coffee cup on the table and sat in the other chair. "How chatty?"

His brother gave him a long, assessing look. "You don't remember anything you said, do you?"

"What the hell did I say?" He wasn't sure he wanted to know. "If you're messing with me, I will kick your ass." But any attempt at being intimidating was doomed to failure from the overwhelming pounding in his head. He reached up, pressing his palms against his temples and closed his eyes.

"In your current condition? I'd like to see you try it." Angus sighed. "Just cool it or you'll end up throwing up."

Dougal didn't argue. Throwing up was a very real possibility.

"Savannah talked to Emory this morning—"

"What?" He risked opening one eye. "Why?"

"Just about the party but, somehow, you came up. Since you're under the weather, Emory said not to worry about coming over today."

He didn't care about the details—only that he didn't have to be sociable today. He wasn't sure it was something he could manage.

Angus went on. "Instead, she'll be coming out here to get a lay of the land."

Both his eyes popped open now. He grabbed his cup of coffee and swallowed it down. "When?"

"Three."

Dougal glanced at his watch, then again. "It's one? In the afternoon?"

"Yeah, well, after last night, it didn't feel right to start pounding on your door at six in the morning." Angus sighed. "Don't say I never did anything for you."

Dougal grunted.

"Chances are, you won't even see her." Angus tipped his hat back. "That's what you said last night. That you didn't want to see her anymore."

He faced his brother, frowning. That didn't sound like something he'd say—especially since it wasn't true.

"You said you were afraid to see her." Angus shrugged.

"Go on…" He braced himself.

"Because you like her." Angus smiled then. "Actually, your exact words were you thought she was the woman you were going to marry and that scared the crap out of you, so maybe it was better if you didn't see her anymore."

Dougal swallowed, wracking his brain to see through the clouds blocking any memories from the previous night. "I did not say that." Even drunk, he'd know better, surely? Maybe his brother was fishing around, hoping he'd say something stupid?

"You don't have to believe me." Angus kept on smiling. "But Buzz and Trace will tell you the same."

Dougal swallowed again, the churning kicking in and going into overdrive now. "I'm guessing that's not all?"

Angus shook his head. "You sure you want to know?"

No. Hell, no. He nodded.

"You've been writing her poems and letters and sneaking them into the mailbox. You don't know why

she's sad, but you can tell she's been hurt and you want
to cheer her up." Angus took a deep breath and said,
"You want her to know the poems are from you but
worry she'll expect you to say things like that and you
can't—you can only write them."

He ran a hand over his face, silently cursing himself.
And the whiskey. He'd spent the better part of his life
keeping his poetry to himself, but a couple of shots and
he was spilling everything.

"You also said you couldn't stand knowing Lucas
was staying under the same roof as her." Angus sighed
then, his smile fading. "I was thinking we could talk to
Emory tonight—while she's here." He held up a hand
before Dougal could argue. "You said last night you
didn't want to put all that on Emory, but you were real
upset—I mean real upset—about Lucas. Trace, Buzz
and I think it'd be better to tell her and get it over with.
So you don't cry again."

Dougal blinked once, then again. "I did not—"

"You did. Lucky for you, they were both too shocked
to think about recording you for blackmail." Angus
leaned forward and patted him on the thigh. "Last night
was…something."

"I got that. I made an ass out of myself in front of you
and Buzz and Trace." He propped an elbow on the table
and rested his forehead in his hand. "And I'm sure the
three of you will never let me hear the end of it."

"I'm not gonna lie, it was funny." Angus chuckled.
"But nothing you said was all that bad. Well, unless
Lucas turns up dead in a field somewhere then you said
some things that would put you at the top of the suspect list."

Dougal frowned at his brother.

"Other than that, you told it like it was. You hate Lucas—though I managed to shut you up before you told them why. You're taking Gertie because I've been ignoring her and she deserves better. You write poems and you're pretty good at it because you've had a few of them published but you figured we'd tease you. And you're on your way to being in love with Emory Swanson but you don't know the first thing about courting her and would rather write poems and letters than run the risk of rejection or, somehow, hurting her."

Dougal took a minute to respond. "Make me a promise?"

"Shoot."

"Don't ever let me drink whiskey again."

"Deal." Angus chuckled. "Beer only from here on out."

"Appreciate that."

"But, for the record, no one would laugh at you about your poetry. None of us did. Maybe we were a little shocked at first but, hell, it's impressive. My brother. A published poet." He paused. "And, you're right about Gertie. She's my first girl, but she's gotten lost in the chaos with the kids and Savannah. I don't want her to be sad or lonely or squashed or harassed by the kids." He sighed. "If you and Willow have room for her, I think she's happier here."

Dougal nodded. He'd gotten fond of the scruffy mutt, her fearless trot and crooked underbite. "She pretty much follows Willow everywhere anyway, so it's not a problem."

"What about this thing with Emory?"

"There's no thing with Emory." He shook his head. "Nothing that needs talking about."

"No? You sure as hell had a lot to say about her last night." Angus cleared his throat. "She's a widow. Her husband died in a car accident a while back. That could explain her being sad."

Dougal stared at his brother. "You playing detective now?"

He shrugged, completely unapologetic. "If my brother is going to get involved with someone, I'm going to find out what I can about her." He stood, grabbed the coffee-pot, brought it back to the table and filled up Dougal's mug. "You should probably eat something. There's some of Mom's chicken noodle soup in the fridge."

"I appreciate it, but the coffee'll do." Dougal's stomach rebelled at the idea of food. If there was any way he could undo some of the damage he did last night, he had to at least try. "And I mean it about Emory. There's nothing going on. No one is getting involved. It's just… Nothing."

"Deny it all you want, but I know better." Angus chuckled again. "There's nothing wrong with having feelings for this woman. The only thing that would be wrong is you not doing something about it. She could end up with Trace or Dean Hodges or…some jerk like Lucas."

Dougal glared up at him. "You're enjoying this, aren't you?"

"Kinda." He replaced the coffeepot. "I figure you should consider how you'll feel when someone else sets their sights on Emory."

It would suck. He didn't like thinking about it. "Are

you done talking at me or are we going to get some work done?" He finished off his coffee, grabbed his hat off the hook by the front door and held the door open. No point sitting here, feeling like death when he could be in a saddle feeling the same.

Angus was shaking his head as he left, taking the stairs down and pushing through the door that separated the barn from Dougal's living quarters.

Until today, Dougal hadn't realized just how bright—and painful—the sun could be. Then again, he'd never had a hangover before. The glare of the sun was only part of the problem. The pulsing throb clamping down around his head intensified, and a steady trickle of sweat broke out along his brow and down his back.

He spent the next couple of hours in the paddock with the new horses, gauging the reaction to his presence, then separating them. Bonding was essential for a good cutting horse. They needed to trust their riders the same way the rider trusted his horse. There was nothing better for bonding than grooming.

Belle, a large buckskin, settled in beneath his touch. He ran the bristle brush over her back, then smoothed over her coat with his hand. This was an easy way to check for bumps or knots or areas sensitive to the touch. Belle's eyes remained closed through the brushing so Dougal didn't have anything to worry about on that front.

"Good girl," he murmured, running a hand along the horse's neck. "You're a sweet thing, aren't you?"

Belle's ears flicked forward.

"How about we check out your feet?" The way his

head was pounding, he didn't relish the idea of bending over for long but there was no hope for it.

He ran his hand down the horse's shoulder, down her front leg until he reached the fetlock. A slight amount of pressure and Belle shifted, letting him lift her hoof up. "Good job," he murmured, using the hoof pick to clean out any rocks or sticks that might cause discomfort. When all Belle's hooves had been taken care of, Dougal was leaning against the fence and taking long, deep breaths to ease his nausea.

"Dougal." Chelsea called out, too loudly, as she headed for him. "You're looking a little green around the gills," she said once she got closer.

He nodded.

"Aren't you sick? Should you be out here, working?" Chelsea patted the buckskin horse's flank.

"Better to keep busy." He used his handkerchief to wipe the sweat from his brow.

Chelsea was watching him. "I have a bone to pick with you."

"You can tell me about it tomorrow." He untied Belle's lead rope and led her back to the paddock gate. Dammit all, Chelsea trailed along after them. He led Belle into the paddock, then pulled the rope halter down and off the horse's nose, giving the horse a final pat before closing the gate behind him. "Let's get it over with, then."

"What's the deal with this Emory chick?" Chelsea's eyes narrowed as she stared up at him. "Why did I have to eavesdrop on my sister's conversation to hear you have a thing for this person?"

Dougal shook his head and walked past her.

"You're not going to say anything?" She caught up to

him. "For a solid year, I tried to get your attention and nothing. What is it that makes her so special? What do you even know about her? I mean other than she's pretty and she can cook?"

"Hold up." He stopped and faced her. "Do you still want *my* attention, Chelsea?" He knew the answer, but he didn't know what this was all about.

She snorted. "Of course not. Not now that I know you, know you. I mean, that would be weird. But I'm trying to understand why her and not me?"

He didn't know what to say to that. "Stop eavesdropping on other people's conversations. Maybe try minding your own business, even." He headed for the barn.

"Fine," Chelsea called after him. "I guess you don't care that she's here."

He almost faltered. "Nope," he called out. "Bye." He didn't give himself time to think or talk himself out of doing what he was doing. Instead, he headed upstairs, took some pain relievers, a long shower and shaved. He put on some clean clothes and knocked the dust from his hat. "How do I look?" he asked the two dogs sprawling across his couch.

Willow's tail thumped but she didn't move.

Gertie sat up, yapped once, then jumped down to stand by his feet.

"I still don't carry treats in my pocket." He stooped and gave the dog a scratch behind the ear. Gertie jumped into his arms, sniffed along his shirt and neck, then lay back in his arms like a baby. Angus had carried her around like this. "You need to be babied a little?" he asked, smiling at Gertie's contented slow blinks. "You're a mess, you know that?"

He sat on the couch beside Willow.

"Who am I kidding?" He shook his head. "I'm the mess." What was he doing? If he showed up at the main house, showered and shaved, people would notice. And talk. He rested his head on the back of the couch. Was he really going to go make a fool out of himself? Again? He'd be better off staying put, with Willow and Gertie, out of the judgment zone and away from Emory. "Hell, maybe I should take a lesson from drunk me and try to stay away from her, period." But, even as he was dozing off, he knew better. At the very least, he had to warn Emory and Ruth about Lucas. He had to. The thought of either one of them falling prey to that bastard had his blood boiling. He didn't know what Lucas Baumgarten was up to, but there was no doubt he was up to something.

Chapter Nine

The McCarrick home was impressive. The sprawling ranch house had large windows, stone arches and a wide, covered wraparound porch. And every bit of it was covered with Christmas lights. Every roofline, every window and door frame, the columns around the porch—it didn't matter. There were red-and-white lights wrapped around two of the large oak trees out front—massive ornaments hanging from the branches.

She lifted her hand to knock on the front door when it opened.

"No knocking. The triplets are asleep." Chelsea Barrett whispered, waving her inside. "Believe me, you do not want to wake them up early." She made a pained face and pressed her finger to her lips.

Emory nodded.

"Come on into the kitchen while we wait for Savannah," Chelsea whispered. "She's still rocking Henry. He's the stubborn one." She walked off, leaving Emory to follow her.

The main room had a vaulted, wooden beam ceiling. There was a towering Christmas tree in one corner. Its limbs were weighed down with a mix of homemade ornaments, glass bulbs and multiple strands of candy-colored lights. It made Emory smile.

A massive stone fireplace was centered on the back wall, an assortment of stockings hung from the wooden beam mantel. The large picture windows on either side were bedecked with more Christmas lights, but they didn't detract from the view of the rolling hills outside. She paused. As rugged as this country was, it was beautiful all the same.

"It's a lot. Lots of nothing," Chelsea said, staring out the window alongside her. "I don't think I could live in someplace so remote, do you?" she asked, watching Emory closely.

"I don't know," she whispered. "It is remote. But I guess that wouldn't matter all that much if you have your family with you."

Chelsea's brows rose. "Uh-huh." She spun and walked off.

Once again, Emory hurried to keep up with her.

The kitchen wasn't what she expected. It was shiny and new and state-of-the-art. One step inside and Emory had to stop and take in every little detail. "Oh my goodness." She was in awe. "This is…this is the perfect kitchen."

"Is it?" Chelsea shrugged. "I don't cook."

The kitchen in the Baumgarten Bed-and-Breakfast was sufficient for its purpose but this room, this space, was made for a serious chef—or a very big family. She eyed the eight-burner top gas stove with envy. There were double ovens, a convection oven and warming tray. The extra-large farmer's sink took up a good portion of the back wall, but there was a second, smaller sink in the marble-topped kitchen island as well. A wine fridge.

An oversize subzero refrigerator. She was so enamored with the appliances and layout, she didn't realize Chelsea Barrett was staring at her. Not right away. Once she did, there was no ignoring it.

"So, you're new to Granite Falls?" Chelsea's head-to-toe inspection was neither welcoming nor hostile. More like—assessing.

"I've been here a few months now." If Chelsea was going to give her a once-over, it seemed fair that she do the same. But it didn't do a thing for her self-confidence. Chelsea Barrett was everything she'd never be. For starters, she was probably a size four—maybe a two. She was tall and willowy. She had great cheekbones, a long elegant neck, big eyes and an overall model-like appearance. Emory felt shorter and rounder than ever. She smoothed the front of her green plaid blouse. "It's a sweet little town. Everyone is nice."

"Everyone is nice, I'll agree with that. It's just a little too small towny for me. Are you planning on staying?"

"For now." She shrugged. "I'm sort of taking it day by day." It was getting easier but thinking too far ahead reminded her that the future she'd planned for no longer existed.

"Day by day?" Chelsea's brow furrowed. "Is that part of the twelve-step program? Good for you for getting sober."

"No, no… Nothing like that." She wasn't secretive by nature, but she wasn't one to share her entire life's story after five minutes with someone.

"So you're starting over in Granite Falls. You're a chef. You live with your aunt." Chelsea counted each item off on her fingers. "No someone special?"

She shook her head. "That's about it."

"Any kids?"

Emory shook her head again, ignoring the kick to her chest the other woman's question caused.

"I know, what's with all the questions? It's instinct. I'm very protective of my family. Growing up a Barrett in Texas meant people were always after your money. Or connections. I'm still a Barrett, but I'm a McCarrick by marriage and the McCarricks tend to be entirely too trusting."

Emory wasn't sure what that meant but felt the need to defend herself. "Savannah called me to cater her party."

"Sure. Of course." Chelsea's smile was brittle. "And what about Dougal?"

Dougal? That was out of nowhere. "Excuse me?"

"I'm not sure how well you know the man, but he tends to shy away from people and conversation at all costs. But, for some reason, he took the time to recommend you to Savannah. It's…odd, that's all." Chelsea shrugged. "They do say the way to a man's heart is through his stomach, so he must have loved your cooking." She paused, her smile still sharp around the edges. "If I didn't know better, I'd say there was something going on between the two of you."

If she didn't know better? If Chelsea and Dougal were a couple, wouldn't it be easier to just say that instead of doing whatever this was? But what if they weren't and this was Chelsea's not so subtle way of staking her claim. Was that what all of this was about? She was interested in Dougal? She shoved aside the flare of jealousy and asked, "How is Dougal feeling? Savannah said he was sick?"

"He was fine when I was with him earlier. Busy. As always."

"Good." She adjusted the strap of her purse on her shoulder, done with the entire exchange. "Is there a bathroom?"

Chelsea nodded. "Back the way we came and to the right of the front door."

"Thank you." She made her escape. She tiptoed, wary of disturbing the triplets, and gently pulled the door closed behind her. Her reflection was red-cheeked. *Because that* was *just...awkward.*

She didn't leave the bathroom until she heard voices. As in, she wouldn't have to face Chelsea alone. Only then did she tiptoe back to the kitchen.

"Emory." Savannah gave her a quick hug. "I'm sorry. Henry must be on the cusp of a growth spurt. He's fighting sleep, which makes him a bear—because he's tired all the time." She shook her head. "Sorry. Mom problems. Sometimes I forget that not everyone lives around their toddlers' schedule."

Savannah was so nice—how could her twin be so different?

"If you're ready, we can drive out to the barn? It turned out so beautiful."

"Because you have a good eye." Chelsea smiled at her sister. "All those years of managing PR and events for Daddy weren't a total loss."

Savannah rolled her eyes. "Are you coming?"

Emory was relieved when Chelsea passed. Since it was just she and Savannah, the ride was pleasant enough. Savannah had a whole slew of ideas about how she wanted the party to go—and she wanted the barn to look just right.

"It's not just a Christmas party. My dad is coming and he's bringing some of his important friends. That means there will be some potential clients for the ranch. Angus and Dougal love what they do, but they're always working so hard. My goal is to have people lining up to get their horses in with them. I don't think it'll be that hard—they don't have a single dissatisfied customer—it's just getting the word out there."

"Building a client list is a never-ending process. I guess that's the same no matter what industry you're in." She glanced at Savannah. "Is it a competitive field? Training cutting horses, I mean?"

Conversation was easy between them. Once they got to the barn, they both had notebooks out and were exchanging ideas and making notes. Emory was all about the notes—and the lists. When they were headed back, they'd come up with a snowfall and starlight theme.

"I should have been doing this for months." Savannah parked the large SUV alongside the main house. "It's just, and I'm not complaining, the kids are a full-time job. There's not enough hours in the day to do or think about much else." She sighed. "I know I don't have to do this but my dad… We've been on rocky footing since I married and I really, really want him and Angus to get along. Something like this? It's what he expects. He is who he is, you know?"

Emory didn't know, exactly, but she understood wanting family to get along. She'd never had to worry about that. Her parents had adored Sam. "I'll reach out to my friend in Dallas and see what she has in the way of snowflakes and stars." Savannah wanted blown glass or crystal snowflakes and stars—Emory didn't know how easy those would be to come by at this late date. "I'll let you know."

"Thank you, Emory. I don't know what I'd do without you."

Emory was walking from Savannah's SUV to her car when she saw movement from the corner of her eye. It was Dougal, walking away from her. And what a view. His jeans were snug and showcased a mighty fine rear. Someone called to him so he turned, putting him in profile. He looked every bit the handsome cowboy in his jeans, pressed button-down shirt, boots and cowboy hat. There was no denying the heat he stirred in her blood or the ache that settled low in her stomach.

When his gaze met hers, time stopped.

Could he see how red-cheeked she was? How she was all but drooling over him? It's not like she could help it. She was just about to raise her hand and wave when he spun on his heel and headed rapidly away from her. He'd seen her. They'd made eye contact. And he'd ignored her.

The drive back to town was long enough for her to replay most of her visit. Things had been fine with Savannah but... She couldn't decide which was worse: the frustration Chelsea's interrogation had caused or the hurt from Dougal snubbing her.

Dougal had seen Emory and locked up. She was here and since he needed to talk to her about Lucas it should have been a good thing. Plus he was happy to see her. So happy that the lingering remains of his headache disappeared the minute their eyes locked. She did that to him. Shook up his insides—turned him from a rational man into a damn fool. That's why he'd panicked and walked back to the barn.

Where, unfortunately, Angus had seen the exchange. "What the hell was that?" he asked.

Dougal shook his head. Like he knew? After he'd poured his heart and soul out last night, shouldn't his brother have had a better understanding of just how much this woman got to him? *Guess not.* He messed up. He knew it. He didn't need to talk about it or to have his brother rub his face in it.

"Whatever." Angus sighed. "Weather alert came in. Here, take a look. Coming in tonight. It's going to be nasty." Angus pointed at the screen on his smart tablet. "Gonna get below freezing, too. We need to make sure we're ready for it."

The weather forecast for the next three days was rain and plummeting temperatures. Rain was a good thing but when it came hard and fast like the forecast was showing, it tended to cause flooding. With the temps dropping, the chance of ice made things dangerous for livestock.

"I'll get Jesse to start weatherizing things." Dougal nodded. "I'll have him start at the house, then move to the barn. Harvey and Clay should go bring in the cattle."

"Just sent them." Angus ran a hand along the back of his neck. "If this is right, we have time to get it all done. Good thing we've finally got so many hands on the place."

It had taken time for them to assemble the crew on the place now, but it was worth it. For the last few years, the place had been running like a well-oiled machine. If something needed doing, it got done. They didn't need to panic if things got bad because there was firewood chopped, gas in the generators and plenty of essentials for a potential power outage.

There are no squeaky gates or uneven paving stones to worry about out here.

The sky was a gray-blue, but there was no hint of what was coming—not yet. Still he knew and the building pressure there had him pondering what to do next.

Ruth and Emory were both smart, capable women. They'd know to wrap the pipes or drip the faucet, wouldn't they? If it froze and a pipe burst, it'd be a pricey repair that could potentially close down the bed-and-breakfast.

Were they stocked in case it turned into a winter storm? Things to stave off the cold? Plenty of food and water and candles? With Texas weather, things could go from bad to worse in a matter of minutes.

Plus he felt like an ass for treating Emory that way. There was no arguing he was an awkward son of a bitch. But he'd been outright rude to her. It bothered him.

"What are you thinking?" Angus asked.

He shook his head.

"Spit it out."

"I need to go into town." He glanced at his brother. "I... I need to do something."

"Go on." Angus nodded. "But don't be surprised if Savannah or Mom send you a grocery list and expect you to go shopping."

Dougal nodded and grabbed his truck keys. He whistled and Willow and Gertie came barreling down the stairs to the truck. "Let's go." He held the passenger door open so the dogs could jump up and into the truck. Gertie backed up a good ten feet before she took a running leap—and landed on the seat by Willow. "Good job." He grinned as he slammed the door shut.

"Got your phone?" Angus asked.

Dougal patted his shirt pocket, jeans pocket, then looked at Angus.

"Yeah." Angus held out his phone to him. "You sure you're good to drive?"

Dougal took his phone. "Yep." He ignored his brother's laughter, made sure he had a shovel, then started the truck and headed into town. He was halfway there when he realized he might encounter Lucas. If the bastard was there, then what? He'd promised Rory he'd control himself, so no matter how hard it might be, he wouldn't break his promise.

Both of the dogs were wagging their tails as he pulled up and parked in front of the bed-and-breakfast. He took a deep breath. "Here we go."

"Dougal." Ruth waved from one of the rocking chairs on the front porch. "What brings you into town?"

"I figured I'd see if y'all needed help getting ready for the storm." Willow and Gertie ran through the front gate and he pulled it closed behind him.

"Storm?" She stopped rocking. "I heard we might get some rain, that's all."

"Yes, ma'am. A lot of it, too." He paused on the bottom step, his hat in his hands. "It's gonna get below freezing tonight. That's when it gets tricky."

"It is?" Ruth shook her head. "I had no idea." She turned as the front door opened. "Did you hear that, Emory?"

"I did." Emory didn't so much as look at him. "It's so warm today, it's hard to imagine that big a temperature drop."

Before he could say a word, Frosty came barreling out the front door and down the steps to Willow and Gertie. The three dogs barked and pounced and circled one another, causing such a racket that conversation was impossible.

Dougal was fine with that. He needed a minute. Emory was laughing at the dogs' antics, and she was so damn beautiful he could barely breathe. That smile of hers. The way her blue eyes lit up. He needed a minute just so his fool heart would steady.

"It's awful kind of you to offer your help, Dougal." Ruth stood. "I'd ask Lucas, but he won't be back for a bit."

Knowing that eased some of the tension from his shoulders.

"Emory, why don't you take him to the carriage house first. We haven't had a hard freeze since it was reno-vated, so I'm sure the pipes will need to be wrapped." She tapped her chin. "I don't even know what supplies we might need. I *think* Lawrence kept all that in his workshop. I'll go get the keys—if Lucas didn't keep them. Said he and his dad had made all sorts of memo-ries together in the shop." She headed inside.

He didn't give a damn about Lucas or his memories. He did care about Emory and setting things right. He thought of a half a dozen things to say to Emory but they all stuck in his throat. She stayed quiet, her attention fo-cused on the dogs—ignoring him altogether.

When Ruth returned, she had a set of keys in her hand. "Here. I never go in there so be careful. That was Lawrence's shop so it's likely a mess. I always gave him grief. Heavens knows how much money is out there, with all that fancy equipment. You'd think he'd have made sure it was all orderly." She smiled. "I'll have some hot chocolate and cookies for you when you're done. Don't worry, I didn't bake the cookies. Emory did. I wouldn't want you to break a tooth or anything."

Emory glanced at him. "I'll show you."

It had been a while since those blue eyes were troubled, but they were now. He knew better than to think he was the cause. The chances of Emory seeing him as anything other than a big, bumbling idiot were slim and it was his own damn fault. His mind automatically went to Lucas… And the need to protect and defend Emory, and Ruth, slammed into him. No more delaying it—he'd tell them everything about Lucas over their hot chocolate and cookies.

He followed Emory along the flagstone path that wrapped around the large old house, past a dormant rose garden and down a slight hill to the carriage house in back. Since he rarely poked around the neighborhoods in town, the last time he'd seen the building it'd been on the dilapidated side. Now the cream paint and blue-gray shutters and trim work matched that of the main house. And, like the main house, it had a white picket fence surrounding a postage-stamp-size yard.

Emory opened the front door. "Excuse the mess. I didn't know I'd be having company."

"This… You live out here?" He paused in the doorway. Until now, he's assumed she'd lived in the main house with Ruth—and Lucas.

She nodded, her eyes darting his way. "Aunt Ruthie wanted me to have my own space."

And, damn, but it was a relief. Was Lucas still too close? Hell, yes. But he wasn't right down the hall from her, and that was something. "That's nice."

"My aunt is one of the kindest people I've ever met." She stepped inside.

When he brushed past her, her scent and warmth almost had him reaching for her. The urge was raw and intense and damn near had him running back out the door.

"Dougal…" There was a hint of irritation in Emory's voice.

He turned. She was too close, dammit. He took a step back.

Her eyes widened and then she was frowning up at him, a crease between those blue eyes. "Did I do something? This morning…" She stopped, staring at him.

"No." He cleared his throat. "I…" He what? "You…" He cleared his throat again. *Dammit.* "I'm sorry for earlier, Emory. I'm not so good at…being sociable."

She studied him for a moment. "Is it Chelsea?" She wrapped her arms around her waist. "I got the impression that she and you are an item."

"What?" He was frowning now. "Hell, no… I mean. No. We aren't. Never have been. Never will." He hoped she believed him.

She seemed to be studying him. The longer she looked at him, the harder it was to ignore the urge to reach for her. Finally, she asked, "Does she know that?"

He nodded. "What did she say to you?" When he got home, he was going to put Chelsea Barrett in her place. He didn't need or want anyone meddling in his life—something he thought he'd already made perfectly clear.

She opened her mouth, then closed it. "I think she picked up on the fact that I'm attracted to you."

All he could do was stare at her. She… How… He hadn't heard that correctly.

She stared back. "You've let me know you're not interested so—"

He wasn't thinking; he couldn't. Closing the gap between them was instinct. An instinct he was entirely unfamiliar with. "Emory... I'm interested." That was it. That was all he could get out. He let instinct take over and reached for her.

His hands slid slowly around her waist and pressed flat against her back before tugging her close. She felt like heaven against him. It was a comfort to see she was just as affected. The way her gaze widened, then dropped to his mouth, had blood roaring in his ears. Her breath hitched, a shudder ran through her and the fire in her eyes likely mirrored his own.

This was good. This was right.

Her hands went from resting on his chest to gripping his shirt front and tugging. He understood. He'd never felt this sort of need before. Flooding every single cell with pure hunger. And so much more.

Even on tiptoe, she couldn't reach him. He wasn't about to leave her waiting. He bent his head with newfound confidence. She wanted him. She was breathing just as hard as he was. And holding on to him with a fearsome grip—eager for his kiss.

And, damn, but her lips were soft beneath his. Sweet at first. Then clinging. The muffled moan that spilled from her mouth tore free any lingering restraint he had. He would take whatever she offered him.

Chapter Ten

Emory was rapidly melting into Dougal McCarrick. She was standing on her own two feet, but his embrace was the only reason she was upright. His thick, strong arms wound around her and crushed her against him. And still, she wanted to be closer to this gentle hulk of a man. That's all she wanted—nothing else.

There was no hesitation or stopping this. Even if she could, she wouldn't. She didn't want this to stop. His touch made her feel alive.

She didn't know who was moving who but they slammed to a stop when his calves hit her couch. For a split second, there was space between them. Then she pushed him onto the couch and climbed into his lap.

His hands cupped her face, cradling her close as his mouth sealed against hers.

For a man with little to say, he knew how to communicate in other ways. The caress of his hands and the sweep of his tongue along the seam of her lips said more than enough. And he had her quivering.

She gasped when his tongue slid into her mouth. It was a welcome invasion. One that had her wriggling against him.

"Emory," he groaned. His hold shifted, gripping her hips tightly.

The gruff sound of her name from his lips only fanned the already out of control hunger blazing inside of her. That was why she turned and straddled him. That was why she leaned forward, her breasts against the wall-like expanse of his chest. She wanted to get lost in this—in him.

Their kisses grew less exploratory and more frenetic yet the slide of his fingers through her hair was oh so tender. That was Dougal—as big and brusque a man as he was, he was just as gentle. Not that there was any-thing gentle about the situation.

Impatient was more fitting. Frantic, even. The way she craved this man was an entirely new experience.

The vibration of his phone was a jolt. Mostly because his phone was in his shirt pocket, which happened to be pressed against her breast. It vibrated and vibrated, but she didn't want Dougal to stop. He was currently nuz-zling her ear and it was delightful.

When he reached between them, she braced herself. This intrusion would be the end of this sensual chaos they'd been descending into.

He was breathing hard as he pulled the phone from his pocket—and tossed it aside. He didn't even look at it. His jaw muscle clenched tight as his eyes locked with hers.

Oh... She couldn't breathe. She couldn't. That look... She was done for. Desperately aching for this man. She wanted to be the one to quench the fire in those eyes. Right here, right now, if she had it her way.

He moved and she went from straddling his lap to laying on her back. The sight of Dougal looming over her did nothing to help her catch her breath. His strong arms braced himself over her but he didn't move. Instead, his brows rose.

Was he asking for her permission? Did he doubt that this is what she wanted? The tug in her chest took her by surprise. This was about urges and needs, nothing else.

"Yes." She nodded quickly, grabbed ahold of his shirt collar and tugged.

He smiled.

Oh, oh... Her chest caved in. Dougal smiling was... Everything throbbed. So much.

As he lowered himself, she savored the feel of him on top of her. Big, yes. Strong, too. Warm. So very warm. He propped himself on his elbows, his lips parting hers and his tongue stroking deep.

Her arms slid around his neck and her fingers twined in his thick, dark hair. It anchored her there, in place, beneath him—right where she wanted to be.

She didn't care about the vibrating phone or that things were going at a breakneck pace or that this man made her so out of control. None of that mattered. His touch. His kiss. His body... She was happy.

Until a large tongue tracked along the side of her face. A tongue that was very definitely not Dougal's.

"Willow." Dougal grunted. "Behave."

The licking stopped and Emory turned her head to find Willow, Gertie and Frosty sitting, watching, not two feet from them. All three of them had their ears cocked up and their tails wagging, curious and alert.

She giggled; she couldn't help it.

Above her, Dougal laughed, too.

She blinked, staring up at the man still braced above

her. She was instantly flooded with sensory overload. Some she welcomed, some she refused to acknowledge. Even with sanity returning, she had not one ounce of regret about what had happened. She also had no doubt about what would have happened if they hadn't been interrupted. If anything, she was disappointed they'd been interrupted.

Now that he was staring down at her with somewhat clear eyes, she hoped he felt the same.

"I guess I should have closed the door?" she murmured.

He smiled, then pushed off the couch to stand.

She smoothed her blouse back into place, mortified that it had risen up to show off her less than toned stomach, and took the hand he offered her—pulling her to her feet in front of him.

"Next time," he murmured, smoothing the hair from her shoulder.

Next time? She blew out a shaky breath. *Yes, please.*

"Uh, yeah, hello?" Lucas Baumgarten knocked on the door frame. "I didn't mean to interrupt."

Emory jumped back, almost tripped over Willow, and wound up sitting on the couch again. "Lucas."

"Ruth said you might need some help with winterizing the house." He leaned against the door frame.

Emory stood, carefully, and risked a glance at Dougal.

He was ramrod stiff. Any semblance of warmth or tenderness was gone. In its place was unguarded hatred. Or something like it. The way he was looking at Lucas scared her a little bit.

Lucas didn't look concerned. He was smiling at Dougal—smugger than anything.

"It looks like you don't need my help getting things

warmed up in here." Lucas's smile grew. "Been a while, Dougal."

Dougal was silent, his nostrils flared and his jaw clenched tight.

"Not exactly the way I imagined seeing you again." The way he looked between she and Dougal had Emory's face burning.

"How's the family?" Lucas asked. "If you see your cousin Rory, give her my best, will you? I always liked her." There was something about his smile that made Emory uneasy. "I was thinking I'd reach out in person. Catch up. You know, talk about the old days."

Emory had never seen a person move so fast. One minute, Dougal was a statue, the next he was across the room and toe-to-toe with Lucas.

"You want to stop while you're ahead." Every one of Dougal's words was a warning.

Lucas's brows went up but his smile didn't waver. "Or what?"

"You want to find out?" Dougal's voice shook—his fury barely controlled.

What was happening? She had never seen such hostility between two people—never felt it. At the moment, it seemed likely that Dougal would hit Lucas. Lucas. Who was sick. *Dying.*

"Dougal." She ran across the room and forced herself between the two of them. "Lucas." She shook her head, trying to diffuse the ever-mounting tension. "Calm down, please."

Dougal instantly took a step back, but his expression remained cold and hostile.

"You're right, Emory." Lucas held up his hand. "I…

I don't know what I said. I didn't mean to get anyone upset."

Dougal's snort said otherwise.

Emory didn't exactly believe Lucas, either, but diffusing things took precedence. From the way the two men were staring at one another, something told her this wasn't going to end well.

"I should go." Dougal's announcement was gruff.

She didn't want him to leave but, all things considered, she understood why he might want to go. "I appreciate you stopping by." She glanced at Dougal. "And your offer to help."

His gaze bounced from her to the floor. His jaw clenched tight before he said, "I told your aunt I'd help winterize things—"

"I can do it." Lucas cut him off, causing Dougal's nostrils to flare.

"No, you can go help Aunt Ruthie, Lucas. I can handle it out here." Emory frowned at both of them. "And if I have any questions, that's what the internet is for." She didn't miss the goading grin Lucas shot Dougal or the narrow-eyed look Dougal leveled at Lucas. And she didn't like it.

Dougal's voice was low as he said, "Emory, there's something you need to know." His eyes met hers. "It's important."

Lucas crossed his arms over his chest. "I guess I did sort of interrupt your *conversation*, didn't I?"

Dougal pressed his eyes shut.

Emory could tell his patience was waning. "Later, Dougal." She waited for his gaze to meet hers. He was struggling and, for whatever reason, Lucas was the cause. "Please."

He nodded, grabbed his phone and left, brushing past Lucas as he did so—all three dogs trailing him.

Emory stared after him, hoping she did the right thing.

Lucas took a deep breath. "I appreciate you stepping in, Emory. If I remember, he packs a solid punch."

"What?" She stared at the man. It was obvious Lucas and Dougal had a history, but Lucas's words were still a surprise. She had a hard time imagining Dougal going around punching people.

"Well, it wasn't always this one-sided." Lucas's smile was apologetic. "But we were dumb kids back then."

Emory had no response for that.

Lucas smiled at her. "So, are you two…" He let the sentence hang there.

She wasn't going to let his earlier comment drop. "Why did you two fight in high school?"

Lucas shrugged. "Mostly, he didn't like me because I was a smart-ass. I went out of my way to get under his skin. I did. I fully admit to instigating ninety percent of our disagreements." He shook his head. "If I could go back and change things, I would." He sighed. "He didn't like me dating his cousin Rory. I tried to fight against my feelings, believe me. It's not like I meant to fall in love with her." He shrugged, and winced. "Then she dumped me and broke my heart so you'd think that'd be enough for him. I guess not."

She wasn't satisfied with that explanation. "That's why he got upset when you asked about his cousin?" It didn't make sense.

"I guess so. I guess time doesn't heal all wounds."

Lucas looked her way. "I am sorry about today and this might be overstepping but, after everything you've been through, don't get involved with someone like Dougal. You deserve someone that will treasure your heart and Dougal... Well, you saw how he was just now. He's a hard man." He shrugged. "I'll get out of your hair." And, with another blinding smile, he left.

Emory's head was spinning. The last thirty minutes had left her with a lot to sort through. First, she had no interest in letting anyone into her heart. Second, she sensed there was more to the story than what Lucas had told her. And lastly, her feelings for Dougal were purely physical. Was she concerned about the conflict between him and Lucas? Yes. Was she curious to hear what he had to tell her? Definitely. But that was it. No matter how tempting Dougal was, she had no right to affection or pleasure—however fleeting.

"Everything okay?" Ruth Baumgarten was putting sheets over her flower beds when he came around the side of the house.

He was not okay. He was pissed off—at himself. Lucas had goaded him, but it was on him for almost taking the bait. After years of holding back, he'd almost lost his temper and taken his first shot at Lucas in front of Emory. "I'm..." He nodded, too worked up to say more.

"You want that hot chocolate now?" she asked, dusting off her hands. "Emory's gingerbread cookies can't be beat."

He drew in a deep, slow breath. "I should take a rain check." He tried to smile at the woman, tried and failed.

"You don't like Lucas all that much, do you?" Ruth

looked him squarely in the eye. "When I asked you about him before, you were quicker than a cat on a hot tin roof to get away."

He pressed his lips together, holding back the barrage of hateful words fighting to get free. Holding on to anger didn't do a thing to Lucas—it only ate at him.

"He's sick, Dougal. Cancer. He doesn't have much time left." Ruth sighed. "That's why he's here. I think he's trying to make amends before he leaves this world for the next."

It was a shock. A big one. But there was a part of him that had to wonder if this was true. While he'd like to think the man wouldn't lie about something that serious, after what Lucas had done to and said about Rory, he couldn't dismiss the possibility.

But, if it was true, he'd almost punched a terminally ill man. *That makes me the bigger bastard.*

His thoughts were all over the place.

If Lucas was ill, was telling Emory and Ruth about Lucas's past the right thing? He'd meant for them to keep their guard up—just in case. But if the man was dying, he deserved to be surrounded by love, not judgment or condemnation. Dougal didn't like the man, but he wasn't heartless.

"I know he's caused a lot of trouble, though Lawrence never went into the details. But I'd like to think he's changed. If someone gave me months to live, I imagine I'd be making changes and reaching out to people, too."

"I guess so." He nodded. Had Lucas been serious about reaching out to Rory? Would he, after all these years, try to make it right? And if he did, Allana would know who her father was—only to say goodbye to him.

Dougal didn't know how to feel about that but, dammit, he did his best to calm down. "How long has he been back?"

"Oh, he said it's been almost two weeks now." She grinned. "About as long as Emory's been getting those letters. He's said a few things that make me think it's him, anyway."

A surprised laugh slipped out. *This day just keeps getting better and better.* "Oh?" He shoved his hands into his pockets.

"I can't say I'd be happy about it, though. Emory's already lost so much, I'd rather she didn't get involved with someone there's no future with. Still, it's never bad to take a chance at love. You don't need a lifetime for a lifetime of love with someone." Ruth shrugged. "I take a chance on it whenever I'm given the opportunity."

Dougal surprised himself by asking, "How long ago did Emory's husband die?"

"Almost two years now?" She paused, then nodded. "Still newlyweds, mostly. Sam was a decent enough fellow. They weren't fiery, the way I like my relationships. They were just…comfy. If you know what I mean." She smiled up at him. "Why do you ask?"

He swallowed. "I… I don't know."

"No? You sure about that?" She winked. "I'm sure you'll figure it out. Until then, it's nice that you drop by and visit. I think it makes Frosty, and Emory, happy." She nodded, still smiling. "All I'll ask of you is to give Lucas some grace when you're here. The past is the past and, since he doesn't have a future, the present is all he's got."

He'd given Rory his word, and that had been an epic

failure. "I'll try." A gust of wind blew across the yard, rattling the shrubs and making the wind chimes sing.

"That's all any of us can do." She shivered. "That wind has a nip in it. Best break out the extra quilts and bring in some firewood."

All things he'd wanted to do for them—until Lucas showed up. After that, the best thing he could do, for all of them, was leave. "If you need something, call me." He pulled his wallet out and handed her his business card.

Ruth took the card. "That's kind of you."

That's me. Kind. Unless he was on the verge of punching someone with cancer. Then he was a straight up ass. He paused. "Please tell Emory I'm sorry. I am. She'll understand." But that didn't mean she'd listen.

"I can do that." Ruth patted his arm.

"I'm headed to the store. Text if you need something." He glanced at the carriage house. What was he hoping for? That Emory would come running after him? She wouldn't. And he had no one to blame but himself.

"Will do. Stay safe, Dougal."

"You, too." He nodded, whistled and headed for the gate. Poor Frosty barked up a storm, dancing back and forth inside the gate and whimpering as Willow and Gertie loaded into the truck.

The whole damn day had been a roller coaster ride, and it was his fault. How the hell was he supposed to fix this? With Emory and, dammit all, with Lucas, too. He'd never hit a man when he was down. It sounded like Lucas couldn't get any lower.

The grocery store shelves were pretty picked over, but he managed to get everything on Savannah's list. He grabbed an extra box of diapers, just to be safe, and was home before dinner. Instead of retreating to his place, he ate with the family and spent time playing on the floor with the triplets. Spending time with the critters always made him feel better about life.

"Unca Doo." Tabitha had been bringing him board books for almost an hour now. They'd read one, she'd put it back in the bookshelf and come back with a new one. Over and over.

"What's up, Tabby-cat?" he asked.

She sat in his lap. "Book." She smiled up at him.

He grinned.

"Weed peez." She patted the book she'd brought to him.

"Yes, ma'am." He was pretty sure they'd already read this one. It was about a caterpillar that ate a hole in all sorts of foods, but, if she wanted to hear it again, who was he to complain?

As soon as Tabitha had gone in search of their next book, Henry jumped on Dougal's back and roared in his ear. Henry was as obsessed with dinosaurs the way Tabitha was with books. Dougal grabbed his nephew and lifted him in the air, causing the boy to squeal with delight.

"Dougal," his mother chastised. "It's getting a little late to get him riled up like that."

"Right." Dougal set the boy back on his feet and roared, softly, at him.

Henry giggled then crawled away, growling and snorting as he chased Emilia around the couch.

"You're going to be a good father one day." His mother sat on the couch and stared at the Christmas tree. "Goodness, so many memories are on that tree."

Every year they pulled down the red buckets full of decorations, and every year his mother and aunt would tell the same stories as they unpacked the ornaments. When he was younger, he'd roll his eyes and get impatient. Now he didn't mind. He was lucky to have that. The family and the memories and the traditions passed down through the years.

He didn't like it but Lucas came to mind.

How would it feel to know this would be his last Christmas? Dougal would want this, right here. All the family and traditions. On the one hand, it made sense for Lucas to be here and spend the holiday in his childhood home. But, on the other hand, why wasn't he with his mother? The sliver of doubt refused to go away. There were too many ifs to ignore.

He waited until he and Angus were alone to fill his brother in on what he'd learned.

As expected, his brother's first reaction was disbelief. "He's full of sh—crap, you know that, don't you?"

"He was, yes. But that doesn't mean he still is. What if he's not lying this time?" Dougal shrugged. "And what's with the self-censorship?"

"Savannah pointed out the kids are learning new words all the time." He chuckled. "Can you imagine Richard Barrett's face if one of the kids started swearing. I think it's hilarious. Savannah? Nope."

"I'm with Savannah on this one." Dougal dried off the dish Angus had washed.

"Whatever." Angus went back to scrubbing the dinner dishes. "What the hell do you think he's after?"

He'd been wondering the same thing. So far, it didn't add up. "What if he came here to make peace?"

"With the stepmother he's never met before?" Angus snorted. "That makes no sense."

Which he agreed with, too. "Neither does lying about having cancer. What's there to gain from that?"

Angus grunted but kept on washing.

While Dougal dried and put things away, he mentally sorted through all the things he'd seen or heard firsthand. The only thing that stuck out was Lawrence's workshop. It was a stretch but not altogether implausible. "Money?"

Angus glanced at him. "Okay. How and why?"

"Ruth said Lawrence had a lot of money sunk into his workshop—his cars and tools. She never went in there but she's given Lucas the keys. Something about how he'd made good memories with his dad there."

"Except we both know he hated shop class in high school." Angus shook his head. "You think he's going to sell Lawrence's stuff?"

He shrugged.

"And the reason?" Angus shook his head. "Never mind. It's money." He frowned. "But why lie about it? Why not just ask Ruth? She seems like the sort of person that'd give him money."

Dougal shrugged again. "Maybe he is sick and we're being jerks—"

"It wouldn't be the first time." Chelsea came into the kitchen. "What are you being jerks about now?"

"What's wrong?" Savannah headed straight for Angus.

"Nothing. Now." He wrapped his soapsuds-covered arms around her waist and pulled her close. "They all asleep?"

"The girls are. Henry's singing in his crib." Savannah kissed his cheek. "I guess it's better than screaming in his crib."

"The boy does have healthy lungs." Chelsea sat on one of the bar stools. "Anyway, what nonkid-centered discussion were you two having when we walked in?"

"What did you hear?" Angus asked, wiping his hands on the kitchen towel Savannah gave him.

"Something about Ruth giving a guy money if he asked for it and then Dougal saying you were both jerks because the guy might be sick." Chelsea sat back. "Not enough for it to make sense." Her smile was unapologetic.

It had been a long day, and Dougal's patience was at an end. Seeing Chelsea sitting there, excitement lighting her face, snapped something inside of him. "Pretty sure I said something about you minding your own business earlier today."

"Did you?" Chelsea ran a hand over her hair and batted her eyes, all feigned innocence. "I don't remember."

"I guess you don't remember talking to Emory about me, either?"

"Chelsea." Savannah spun, staring at her sister. "What did you do?"

"I didn't *do* anything." Chelsea sighed. "I just wanted to get to know her a bit."

Savannah's groan said it all. "Chels, I like her. And she's super talented. If you cost me a potential friend and world-class caterer—"

"Whoa, whoa, nothing happened." Chelsea rolled her eyes. "Dougal is overreacting."

Dougal turned to his brother. "We can finish this conversation at my place—where the walls don't have ears."

Angus nodded.

"Oh, come on, Dougal." Chelsea slipped off the stool. "You can't stay mad at me. Please, please. I'm sorry." She smiled up at him, all mischief and no remorse.

"No, you're not." He looked her straight in the eye. "Seeing as you're Savannah's sister, I have to put up with you. Don't push it." And he brushed past her, whistled and opened the back door. It wasn't a long walk from the main house to the barn, but it was enough to ease his temper. Maybe he'd been a little hard on Chelsea, maybe not. But, dammit, he didn't need her help making a mess of things with Emory.

Emory.

Even the dropping temperatures couldn't cool the fire in his blood. He'd never gotten so lost in a person, so consumed by their scent and touch. But with Emory, everything else faded into the background. Her sighs and moans. Her soft curves. The way her full lips clung to his, as if ending their kiss was unbearable—at least, that's how it was for him.

He rubbed his hands together. If he'd been smart, he'd have brought his coat and gloves with him when he'd run off to Emory's earlier. All that had occupied his brain was getting to her. And now?

I hope I didn't end things before they got started. He glanced up at the darkening sky. No moon. No hint of the star-filled skies he'd often sit outside to watch. Instead, the distant flash and flicker of lightning illuminated the growing clouds. "It doesn't look good." That could apply to the weather and, potentially, his would-be relationship with Emory.

Chapter Eleven

Emory put the finishing touches on the iced sugar cookies. It had been two days of nonstop raining and, with the temps hovering at freezing, the roads had gotten slick. As a result, the bed-and-breakfast had a lot of cancellations.

Burt and Kathy White were celebrating their twenty-fifth wedding anniversary. Lisa Zimmer and Sonja Montoya had been college roommates and liked to get together for a girls' weekend a couple of times a year. Now the four of them were becoming fast friends over holiday treats, copious amounts of hot chocolate and coffee, board games, holiday movies and Aunt Ruthie's astounding knowledge on all things Dolly Parton–related.

Lucas had gone to a doctor's appointment shortly after his run-in with Dougal. His doctors were in Houston and, with the bad weather, there was no way he could get back to Granite Falls. Honestly, Emory didn't mind. She understood why Aunt Ruthie was letting him stay but there was just something…off about the man. The encounter between him and Dougal had only added to that feeling.

Tonight, they'd decided to have a movie night. Aunt

Ruthie had sent her off in search of the vintage reel-to-reel projector and films. It was either in the attic or the oversize closet in The Sweet Magnolia Tree suite—where Lucas was staying. Since she didn't relish climbing into the unheated attic, she'd start in Lucas's room.

Frosty, ever at her heels, immediately hopped onto the bed. He made a chirping sound, spun around and curled into a white ball.

"By all means, make yourself at home." She smiled at the dog, then surveyed the room. "He's not exactly the clean and orderly type now, is he?"

The room was, quite simply, a mess. He'd insisted he'd take care of it himself. Since Ruth was letting him stay there for free, the least he could do was clean up after himself. Considering the state of the room, she wasn't sure what cleaning he'd done since his arrival.

Another chirp. "Do you have the hiccups?" she asked Frosty—who appeared to be sleeping. "If so, I guess it's not bothering you."

Food wrappers and trash littered the top of the antique wooden writing desk. The bed was unmade, the blankets and sheets hanging off one side and resting on the floor. Shoes and boots were scattered all over the floor, and there were clothes piled in the mauve velvet wingback chair in the corner.

"Not my problem." She shrugged and stepped over a duffel bag to get to the closets. There were two. One for the guests to use and one, locked, for storage. Emory unlocked the closet and pulled the wooden door wide.

Frosty chirped again and Emory laughed. The little dog never failed to surprise her. He was a character. He'd learned to stare at her until she picked him up, to put one paw on her arm or foot when he wanted pets and to carry his food bowl to her when he was hungry—even if he's just been fed. The chirp was new.

Even though the closet was stacked high with boxes, they were labeled. "I don't see it." She scanned the boxes again, sighed, then closed and locked the closet. "Great."

Aunt Ruthie had used underbed storage containers in some of the rooms so Emory dropped to her knees. "Yes." The projector was there. She reached under the bed and tugged, the wheeled container sliding out with ease. It was almost free when something shifted and caught on the bed frame. A few swipes and she'd knocked it free and pulled the plastic-wrapped parcel out. "What…" Emory stared at the shrink-wrap block of money.

"Oh, Aunt Ruthie." She knew her aunt was eccentric, but this seemed a bit extreme. "This should be in the bank earning interest, where it's safe." She could only hope this was the only room her aunt had a stash in. What if one of the guests had found it? "Can you imagine, Frosty? This beats taking home a tiny bottle of shampoo or scented soap souvenir."

Frosty chirped again.

Only it wasn't Frosty.

The noise was coming from the slim drawer of the writing desk. She sat up on her knees and opened the drawer.

"Lucas forgot his phone…" But he hadn't. He'd been talking to his doctor's office as he was headed out the door. "Whose is this?" She took the phone. It was newer. It must belong to one of their recent guests. Odd that no one had called about it.

She swiped up to see if there was an emergency contact.

Susan Baumgarten.

Susan was Lawrence's ex-wife. Lucas's mom.

"Why does Lucas have two phones?" Something hollow and cold sank into her stomach. She'd felt guilty for being suspicious of Lucas but this... *This* was suspicious. Most people didn't have two phones. "At least, no one I know does."

She sat back, the phone in her lap, and glanced at the cash. The day he'd told her he was sick, he'd been on the phone with someone about money. Medical debt collectors he'd said. The sinking feeling expanded. Was the money her aunt's? Eccentric or not, her aunt had a good head on her shoulders. Leaving this sort of money to be discovered wasn't Aunt Ruthie's type of behavior.

But Lucas... He hadn't wanted anyone in here—even for clean sheets or towels. He'd wanted to be considerate. *Or hide something.* But what, exactly, did this mean?

A door closed downstairs and Emory sprung into motion. She was shaking as she put the phone back in its original place, pulled the projector from the bucket, then slid it—and the cash—back under the bed. Her heart was racing by the time she stood on the top of the stairs, a groggy Frosty in one arm and the projector bag under the other.

The lights flickered once, then twice, before the house went dark.

Emory giggled, her nerves strung taut. *Go figure.* She took a deep breath.

"Emory?" Aunt Ruthie called up. "We lost power. Can you make it downstairs okay?"

"I'll be careful." She set the projector down and pulled her phone from her pocket. "Lights." She turned on the phone's flashlight and carried Frosty downstairs and into the parlor. "Everyone okay?"

There was a fire crackling in the fireplace, and Aunt Ruthie was lighting candles. "It might be a little gloomy without the lights, but we've got gas for cooking and hot water and heat—plus fire for extra warmth—so I'd say we're set." She paused. "With any luck, they'll get the power fixed up and we won't have to use the solar power backup. Lawrence never showed me how to turn it on or how it works."

"It's fine, Ruth. We can still see enough to play the game," Lisa, one of the old college friends, said.

"If anything, it's like stepping back in time. It's nostalgic." This from Burt White.

"Food. Drink. Heat." His wife, Kathy, smiled. "Nothing to complain about."

"As long as there are cookies, I'm happy." Sonja laughed.

At least the guests were content. That was what mattered most to Aunt Ruthie.

Emory's phone vibrated, startling her. Other than her parents, she rarely got phone calls. And since her parents didn't text, she wasn't sure who'd be reaching out.

"Everything okay?" Ruth asked.

"Yes." She put Frosty on his dog bed in front of the fire and sat on the hearth to look at her phone. It was Savannah.

Emory was relieved to hear Savannah had changed her mind about going the fancy route. Between the weather and the tight timeline, it would have taken a miracle to pull it off. Instead, she'd decided to go with a more rustic Christmas theme—and use all the appetizers they'd sampled for the menu.

That sounds great to me, Emory texted back.

Great. Thanks for rolling with the change. Three dots bounced until Savannah asked how things were there. Dougal wants to know if you and your aunt are all right?

Emory hesitated. The last forty-eight hours, Dougal McCarrick had been on her mind. A lot. And no matter how hard she tried not to think about the way he'd held her, kissed her and generally rocked her world, it always went there. What happened between them had kicked open the door for an entirely new sort of craving—for Dougal. A craving that was even stronger now.

Now that she'd decided that could never, ever, happen again, those memories were torture.

But now, especially with today's discoveries, she wanted to talk to Dougal. Please give him my number and ask him to call me.

The three dots bounced and bounced and bounced.

Emory frowned at the screen.

Okay. Done. I'll try to get him to call but he doesn't like phones.

She'd barely finished reading the text when her phone started ringing. "Hello?"

"Emory?" His voice had her toes curling.

There it was. That gruff, raspy voice. It sounded just as delicious in person as it had the last two nights—in her dreams. "Hi, Dougal." She was not going to get hot and bothered in a room full of people. She stood, wrapping one arm around her waist and tried not to think about his lips on her neck. "How are things there?" She smiled at her aunt and left the room, heading into the kitchen.

"Fine. Cold." There was a pause. "You need something?"

You. Your body. She swallowed, shaking her head. *No. No. Absolutely not.* This was important. *Focus.* "I need to talk to you." She swallowed, choosing her words with care. "About Lucas. It's just… I have questions."

There was a bunch of rustling. "I'm headed into town for a few things. I can stop by."

"You're going to drive? Aren't the roads covered in ice?" According to the local news, most of the roads were a hazard, and only a handful of essential businesses were currently open. She didn't like the idea of him taking such a risk. "Is it safe?"

"Four-wheel drive." He didn't elaborate.

"Are you sure?"

"Yes." And he hung up.

Emory stared at her phone. She was smiling. And she couldn't stop. She'd be lying if she said she wasn't happy he was coming. *Because I need answers.* Throwing herself at him was not on and never would be on the agenda. All she had to do was think about Sam to know she had no right to be happy. And, even if she wanted to try again, was there enough of her tattered heart left to feel love?

"You're serious?" Angus followed him from the living room. "You want to end up in a ditch somewhere? Freezing to death?"

Dougal grabbed his Carhartt jacket and gloves off one of the hooks in the mudroom. "I'll be careful."

Angus grabbed his arm. "Dougal… I think it's great that you care about this woman, but I'd kinda like to keep you around. Have you watch my kids grow up so you can embarrass them—that sort of thing."

"That's the plan." He headed back into the great room to find all eyes on him. His mother. His aunt. Savannah. Chelsea. The dogs. Even the triplets were watching him.

"What?" He tugged on his coat.

Aunt Nola snickered. "Oh, nothing."

"Fine." He sighed. "Let's get this out of the way. I… like Emory Swanson." He paused, looking at each one of them. "Wait to talk about this until after I'm gone."

Willow and Gertie jumped up and ran to the front doors.

"Nope. You two are staying here." He stooped and gave them both a pat.

"You're worried about the damn dogs' safety, but not your own?" Angus grumbled.

"Watch your language." Dougal stood. "Stay."

Willow's tail drooped and Gertie let out a low growl.

"No, ma'am. No arguing." Without another word, he left.

The wind sliced through him, regardless of the layers he wore. He stepped cautiously, dodging ice and puddles until he was in his truck. By the time he was halfway to town, he was second-guessing himself. The roads were so bad, he found it easier to drive along the shoulder. So he did, at a snail's pace. He had his heater blasting and the radio on to distract himself, but he had knots in his shoulders by the time he parked in front of the bed-and-breakfast.

Power's out. He stared at the dim windows. So far,

the ranch hadn't lost power. He pulled up the collar of his coat, and carefully made his way to the wrought-iron gate. His boots slipped on more than one of the paving stones, but he windmilled his arms and managed to stay on his feet.

"You're here." Emory opened the door before he could knock. "Come in. Get warm." She shivered as a sudden gust of icy air buffeted them.

He stepped inside and closed the door, relieved to be here—with her.

Not staring at Emory was like not breathing. It had to happen. He tried not to be too obvious about it, but he couldn't help it. She wore a pale blue sweatshirt that had the words *Fluffiness Is the Key to Happiness* on the front and that made her eyes bluer than ever. If that was possible.

Her cheeks were a rosy pink. "What was so important that you had to drive into town?"

He should have thought of that before he got here.

"Diapers?" she asked.

He nodded. That made sense. "Yeah." He looked around. "How long has the power been out?" It wasn't cold inside, so he suspected it was a relatively recent occurrence.

"An hour, maybe?" She hesitated. "The house runs on gas so, really, the only thing we're missing are lights. Everyone's in the front parlor, playing games. Aunt Ruthie and the guests, I mean. We only have four guests but they're stranded here."

Which was four more than he was expecting. He hung his hat on the coat tree.

"We can go to the study to talk."

"Okay." He'd planned on practicing what he had to say on the way here, but the icy road had required all of his attention. Now that he was following her, the sway of her hips prevented any productive thoughts from developing.

Even with a wall of windows, there was a wood-burning stove to keep the room cozy. He took in the bookshelf that lined another wall and the collage of photos and newspaper clippings while she closed the door.

"Emory..." He turned, but couldn't look her in the eye. Not until he got it all out. "I am sorry for what happened. I shouldn't have let him get to me like that." He shook his head. Lucas was an ass, but he was the one who'd reacted the way he had. "I shouldn't have come that close to losing control like that."

Emory sat on the love seat, watching him. "He said it wasn't the first time you two had fought."

He ran his fingers through his hair. "We didn't like each other, but I never laid a hand on him—or anyone, for that matter. I knew better." He shook his head. "I still do."

"You never..." She paused, her gaze fixed on his face. "What did you want to tell me?"

He swallowed, paced the length of the room, then turned and did it again. "My cousin Rory stayed with us when her mom was deployed. She went to high school here—sweet and smart. Good kid." He glanced her way. "She's a couple of years younger than me."

She nodded, her brows dipping. "And she and Lucas dated?"

"Yeah." He sighed. "Angus and I tried to warn her off of him, but she didn't listen. When she got pregnant, she took it pretty hard. She had a goal. Good grades, scholarships, college, all that." He sat on the other end of the love seat and rested his elbows on his knees. "It was Lucas's. There was no one else."

Emory swallowed.

"Lucas said it wasn't his." He sat back. "He said she'd cheated on him." He pushed off the couch and went back to pacing. "Lucas was a local and his dad was honest and hardworking and well-respected. Folks believed him." He ran his fingers through his hair again, sticking to the facts. "Rory still loved him, and she went to talk to him. I don't know what he said to her, but she came home and...tried to hurt herself. Her mom came home and they left Granite Falls." He cleared his throat.

Emory covered her face with her hands. "And then he said... What he said to you..."

"Yeah. I reacted."

Emory peeked through her fingers. "Is Rory okay now? What happened to her? To the baby?"

"Rory's happy. Allana is a good kid. She hasn't asked about who her dad is yet. Maybe she won't." He hoped she wouldn't. He sat again. "They're good, they've moved on, but I still let him get to me anyway."

Emory was staring at him, her mouth open. "Dougal, you can't be serious? It makes sense..." She reached over and took his hand. "What he did was awful. And, that day, it seems like he was goading you." A garbled, frustrated sound slipped out. "I'm not sure I'd have stayed as calm as you'd been."

"Was I calm?" But he chuckled, his thumb running along the back of her hand before he could stop himself.

"Is that why Lucas went to live with his mom?" Emory didn't let go of his hand.

"I don't know. Lucas caused a lot of problems. Crashing a friend's car. Breaking into the grocery store for beer. Dragging tire spikes across the highway and causing one hell of a traffic pileup. He was a piece of work—somehow he never got caught. He was good at lying. Did it all the time. Who knows what was true." He glanced at her. "Ruth told me about his cancer and I'm sorry for him but... Well, him showing up strikes me as odd."

"Me, too." She paused, studying him for a long while before she said, "I overheard him talking to someone about paying something off. He said it was a debt collector but... Then, today, I found another phone in his room. And...there's money under his bed." She lowered her voice. "More than the average person would have on hand. It's weird, isn't it? All of it."

He nodded. "He's hiding something."

"I think so." She seemed to realize they were holding hands now and gently tugged free of his hold—tucking a strand of hair behind her ear. "If I hadn't been looking for the projector for Aunt Ruthie, I wouldn't have found the cash. But it was under the bed, with the money. And I thought Frosty was making a weird sound, but it turned out to be his phone chirping. He has some messages. I couldn't unlock the phone, but I know it's his because his mother is his emergency contact."

They sat there in silence. Dougal was working through everything she'd said; he figured she was probably doing the same. It didn't add up.

Emory nibbled on her lower lip. "This is horrible to say but... What if he's not sick? What if he's here for something else from Aunt Ruthie? More money?" She shook her head.

"If it makes you feel any better, Angus and I were wondering the same thing." He sighed. "Has he asked her for money?"

"I don't know." Her gaze met his. "But they have spent a lot of time together, Dougal. Without me. If he did ask her, she might not tell me." She was whispering when she said, "I've never seen that much money in my life. Why would he have that? And still have debt collectors calling him? What if…what if he's involved in something dangerous?"

He didn't like seeing fear in her eyes. "Hey." He tilted her chin up. "It will be okay." Somehow, some way, he'd figure this out and send Lucas Baumgarten packing. He was done letting the bastard torment the people he cared about. And he cared about Emory—who was he kidding? It didn't make sense but the truth was he was falling for Emory. And he'd do everything in his power to protect her from further hurt.

Chapter Twelve

The way Dougal looked at her, so confident and determined, she was tempted to believe him. Maybe, thanks to Aunt Ruthie's penchant for crime shows and murder mysteries, her imagination was getting carried away. Maybe the phone and money and odd phone call would turn out to be nothing. Maybe, just maybe, she was making too much out of things and it would be okay.

But there was a tiny voice in the back of her head that told her otherwise.

It was the same voice that had warned her about Sam—the same voice she'd ignored. She knew now it was better to face the truth, no matter how hard that truth was, than willfully pretend everything was fine. If she and Sam had called it off instead of having the same fights, over and over, would he still be alive? If that last horrible fight hadn't happened, there would have been no reason for him to be so angry that he'd lost control of the car.

"Emory." Dougal's hand rested against her cheek.

She blinked, bringing her back to the present. Here. With Dougal. She met his gaze and saw the concern on his handsome face. "Sorry."

His thumb stroked along her cheek, searching her face. "Where did you go?"

She was not going to talk to him about Sam. "I…nowhere…" She should lean away from his touch. It was too warm, too gentle.

He frowned, but didn't push. It was one of the things that drew her to him. His quiet, steady presence. Even when she'd been sobbing in the vet hospital, he'd stayed by her side. It was unexpectedly sweet. *He* was unexpectedly sweet.

Instead of pushing his hand from her face, she covered his hand with hers, pressing it to her cheek. He was warm. His presence was solid. She closed her eyes and took a deep, steadying breath, drawing in his delectable scent of leather and minty aftershave. *I am in so much trouble.*

"Emory?" Aunt Ruthie called out. "I think Frosty needs to go out."

"Oh." She was instantly up. "Dog mom duty calls."

Dougal stood, too, towering over her.

It took everything she had not to slide her arms around his waist. Not just to touch him but to lean on him…to take the strength she knew he'd give her.

That realization unnerved her. There was a huge difference between being attracted to someone and wanting to rely on them for emotional support. She was okay with the attraction, but getting emotionally attached to Dougal was…well, it was ridiculous. They barely knew each other.

"Emory?" Aunt Ruthie called again.

"Coming." She ran past Dougal and out of the study, grateful for the interruption. Frosty met her at the front door, whimpering and turning in circles. "Okay. Let's go." She tugged on her coat and followed the dog onto the front porch. Not only had the rain turned to sleet, but the winds were gusting—snapping tree branches and icicles free.

When Frosty was done, she and the dog headed into the kitchen. It had always been her sanctuary and that's just what she needed—someplace safe to collect herself.

Aunt Ruthie was waiting for her. If she noticed anything amiss with Emory, she didn't say so. The only thing on her mind was making sure there was plenty of food for dinner. Normally the bed-and-breakfast only served breakfast and an afternoon snack. But, normally, guests were out and about for dinner, shopping downtown, and whatever festivals or rodeos taking place in the evening.

Aunt Ruthie opened the pantry. "Do we have enough food?"

"We always have more than enough food." Emory opened the refrigerator to take stock of their options. "I can make a beef and potato stew with veggies, chili, or...spaghetti and meatballs."

"You are an angel." Aunt Ruthie clapped her hands. "I'll ask the guests?"

"Sounds good."

"Oh, there you are Dougal." Aunt Ruthie patted his arm. "You're staying I hope? It's nastier than ever out there."

Emory agreed. "You're staying." The thought of him driving in this weather was terrifying.

He nodded, his gaze lingered on her for longer than

necessary—just long enough for her insides to soften. "How about I get the generator started?"

"We don't have one. Lawrence was all about the latest bells and whistles, so he had some batteries installed for the solar panels. I don't know how it works or how to turn it on." Aunt Ruthie pulled open one of the kitchen drawers. "He has all that out in his workshop. One thing I did do before I gave up on the place was get him a filing system for all his manuals and warranties and all that." She handed him the keys. "I'm sorry, I imagine it'll be cold out there."

"I'll see what I can figure out." Dougal took the keys and went out the back door.

Aunt Ruthie headed to the parlor to establish the dinner menu and Emory took inventory of the holiday cookies.

"Almost out of gingerbread." And since reminding herself of all the reasons why she needed to resist this ache for Dougal wasn't working, she might as well be productive and bake. "I do already have dough in the refrigerator."

Frosty barked, sitting at her feet.

She ignored the piles of iced sugar cookies, peppermint brownies and snowball cookies. As well as the platters on the kitchen table laden with molasses cookies, eggnog cookies, raspberry and apricot thumbprint cookies, and peanut butter blossoms. "You can never have too many Christmas cookies, Frosty." She pulled a chewy bone from the cookie jar on the counter. "A treat for you."

Frosty took the chewy to his bed in the corner, wedging himself between the cats. Loretta and Tammy had definitely accepted her pup because neither of them put up a protest.

Then she got an idea. She rolled out some dough, cut out a myriad of festive shapes, then put the pan in the oven. Next, she collected all the Christmas cookie cutters, bags of cinnamon dots and raisins, filled piping bags with colored icing and put everything on the kitchen table. "I'll be back," she said to Frosty. She peered into the front parlor to find the five of them still gathered around the card table, intent on their game.

"When you're ready for a break, I could use some help cutting and decorating cookies."

The next hour was spent in the kitchen. The double batch of gingerbread dough made several dozen cookies. Each and every cookie was decorated.

"My, oh my, look at all the edible works of art." Aunt Ruthie was perusing the afternoon's work.

"I don't know about art." Kathy White pointed at one of her husband's cookies. "This looks like something our grandson would have made."

Burt picked up the cookie and took a bite. "Tastes delicious."

All of a sudden, the lights came on.

"Looks like Dougal figured it out." Aunt Ruthie smiled.

A minute later, Dougal came inside.

Emory took one look at him and frowned. "Oh, Dougal." His cheeks were deep red. So was the tip of his nose. And his ears. She poured a cup of hot chocolate into a mug and pressed it into his hands. "You're freezing. Drink that and warm up."

He nodded and sat at the table, cradling the mug.

Frosty came running, jumped into Dougal's lap and curled up.

"Good boy. Poor Dougal's cold, isn't he?" Emory smiled at the picture they made.

"I'll wait on introductions until Dougal here isn't a human Popsicle." Aunt Ruthie was exceptional at playing the hostess. "I appreciate you getting the lights on for us. I hope you didn't catch a cold out there."

Dougal shook his head. "It's not so bad."

Burt chuckled. "I take it this is your better half, Emory."

"I remember when Steve used to do sweet things like this." Lisa shook her head. "Now he'd probably hand me my coat and expect me to go do it. I mean, I'm perfectly capable but it's the thought that counts."

"A man should never stop romancing the woman he loves." Burt dropped a kiss on his wife's cheek.

For some reason, Emory felt the need to set the record straight. "Dougal is *not* my boyfriend." Why had she said it like that? So aggressively. Almost defensive.

The kitchen went quiet.

"He's my... He's a friend of the family." She glanced at her aunt for help.

Aunt Ruthie's brows went up as she glanced between the two of them. "Yes, he's a dear soul. And a very good friend. Clearly. To come and check on us in the middle of a storm."

Her aunt's words only added to the awkwardness of the whole situation. That was why she felt the need to explain why, exactly, he was here. "Oh, he didn't come for me—us. He'd already been planning to come into town. You had to get something, didn't you?" She looked at Dougal.

Why was he staring at her like that? What did that look mean? Was he mad at her? The muscle in his jaw was taut. He was mad. But why? Everything she said was true.

"I came to check on you." He took a slow sip of his hot chocolate, then another. "And Ruth."

But he'd said... Why would he... Her heart rate tripled and the sudden rush of heat to her cheeks had her panicking. Why had he said that? Why would he do that? No, she wasn't going to go there. Instead of standing there, staring at him with her mouth hanging open, she needed to do or say something. She managed, "It's so nice of you."

And then she headed around the kitchen island to wash her hands—as if washing her hands was of the utmost importance at that very moment. But, really, she needed a minute. She ignored the chatter and laughter behind her and began to tidy up the cookie decorating mess. When that was done, she stared around her for something else to do.

Dougal was watching her.

She tore her gaze from him.

"Oh, Emory, honey. I think we voted on stew for dinner." Aunt Ruthie's announcement was almost a relief.

"I'll get started." She started assembling what she'd need, hoping they'd all leave and she could have her sanctuary back. Alone. Just her, Frosty and the cats. And, eventually, everyone did go back to the parlor. Except for the silent mountain-of-a-man sipping hot chocolate—his eyes warm and steady as she worked.

* * *

Dougal rarely got his feelings hurt. Mostly because he kept a tight rein on his emotions. His circle of family and friends was small, and his loyalty and devotion to them was absolute. This whole thing with Emory was a brand-new experience. He didn't know what to do with it—but he did know it hurt to have her dismiss him that way. As if the idea of the two of them being involved was distasteful or offensive. Did she really think that?

Whatever she was thinking, he couldn't tell. She was chopping and peeling and slamming pots around—all with her back to him. He couldn't see her face or read her eyes...

Angus was right. He had no idea what he was doing. That much was obvious. And now that the room was crowding in on him and all the things he'd never expected to feel had him by the throat, he needed to get the hell out of here.

He set the mug on the kitchen table and stared at her back. "I guess I should head out."

She stopped moving, but she didn't face him. "No."

He took a deep breath. "Why?"

She threw another carrot into the large pot and spun to face him. "Because it's dangerous, that's why."

Why was she mad? He hadn't done anything—this time. "I made it here just fine. I'll make it back fine, too." He stood.

"No."

Her tone brought him up short. He didn't know what to make of her.

Her face was bright red as she came around the island. "Dougal." She wiped her hands on a kitchen towel as she walked. "Your family wouldn't want you driving in this." She tossed the towel aside and put her hands on her hips.

"They weren't happy about me driving into town." He couldn't keep the edge from his voice. "They probably won't like me driving back home, either."

"Then why… Why…" She sputtered and shook her head. "You said… You told me you were already coming into—"

"I came here for you." He shrugged.

She froze, her eyes going wide. "I don't understand."

"I wanted to apologize. You said you had questions." He swallowed. "I came."

"While I do appreciate that, it could have waited." She frowned. "Or you could have said so. On the phone. Not driven through that—" she pointed at the window "—to do it in person."

"I could have." But if he'd done that, he wouldn't have seen her with his own eyes—and known that she was warm and safe.

"Then why didn't you?" Her voice was shaking.

She was breathy and flustered and, for the life of him, he didn't get why. "You're awful upset. What happened?"

She pressed her eyes shut. "You…you…" She broke off. "You're making this…hard."

Making *what* hard? He couldn't win. "I'm going."

"No." She grabbed his arm, her fingers tightening as she said, "You're not." Why wouldn't she look at him? "You can't." She let go of his arm—then turned into him to bury her face in his chest.

He stared down at the top of her head, beyond lost

now. But, dammit, she was soft and warm and pressed against him. He wasn't going to resist. His arms went around her. "You're shaking."

She shook her head but she stayed silent.

He ran his hands up and down her back. The push and pull going on inside of him was a new experience. One part of him was all too happy to have her close. The other part was trying to make sense of what was happening.

"Stay." The word was muffled against his chest.

"Okay." If that's what she wanted, he'd stay. But he had to know. "If you'll tell me why you're so upset."

She stared at his chest a full minute before looking up at him. "I'll tell you. But later, please. After dinner—after everything is done for the day?"

He didn't like it but he'd wait. "Okay."

Her blue eyes were searingly intense. "If you tell me why you really came here today."

"To apologize." Hell, he might as well get it all out there. "Mostly."

"Mostly?" It was a whisper.

"It doesn't matter now." He could still hear the way she dismissed the notion that he was her boyfriend—all horrified denial. Fast, at that. "I got my answer." So why was he tangled up in her right now? His hold eased and he stepped back.

When she was too close, things got muddied in his head. Like now. If he kept space between them, he wouldn't serve himself up for more hurt. And he'd get hurt. Guaranteed. He could see it from the wary look on her face. It took effort, but he managed to tear his gaze from hers and step back until there was a few feet between them.

She stood, blinking her big eyes and looking beautiful.

Dammit. He took a deep breath. "I'll go see what else needs doing." He walked out of the kitchen and toward the murmur of conversation at the end of the hall.

Lucky for him, Ruth Baumgarten understood he needed to stay busy. Working on a ranch meant there was always something to do. If he was sitting still, he was eating or sleeping—that was about it. Those days where he was stuck indoors doing paperwork were his least favorite.

Dougal spent the next few hours getting a fire started in each of the occupied rooms. Including, she insisted, the room he'd occupy that night. He didn't let himself think about that. Once the fireplaces were crackling away, he braved the cold to bring in more firewood and delivered logs to each room.

There was nothing left to do, so he took the keys and went back out to Lawrence's workshop. He didn't know what he was looking for but that didn't stop him from looking. He'd been in a rush earlier, so maybe that's why he hadn't noticed the workshop lock itself. It was all scratched up. And, from the looks of it, the metal bar it was looped through had been jimmied at some point.

Someone had been trying to break in? It could have been years ago. Considering Lucas had the keys, there was no reason for him to break in.

Ruth was right about one thing. Lawrence did like to have all the bells and whistles. Not only did the large metal building house a workshop with every tool known to man, there was a man cave in the back—with built-in shelves to show off his substantial coin and baseball card collections.

He figured it was best to start in the workshop. Two things immediately stood out. A 1957 Chevrolet Bel Air and a 1980 Ford Bronco. He wasn't all that into collectable vehicles but even he knew each of these was worth a pretty penny. If he was going to sell anything, that's where he'd start. A quick scan of the workshop's interior was daunting. Lawrence Baumgarten had been a man of means. If Lucas was looking for a way to make cash, he wouldn't need to look far.

Dougal ran a hand over his face. After what Emory had discovered, he had more questions than ever. If Lucas had cash stashed upstairs, why would he need more? Or be in debt? Until they had more information, all they could do was be on the defensive.

He looked inside the file cabinet and did a quick search—both the car titles were missing.

That's good.

Without a title, there was no way to legally sell the cars. Unless, of course, Lucas already had them.

He skimmed the tabbed folders and paused. Two folders, Correspondence and Lucas. He reached for them, then stopped. It wasn't his place to go digging through Lawrence's life. He'd leave this to Emory and Ruth. He closed the cabinet drawer and headed to the man cave.

It was a sizable room. Photos dotted one wall. Family and friends. There was one of Lucas and Lawrence by the Ford Bronco, smiling and happy. He shook his head. What would keep a son from his father? Or a father from his son? He didn't understand it. He'd butted heads with his father through the years but, no matter how angry they got, neither of them ever worried about losing the other's love.

Aunt Nora said some people just had faulty wiring and there was no changing it. He thought that might be the case with Lucas.

He sat in one of the oversize leather recliners and turned on the massive big screen television. If he timed it right, the weather should be on soon—but he hadn't meant to doze off. By the time he headed back inside, it was dark outside. And colder than ever.

He crept into a dark kitchen. There was a single candle burning. Beside it sat a large bowl and a plate with crusty rolls stacked high. He leaned against the counter and ate, devouring every delicious bite. Emory was magic in the kitchen.

And in his arms... Yeah, those were the sort of thoughts he needed to avoid. He washed his dishes, put them in the drying rack and headed upstairs. He was tired. He could only hope he was tired enough to sleep— without his dreams tormenting him.

Since the solar panel batteries wouldn't last forever, he kept his shower short. After he wrapped a towel around his waist, he used the travel-sized toothpaste and new toothbrush that had been placed on his bathroom counter and headed into the bedroom.

Emory sat, curled up in the wingback chair before the fire. But the moment she saw him she was up and staring at him. Why was she here? And why did the firelight have to turn her nightgown all but invisible. His gaze dropped to the carpet at his feet and he dragged in a deep breath. He liked to think of himself as a strong man, but he was rapidly discovering he had one hell of a weakness. Namely, Emory.

"What are you doing in here?" He couldn't help the gruffness to his voice.

"I… I told you we'd talk later."

He saw her bare feet. She shifted from one foot to the other, her toes curling into the nap of the carpet. "Now?"

"It's later." She blew out a slow breath.

It *was* later. But he hadn't considered they'd be talking with her in a nightgown and him in a towel. Still, she was here and he knew he'd listen to whatever she had to say.

"I haven't talked about what happened but now… I want to get it out." She paused. "My parents don't want to hear the truth. I don't want to upset Aunt Ruthie. You've let me fall apart more than once—without judgment. Can I tell you?"

He looked at her then. The rawness of her plea tore at him. She was fragile; he could sense it. If she fell apart, he'd be here to help put her back together.

She took a deep breath. "Sam—Sam was my husband— was a genius. Medical research. He would have done something amazing. Cured cancer or diabetes—he was that sort of genius." She paused. "When we got married, I became part of his five-year plan. We just fit, you know? Seamless… No ripples. No drama. Life went on."

No ripples? He didn't know what that would look like. Since he'd met Emory, he'd been riding on a damn tidal wave.

"When I got pregnant—which hadn't been part of the plan—it got hard. We argued but worked through it. Eventually, I thought he was happy about it. Then I miscarried." She broke off, hugging herself.

This was the pain that still tormented her. Her struggles were beyond his comprehension. That sort of loss…

It was hard to see her struggle and keep his distance. He took a step forward, then another.

"He was detached afterward. I assumed he was grieving, like me. It hurt to deal with it on my own but… In counseling, he admitted he was relieved. He'd worked so hard to get where he was and had so much to do before he could think about having a family." She shrugged. "All I could think about was the baby we'd lost and the hole in my heart. That he didn't want to talk about the baby? I just…" She shook her head. "Somehow, it caused a disconnect between us. We went from arguing to not talking much at all." Her hand was shaking as she plucked at the front of her nightgown. "The night he died, he told me counseling wasn't working for him. Neither was our marriage. I was so hurt I lashed out at him. I was horrible. Called him selfish… Uncaring. And more." The words were rapid-fire, rushing together and blurring so that he had to focus. "He was so angry…" She paused to take a deep breath. "The police report said he lost control of the car. That was why he crashed, because of me. The world lost the next Charles Best or Edward Jenner and it's my fault. It's my fault he's gone." She was shaking now. "I can never tell him how sorry I am or take back what I said. And all the things I should have said haunt me."

It gutted him to know she felt responsible for Sam's death—and that it still weighed on her so heavily. "Maybe it's time to let go, Emory."

"I know it's not the same, but you were mad at me tonight. When I asked you to stay you pushed back and… I panicked." She swallowed, her gaze searching his face.

"Partly because the roads are the way they are, and all I could think about was you crashing…" Her voice broke off.

He'd wanted to give her space but now he found himself wrapping her up in his arms. "I'm sorry about that. I was being pigheaded." He sighed as she relaxed into him.

"You were," she whispered.

Even with his insides twisted up, she managed to make him grin. She'd been through hell. She'd tried to endure it on her own—then chosen to confide how she saw her truth. In time, he hoped she'd see the accident for what it was: an accident. She wasn't responsible for Sam's death. But she probably didn't want to hear that right now. It took a minute to form the words. "Thank you for sharing, Emory. I… I am sorry you had to bear that. All of it." It wasn't nearly enough. All he could do was hold her until he figured out what to say next.

Chapter Thirteen

Emory took a deep breath. Finally. After almost two years, it was out. While everyone had been offering her support and shedding tears on her behalf, she'd been consumed with anger and regret. The world saw her as a victim in need of consolation. But she knew better. She deserved to be punished so she'd punished herself. She'd bottled it all up and held on to it until it colored her every day.

How many times had she replayed everything that had happened? All the loss and loneliness. What she'd done to Sam.

Maybe it's time to let go, Emory.

The idea scared her. Her grief and guilt had become her armor—keeping the world at arm's length, it kept her from getting hurt or hurting others. She'd never be free from the guilt, but she wasn't smothering anymore.

Did she deserve that? To feel lighter?

She'd known Dougal wouldn't cut her off and argue with her. He didn't tell her it wasn't her fault. That's not what she needed. She'd needed to unburden herself freely about what had happened. And the part she'd played in it. And he'd let her do just that.

In the fireplace, a log shifted—followed by snaps and pops. It was quiet. So quiet. The fire. The light thudding of rain and sleet on the roof. And…the rapid beat of Dougal's heart beneath her ear.

She closed her eyes. Counting the thump-thump of each beat, soaking in his warmth, and just breathing. There was something about Dougal. His steady, solid presence. Yes, he was shirtless—well, mostly naked, really as her arms were pinned between them—but, somehow, there was nothing awkward about being in his arms. Nothing. She sighed.

His hand pressed against her back, his fingers splayed between her shoulders.

His breath brushed against her ear. Deep and rhythmic.

She was all too happy to be here. Even her heart…

No. No. No. Her heart would not get involved. Period. She had no right. How could she open her heart to anyone? How was it fair for her to love again?

But she was in no hurry to break his hold. Her heart wasn't the only part of her that responded to him. She ached for him. His touch. His kiss. Every bit of him. And now that she was thinking about the touching and kissing and Dougal, she was burning for him. She'd never burned for anyone before.

His other hand smoothed over her hair and down her back to rest at her waist—amplifying the heat low in her belly.

"I still don't understand why you didn't apologize over the phone." She tilted her head back to see his face. A brother and son, uncle and dog-father. He had people who relied on him and needed him in their lives. To think of him navigating the icy roads into town upset her all over again. "It's not a short trip, Dougal. Why did you risk your safety coming here?"

He blew out a long, slow breath. "I told you." His hands slid down her back and let her go. He took a step backward, dodging her eyes.

"To check on me and Aunt Ruthie?" But he was holding something back. "What else?"

He ran a hand over his face, causing the muscles in his arms and shoulders and chest to flex.

Emory couldn't breathe. It wasn't that she'd forgotten he was only wearing a towel, it was that she hadn't been in the right frame of mind to fully appreciate that fact before. Now, she was. And she was very much appreciating everything on display. The sculpted expanse of his wall-like chest was breathtaking. She was, in fact, having a very hard time breathing.

He sighed, oblivious to her struggles. "I thought there was something here. Between us. I figured it was a stretch to ask you for more. But... I figured I'd ask anyway." He ran his fingers through his hair, his gaze locking with hers. "You made it clear in the kitchen you've got no interest in this." He pointed back and forth between them. "So, it doesn't matter now." His smile was tight.

"I said you're not my boyfriend..." She blinked. *No right to ask you for more.* What did "more" mean, exactly? She swallowed, trying to muster the courage to ask. "But..."

The muscles in his jaw clenched tight. He tore his gaze from hers but not before she'd seen his blazing hunger.

This was Dougal. If she didn't say something, do something, nothing would happen. She could walk out of this room and go to bed, imagining what could have happened, and hope this attraction fizzled quickly. Or… Or she could say something outrageous like, "If, by more, you were going to ask me if I want you to take me to bed and make love to me, then you should ask." The words were out, hanging between them. "Ask, Dougal…"

His head whipped up. For a second, she thought she'd made a mistake. He stood, his hands flexing at his side—then he moved. "I want you in my bed."

No man had ever picked her up before. Dougal had no problem swinging her up and into his arms. Still, it surprised her. "Dougal…" she gasped, staring up at him.

The longing on his face stole whatever words she might have said.

"Do you want me, Emory?" The rasp in his voice triggered a full-body shudder.

"Yes." Her voice wobbled as she said, "Please." She threaded her hands through his damp hair to pull him closer. She wanted him to kiss her.

His lips were surprisingly gentle. Cautious at first. Sweeping over her own once, again, before the kiss deepened and she was clinging to him. The moment his tongue touched hers, she was lost. She arched into the brush of his work-roughened fingers along her neck. When her hands slid down to his shoulders, she marveled at the flex and roll of his muscles.

When they'd reached the bed, she didn't know. But the sight of him over her, braced and breathing hard, made her insides melt. The way he looked at her left little doubt of his desire.

His fingers fumbled with the buttons down the front of her nightgown but he was determined. The low groan that slipped from him as he pulled the fabric apart made her feel beautiful. His gaze explored her bare skin with an almost reverent quality. It was too much, too intense. She reached up, wrapped her arms around his neck and pulled him down for a kiss.

Skin on skin. Mouth to mouth.

"Dougal," she moaned against his lips. She wanted to taste every inch of him. From nipping kisses along his neck to sucking his lower lip, she couldn't get enough of him.

His hands were never still. Where his hands went, his mouth followed. There was nothing rushed about him. His mouth worked over one breast until the nipple was hard and throbbing. Only then did he turn his attention to the other. And it was exciting and frustrating at the same time.

She was frantic when she reached down to tug his towel off.

He paused, breathing hard, and smiled down at her.

She pulled her arms free from her nightgown and sat up long enough to pull it up and over her head.

His strangled groan told her he wasn't as in control as he acted. That, and the weight of his arousal against her thigh, had her murmuring, "Dougal...please."

He froze then, shaking his head as he pushed off of her. "Dammit."

"What?" she asked, stunned.

"I don't carry protection around." There was real anguish in his voice.

"I have an IUD." She swallowed. "And I'm healthy."

"I am, too." He nodded. "You trust me?" There was a vulnerability to him that surprised her. He stood, fully naked and aroused, looking uncertain as he waited for her answer.

"I trust you," she whispered.

He stayed where he was, staring at her. It was hard to stay still while he gave her a head-to-toe inspection. "Hold on… You're beautiful."

And now she felt beautiful. "Come here." She reached for him.

He took her hand and let her pull him down on top of her. His hand trailed along her hip to her thigh, sliding between her legs and hitching her knee along his hip. The whole time, his eyes blazed into hers. Even as he settled between her legs and slid, slowly, inside of her, he held her gaze.

Emory was gasping. The pressure was intense…and blissful.

His nostrils flared and a hiss slipped between his lips as he slid home. He was fighting for control. Fighting hard. His movements were deep and steady and still, he watched her face. It was enough to have her quickly coming apart. She held on to him as her body tightened, covering her mouth as her orgasm slammed into her.

"Dammit," he hissed, the muscle in his neck taut. He moved faster now, harder—until Emory was shattering beneath him again.

There was something wholly empowering about giving this big, silent man pleasure. The way his eyes widened as he fought to stay silent. The flare of his nostrils. The way he gripped her hand as his body bowed taut and he climaxed.

Watching him was the single most erotic thing she had ever seen.

"You okay?" he rasped, easing out of her and lying at her side.

She was panting too hard to speak but she managed to nod. Okay wasn't the right word. Weightless. Bone- less. Powerless. She couldn't move if she wanted to— and she didn't want to. "You?" One word, that was all she could manage.

He grinned. "Never been better." His fingers smoothed the hair from her forehead.

If she'd had any strength, that grin would have had her demanding a repeat performance. He looked so...so... happy. There was no sign of the withdrawn Dougal he showed the world. This Dougal had nothing to hide. He was showing her who he was. He was being open and vulnerable with her. As wonderful as it—this—he was, she'd never been more terrified in her life. How was she supposed to keep this man out of her heart?

Because I don't deserve him. This handsome cowboy deserved better.

That was that. Emory was it. Done. And over. He'd suspected it already, of course, but this erased any lin- gering doubt. She was meant for him. He wasn't fool enough to start declaring his love for her. Hell, not twenty minutes ago she'd been exposing her wounds to him. They were big and deep and a long way from healed. Until she was ready, he'd love her and bide his time. He was in no hurry and he wasn't going anywhere.

For now, he'd enjoy this. Emory. In his bed. Soft and warm and smiling at him. He wasn't sure what to say, so he said the first thing that came to mind. "Thank you for..." For making my world come apart? He swallowed. "The...the stew." He pressed his eyes shut, silently cursing himself.

"You're welcome." She sighed. "Thank you for the orgasms."

That had him chuckling. "Any time." He trailed his finger along her collarbone and down between her breasts. Watching her skin shudder and pucker from his touch was addictive.

She giggled. "Be careful what you offer."

"It's an offer." He raised up on one elbow. "Any time." From this angle he could see all of her. It was a view he couldn't get enough of. Her body was damn near perfection. He liked that she was soft in all the right places. Her curves were made for touching. So he did. He cupped her breast, his thumb dragging across the pink tip until it pebbled. It was gratifying as hell.

"Are you proud of yourself?" Emory sounded a little breathless as she pulled the sheets up to cover her.

"Hmm?" He looked at her face.

"You're smiling at my boob." She clutched the blankets beneath her chin. "What did you expect to happen when you're teasing it like that?"

"You...fascinate me."

She rolled onto her stomach, effectively cocooning herself in blankets and sheets, then moved closer to him. "Is that a compliment? Fascinating?"

He couldn't figure out why she was suddenly determined to hide. "Yes, ma'am."

"Then I guess that's good." But she didn't sound convinced.

He sat up, turning to see her easier. "You don't like me looking at you?"

Her cheeks went red. "I… I… I guess you could say I'm not exactly comfortable in my own skin."

"I like looking at you." He frowned. "You're beautiful. I already said that." He ran a hand over his face. "You didn't mind when we were…"

"I figured you were too preoccupied to notice all my flaws." She sighed. "Let's just—"

"Wait, now. Hold on." He tipped her chin up, so she couldn't avoid him. "I was distracted, all right. By you and your body. All your flaws?" He shook his head. "There was nothing I'd want to change, that's for damn sure."

She blinked rapidly. The tip of her nose went red and she sniffed once, then again.

"Are you…" He let go of her chin. "I'm sorry. I didn't mean to upset you."

"Oh, Dougal." Her smile was brighter than sunshine. "You are… You have a way with words, you know that?"

His laugh was startled. "No. I can honestly say no one has ever said that to me before." But then a tear tracked down her cheek and he wasn't laughing anymore. "What's going on? What did I do?" He leaned forward, brushing the tear away and hoping like hell there were no more.

She let go of the blanket and wrapped her arms around him. "Nothing." She kissed him. "Everything." She kissed him again, her fingers caressing his jaw. "You're going to make this hard, aren't you?"

He had no idea what she was talking about.

"Are you tired?" Her lips moved along his neck.

He shook his head, tugging at the blankets that separated them. Tired was the last thing he was feeling.

"Good." She rose up on her knees, facing him. "Neither am I."

He slid his arm around her waist and pulled her onto his lap. Tomorrow would come and real life with it. Tonight, this was all that mattered. Sliding into her body and being gloved in her heat. Hearing her breath catch and her soft moan. The bite of her fingernails against his shoulder. He'd never get enough of the dazed wonder in her blue eyes.

It was the early hours of the morning before exhaustion won out and her eyes drifted shut. He could let her sleep and deal with the consequences in the morning. Or, do the right thing.

"Emory," he whispered. "Let's get you into your own bed."

"No…" Her eyes popped open. "Oh. Right."

Her pouty frown had him grinning. "You can stay."

She sighed. "I can't."

"I know." He'd have no problem walking into Ruth's kitchen in the morning, planting a kiss on her lips and staking his claim. But he respected her too much to do that to her.

She melted into his kiss—breaking away with a frustrated groan. "That was the shortest night in the history of the world."

He grinned.

She stooped to collect her nightgown and slipped it on. "Sleep well." She paused to shoot him a sleepy-eyed smile before slipping out the bedroom.

"Well…hell." He lay back on the bed, then rolled onto

his side. *Emory.* The sheets smelled like her. The pillows, too. He closed his eyes and breathed deep.

What happened tomorrow? How was he going to stop himself from reaching for her. From kissing her? How was he supposed to go back to acting like he hadn't been buried inside of her?

I'll damn well have to.

He slept hard and deep. As soon as his eyes popped open, he showered and dressed and headed downstairs.

"Good morning." Ruth stood at the check-in counter. "Power is back and the rain has stopped. Even better, the sun has decided to make an appearance. With any luck, next week's holiday activities will be a go after all."

He glanced at the glass-paned front door. Sure enough, the sky was a pale yellow. It was good news. So why wasn't he happy?

Ruth, on the other hand, looked happy. Was it his imagination or was her smile extra big this morning. "Go on into the dining room. Emory's been up since the crack of dawn. She's made a smorgasbord—there's certain to be something for everyone."

He nodded and headed for the dining room.

The three female guests he'd met the night before were sitting around the table, chatting, but there was no sign of Emory.

He must not have been all that subtle in his search because the male guest, who was at the sideboard loading up his plate, whispered, "She's in the kitchen."

He gave the man a nod and headed into the kitchen.

Emory's hair was piled high on her head. Her red-and-white sweater clung to her curves and kicked his pulse into overdrive. They'd spent a night wearing each other out, but that didn't stop him from wanting her.

He came up behind her and slid his arms around her.

"Mr. White, we've talked about this." Emory lifted his arm from her waist.

"Mr. White?" Dougal growled, ready to head back into the dining room.

Emory burst out laughing. "That was too easy." She smiled up at him. "It was a joke." She glanced around him before standing on tiptoe for a quick kiss.

But that quick kiss turned into something else. Before long, she was pressed against the island and he was sucking on her lower lip. She tasted just as good as she had last night. And he couldn't get enough of her.

It was Frosty that set him straight. The little dog scratched and pawed at Dougal's boots until he found the strength to let go of Emory.

She swayed against the island, holding on to the edge like her life depended on it. Damn, but she looked beautiful. Her cheeks were flushed and the fire in her blue eyes had him regretting ever letting her out of his bed to begin with.

"Morning." He all but growled.

"It is." The way she was staring at his mouth left no room for misinterpretation.

It helped knowing she still wanted him because he sure as hell wanted her. "Any time." His whisper was thick.

She nodded, her eyes locking with his. "This is going to be interesting."

That had him grinning.

"What happens now?" She swallowed, tightly gripping a kitchen towel in her hands.

He reached out, took the towel and tossed it on the counter. "The roads will likely be clear pretty quick." He caught hold of her hand. "Which means I'll head home. I'm guessing you'll be heading out to do something for the party soon?" He hoped. "Later today?"

"Today?" She smiled. "Now that Savannah's scaled things back there's no real reason for me to come out again until the day of the party." She let go of him to move the whistling kettle off the burner.

He frowned. The party was a week away.

"Emory." Ruth breezed into the kitchen, a notepad in her hand. "It looks like our last guests canceled. This freeze really panicked folks." She smiled at him. "At this rate, we'll only have Colonel Jimenez until New Year's."

Meaning she'd have plenty of free time? Dougal liked the sound of that.

"I figured we could set up a booth for the festival—give out cookies? Might get you some more business on the side? The Main Street group does it up right. A tree lighting. Santa in the square. Caroling. And a parade. All the local clubs and groups get involved. My favorite is the little cherubs' choir. So precious. All dressed up like angel babies, singing their hearts out."

Emory's smile barely twitched, but he saw it. Hell, he felt it. And since the kitchen island was blocking everything from the waist down, he let the back of his hand rest against hers. A light touch—in case she needed it.

She turned her hand and gave his a squeeze.

"How does that sound to you?" Ruth asked. "We could

do cookies and hot chocolate? Donate all the proceeds to the toy drive?"

"I'd love that. I'm always in the mood to bake." She adjusted the tie of her apron.

"Excellent. I'll try to get us close to Santa. That's where all the traffic is." Ruth glanced at Dougal. "You need to eat, Dougal. I don't feel good about wasting food." And she marched back out the kitchen.

"You *should* eat." Emory leaned close. "Goodness knows I worked up an appetite last night."

He shook his head at her grin. She was enjoying herself. "You wore me out." He loved the way her eyes widened, shocked. "Join me?"

"Okay." She pulled off her apron. "I need to see if anyone needs anything."

He swallowed his sigh. This was her job. He didn't relish the idea of sitting around the table with four strangers or trying to make chitchat. Comfortable silence was his preference. The only upside: Emory's cooking and, even better, Emory's presence.

He followed her back into the dining room and took the plate she offered him.

"Go on." She nudged him, her gaze lingering on his mouth.

"Emory, you're an amazing chef," one of the women at the table said. "Have you ever thought about opening up your own place?"

"You'd do well for yourself," another woman added, nodding. "Actually, there's an empty shop on the sea wall in Galveston. Isn't that right, Burt?"

"That's right, Kathy." Burt peered over his glasses at Emory. "You ever thought about moving?"

"She's only just got here." Ruth came in then, her hands on her hips. "Don't you all go trying to steal her away." She came around the table and hugged Emory close. "Having her here has been a gift, I tell you. One I'm not all that eager to part with."

"Don't you worry, Aunt Ruthie. There's no place I'd rather be." She hugged Ruth back, but over Ruth's shoulder, Emory's blue eyes found his.

He shouldn't read into that look. He knew better. She wanted him, he knew that. But wanting him wasn't the same as loving him. And that was what he was going to hold out for. A future, with Emory.

Chapter Fourteen

Two days. Two days ago she'd watched Dougal climb into his truck. He'd sat there, his gaze locked with hers through the windshield. If she waved him back, would he have come? Was that what she wanted? Not just Dougal in her bed, but Dougal in her life. The thought was too much for her.

"What's got you in knots, sugar?" Ruth sat across the kitchen table, her hair tied up in a bright pink net. "You're awful perplexed."

She shrugged. Aunt Ruthie didn't need to know how scrambled up her head was. But this had given her the opening she needed to bring up Lucas. "I'm worried about you, Aunt Ruthie. Lucas... I found a few things in his room that make me suspicious."

"Emory." Her aunt's disapproval was written all over her face. "I don't need you worrying over me. I certainly don't need you digging around in that boy's things—or his life. I'm capable of taking care of myself and making my own judgments. And I'm not going to hold his past against him. We all have pasts, don't we? We've all made mistakes a time or two?" She shook her head. "I know I have. And now that he's sick and dying? It's not right for me to use that as a means to keep him from finding his own peace."

Everything her aunt said was what she'd expected. Kind and benevolent. Still, she had to try. "But—"

"No buts. I appreciate your concern but I don't want to talk about this, you hear? I've made up my mind—for Lawrence and Lucas. I'm going to give that boy a second chance. If it's a mistake, it's a mistake I'll own."

Emory didn't agree with her aunt's choices but she'd hold her peace—for now.

"And here I thought your mood might have something to do with one Dougal McCarrick? It seems to me you've been a little blue since he left."

She slumped in her chair, stirring cream into her coffee.

"I'm just going to tell you what I think. No, you didn't ask me but that's not going to stop me." She took a deep breath. "You ready? Got your listening ears on?"

Emory propped her elbows on the table, rested her chin on her hands and nodded. "I don't know if I'm ready for this but… Go on."

"I've been married six times, Emory. Six wonderful men and six wonderful marriages. I'm not saying they all ended on the best terms but the beginnings? I wouldn't trade any of those. I decided early on I didn't want to live alone. I wanted a good life with someone I could share things with." She adjusted the linen napkin on the table. "I see how hard you're fighting that and it breaks my heart." She reached across and took her hand. "I love your mother, I do. She was my sister long before she was your mother. She's put Sam on a pedestal—made him into a saint—and that's hard to beat. Might make it difficult to find another man that measures up. The truth is, sugar, he was just a man. A good man. Smart, too. You loved him, I know you did. And that's as it should be." Ruth gave her hand a squeeze.

Emory shook her head. "The truth is, in the end… Sam and I… Our marriage was over." She swallowed against the tightness of her throat. "I loved him, I always will, but… It was broken between us. I broke it."

Aunt Ruthie was quiet for some time. "Well, now, I don't know about that, but I do know holding on to the past will lead to a lonely life." She gave her hand another squeeze. "All you can do is move on and try again. You have to ask yourself if life alone with an empty bed and memories is enough to make you happy? For some folks, it is, and only you know if you're one of them. You've got a lot of long nights ahead of you. And you deserve to be happy, Emory." She cleared her throat. "I get the feeling there's at least one big and brawny cowboy that'd be all too happy to take on the job."

"It's not like that, Aunt Ruthie." At least, that's what she kept telling herself. Considering anything else was too scary.

"Fine, then. If all you're ready for is knocking boots, I bet he'd take care of business. No need to live like a nun." Ruth waved her hand at her. "A person has needs. Women have needs."

Emory pressed her hands to her cheeks. "Aunt Ruthie…" She giggled. Dougal had been oh so good at satisfying those needs.

"Did I scandalize you?" She laughed. "I've been known to do that a time or two. Sorry, sugar. It's just, I figured you might need someone to set you straight. Or, at least, point out that you've got options." She let go of her hand. "My hope for you? You choose to live in the present, not the past." She stood and went to the wall of cupboards. "I think he left this here." She pulled out the handkerchief he'd given her so long ago.

Emory took the handkerchief.

"Maybe you need to take it to him?" Ruth shrugged. "For all you know, it might be important to him."

"It's a handkerchief." But she was already standing up, the handkerchief clutched in her hand. "I'm going to take a shower and get dressed." But her going to see him had nothing to do with love. She was going to see him because... Now wasn't the time to figure that out.

Aunt Ruthie patted her cheek. "You do that." She offered Frosty a treat. "Why don't you stay with me, Tammy and Loretta?"

Emory thanked her and ran to the carriage house. She shouldn't be this excited... But she was. Giddy, even. The sooner she pulled herself together, the sooner she could leave. It took ten minutes. Her hair was still wet when she grabbed her purse and yanked open the door of the carriage house—and froze.

"Dougal?" She gasped. He was here? She launched herself at him, smiling like a fool.

He caught her around the waist and held her a foot off the ground so he could carry her back inside—kicking the door shut behind him. "Going somewhere?" And then he was kissing her neck.

She pulled the handkerchief from her denim skirt pocket and pressed it to his chest. "I was on my way to return this. To you." She caught a glimpse of his smile before his mouth found hers. This...this was the reason she'd wanted to see him. She melted into him with a sigh.

"Your hair's wet." He stopped kissing her and frowned down at her. "You could catch a chill."

"A chill?" She tugged his shirt from the waistband of his pants as she walked him backward to the couch. "I'm pretty sure I'm on fire."

"Damn, Emory." He sat, tugging her down with him.

He smoothed her hair from her face and stared up at her, the heat in his eyes tempered with something far more devastating. Something she wasn't ready to see—or accept.

She focused on removing his thick gray Henley, on helping him unhook her bra. When he scooped her up, she pointed to her bedroom door. There was a trail of clothing from the living room to her bed. When he lowered her onto the mattress, she was wearing socks.

But then he was kissing her and she let herself get lost in him. Her fingers gripped his hips, reveling in the weight of his body against hers. The way they came together on a sigh. His every thrust was deliberate, stroking deep, and demanding her response. What choice did she have? Her body clenched around him, desperate for release.

His kiss fanned her hunger on but it was his gaze, boring into hers, that shook her to her core. Her name spilled from his lips, broken and rough, and she split into tiny blissful fragments. The pleasure rolled on until she was clinging to him and crying out.

He slid one arm beneath her to hold her against him but never stopped moving. Until his release found him. He ground into her, smoothing her hair back to hold her gaze. He was mesmerizing. Once again, he'd given her everything and left her shaken.

They collapsed in a tangle of blankets and limbs and heavy breathing.

"Hi," Dougal murmured against her temple.

She giggled. "Hi. How's your day been? What have you been up to?"

He chuckled then, shaking the bed.

She turned to see him. There it was. A tug. Deep in her chest. Because his laugh was...magic.

"It was a day... Now, it's looking pretty damn good." He paused. "Making you scream."

"I did not." Her cheeks were scalding.

His brows rose. "I'm not complaining." He shrugged. "Nice to know I'm doing something right."

She was laughing then. "If you did that any *righter*, I think you might kill me."

He nodded, a satisfied smile on his too handsome face. "Sounds like a challenge to me."

"Tell me something about you, Dougal." She stared up at him.

"Like?" He ran a finger along her shoulder.

"What...what's your favorite thing to eat?" She rolled onto her side and just out of his reach. He distracted her too easily.

He blew out a long breath. "I don't know. Food. I'm not picky." He smiled at her. "I'm getting pretty partial to your cooking."

She rolled her eyes. "Movie? Book? Vacation? Dream?"

He ran a hand over his face and sat up. "Well... I'm gonna need to think about all that. You?"

"You already know about me." She held up her hands. "Too much. With you, I start talking and don't stop."

He smiled.

"That makes you smile? I'm pretty sure I should be apologizing to you."

"I like that you like talking to me." His eyes narrowed. "I'm not complicated, Emory. Boring, is more like it. This is it. I've got no problem talking about horses or training or teaching someone—or telling someone when they mess up. But talking about feelings and thoughts?" He shook his head. "I'm clumsy with my words. Short is what Angus calls it."

"You're not clumsy with your words." Or boring.

"Not with you." He paused, his gaze falling from hers.

Dougal was a direct eye contact kind of man. When he was talking or thinking or making love to her. That— looking away—meant he was uncomfortable or hiding something.

"*Frankenstein*," he said, his fingers toying with the pom-poms decorating her quilt.

"What?" Where had that come from?

"The book. It's a good one. Read it a couple of times." He shrugged. "Straightforward. Good versus evil, right and wrong." He pointed at himself. "Simple."

"Nope." He'd shown her who he was. A good man. Protective of his family. Hardworking. That was who he was. Thoughtful, kind—with a good head on his shoulders. Handsome, too. No, gorgeous—especially all mussed and naked in her bed, like now. She swallowed. She shook her head. "I don't see you the way you see you."

"Same. I see a strong, sexy-as-hell woman who can

take care of herself. You look after your loved ones and will champion the weak. Frosty is proof of that." He tugged her closer. "A woman I like making scream— even if she denies it."

"I did not…" Why was she denying it? Whether or not she'd screamed, she had made a very loud and pleasure-filled sound. "Whatever. You said you liked it."

He nodded, sliding his arms around her and pulling her beneath him. "Might need to do it again."

And just like that, she was arching into his touch.

He did like making her scream. And, for the second time this morning, it was what broke his control and had him climaxing with her. He could keep this up all day—if that's what she wanted. Though he liked holding her close after. The way she was pliant against him gave him a different kind of pleasure. A different kind of intimacy.

He hadn't intended to take her to bed immediately. Making love to her had crossed his mind, of course, but not that they'd wind up naked in the first five minutes of his visit. She'd looked so damn happy to see him. So eager. He'd never had a woman jump into his arms before. When he'd seen it happen in movies he'd always rolled his eyes… But that was before. He hoped it was the first of many times Emory would jump—knowing he'd catch her.

The last couple of days, he'd thought an awful lot about her. Her laugh. The way she talked to Frosty. The open love she had for her aunt. The sweetness of her smile. The time apart had distilled things in a way he understood. He loved her. Loving her meant caring for her beyond the bedroom. That's when it got tricky for him. The urge to protect wasn't new—being protective of his family was inherent to him. But would Emory appreciate that? She was a strong woman. Independent, too. She might take what he'd done as interfering. The only way to know was to tell her. "I did something." He ran his fingers up and down her arm. "Might make you mad."

She glanced up at him. "I guess we'll have to wait and see."

"An old friend of mine is a Texas Ranger. I asked her to run a check on Lucas—see if he's flagged for something. Anything." He didn't like doing it. He hadn't talked to Maxine Bryant in years so to call her up and ask for a favor was way outside Dougal's comfort zone. And, as a man who liked his privacy, snooping in other people's business went against his nature. But this wasn't about him. This was about Emory. And Ruth. If anyone could find dirt on Lucas, it'd be Maxine. "If I overstepped—"

"You didn't. Thank you. Why would I be mad?"

"Me, butting in." He shrugged. "If I can protect you..." *Dammit.*

The subtle shift in her posture had him cursing his words. She wasn't melded against his side now—her posture was getting more rigid with each passing second. When she sat up, there was a shuttered look that triggered all sorts of warning bells.

"I appreciate the help, Dougal. Aunt Ruthie and I both do. But I'm not your responsibility. You don't have to protect me." She tugged the blankets up, putting up a shield to protect herself—from him.

He understood where she was coming from. And even

though he was taking a big risk, he wanted her to understand the same. "What if I want to?"

Her breath hitched. "Don't."

If only it were that easy. Emory had come into his life and turned everything upside down. And now, being protective of her was part of his new normal. He didn't want to feel this way—he'd been just fine before. But what he wanted hadn't factored in to any of this. When it came to her, it was all need. The need to be with her. The need to touch her. And, yes, the need to keep her safe. But he managed not to say as much.

"Dougal… I can't. I don't want anything more than… this." She was shaking her head as she spoke. "If I did or said something to make you think—"

"This works." He smiled, trying to lighten the mood. "This is good." Even if she never fell for him, he'd take whatever she gave him.

She didn't smile at him. The wariness in her blue eyes said enough.

Better to retreat and change gears. "No sign of Lucas?" He'd meant to ask—but then they'd wound up in bed and Lucas was the last thing on his mind.

"No." She let out a slow breath. "He's sort of disappeared. But I did ask Aunt Ruthie if he'd asked her for money. He has, for his medical bills. She said she's thinking about what Lawrence would want her to do. I suggested she look into everything before giving him money—what with the history between him and Lawrence. She didn't like that. In fact, she told me she was perfectly capable of making her own decisions, and it was no concern of mine."

"You didn't tell her about the phone or the money?"

"I tried. She didn't want to hear it. She said we've all made mistakes and that everyone deserves a chance at redemption. Especially someone who's dying. We didn't argue, exactly, but it didn't go well." She wrinkled up her nose.

That was the real roadblock. Being suspicious of a dying man sounded pretty damn heartless. Lucas could be into something shady and still be here for the reasons he'd stated. He was dying, and he wanted to be close to where he had good childhood memories. But seeing as how he had a small fortune under his bed, why was he asking Ruth for money?

"I guess it's too much to hope that he's gone?"

"That'd be nice, but I'm thinking he'll be back for his money. Max—Maxine said she's real busy, but she'll try to get the info to me in a couple of days. Let's see what she turns up. If anything."

"It would be nice to know before Lucas shows up." She was nibbling on her lower lip. "I don't want to broach the subject again with Aunt Ruthie unless there's something she needs to know. And, if there is, I'd prefer to have that conversation when he wasn't around."

"Are you scared of him?" Because he'd never seen that look on her face before—and it put knots in his stomach.

"He makes me...nervous." She glanced at him.

"Listen to your gut." He was doing his damnedest to stay calm. She didn't need to know how her confession troubled him. "Always."

She nodded. "It doesn't help that Aunt Ruthie only watches true crime, detective shows and police procedurals. Suddenly the most ordinary thing is suspect."

She smiled the first real smile since before he'd stuck his foot in his mouth and damn near spilled his heart.

There was nothing prettier than that smile. He was about to reach for her when his phone started ringing. He wanted to ignore it. But if he ignored it, there would be all kinds of hell to pay when he got back.

"Go ahead." Emory nodded. "We can't stay in bed forever, anyway."

But he was pleased to hear something that sounded an awful lot like disappointment in her voice. "Who says?" he asked, then grabbed his jeans off the floor and fished the phone from his pocket. "Hello?"

"Dougal?" It was Savannah—but it was hard to make much out with all the crying in the background. "Are you still in town?"

"I am. What's wrong?" He turned to sit on the edge of the bed.

"The triplets are sick." The wailing in the background was proof enough of that. "We were waiting for their meds, but they said it would be a couple of hours so we headed home. But the pharmacy just called and their meds are ready so—"

"I'll go get it." Poor kids. Poor Savannah, too.

Savannah's sigh was pure relief. "Oh, thank you Dougal... Hold on." There was a muffled sound. "Go on, sweetie."

"Unca Doo?" Tabitha's little voice wavered.

"Hey, Tabby-cat. You feeling poorly?"

"Owie, Unca Doo." She sniffed.

He started tugging on his pants. "I'll get your medicine and you'll be feeling all better. Okay?"

"'Kay." Another sniff. "Unca Doo weed?"

"I'll read all the books you want." He stood, the phone wedged between his ear and shoulder so he could zip up his jeans. "You rest and listen to your mommy."

"Wuvvoo."

"I love you, too." And he hung up the phone. "I'm sorry, Emory—"

"Don't be sorry." She held out his shirt and he tugged it on. "Here. That little voice was precious." There were tears in her eyes. "Who is Tabby-cat?" She smoothed his shirt in place.

"One of the triplets. Tabitha." Now that he knew about her baby, the pain in her eyes gutted him all the more.

"Unca Doo?" She smiled up at him. "I'm guessing you're her favorite uncle?"

"Only one, so yeah." His hands rested on her shoulders. "She likes me to read to her. Maybe I should have said my favorite book was *Goodnight Moon* or *The Cat in the Hat*. I've read them enough times."

She leaned into the hand he pressed against her cheek. "They're sick?"

"All three of them." He frowned, imagining the chaos—and the noise—that would be waiting for him. "They're going to need all hands on deck."

"Well, don't let me hold you back, Unca Doo." She winked at him. "Go be a superhero and save the day." She gave his rear a pat.

He slipped an arm around her waist and, surprising them both, dipped her. "Yes, ma'am." He kissed her, stood them up and let her go.

"A cowboy hat–wearing-superhero." She picked up the hat that'd been knocked off less than an hour ago. She put it on his head, adjusted it, then stepped back.

"Too bad you don't have a horse—you could ride off into the sunset."

"Not with me. But I have. More than one." He opened the door. "Next time you come out to the ranch, I'll take you for a ride."

Her brows rose. "A ride on horseback? Or…" Her grin was crooked, and her cheeks turned a pretty shade of pink.

He chuckled. "Both." With a final lingering look, he turned and jogged to his truck. He couldn't keep Tabby-cat waiting.

Chapter Fifteen

By Friday morning, there was no sign of the storm that had blown through earlier in the week. The air was crisp, but the warm sunshine kept it from getting chilly. All around Emory, the shop owners and artisans of Granite Falls were setting up a village of old-fashioned wooden booths. Each structure was unique and festive—but once they were adorned with fake snow, lights, tinsel and ornaments, the transformation of the courthouse lawn into a mini Christmas land would be complete.

"I've handed out stamps to all the booth owners." Aunt Ruthie held out the reusable shopping bag. "Now, the kiddos can go from booth to booth and get a stamp. When their card is all stamped up, they can bring it here and get a free cookie." She patted Emory's arm. "Where did you come up with such a brilliant idea?"

"Guess I'm just brilliant. Like my aunt." Emory stood on a stepstool, adjusting the strand of light-wrapped garland around the arch of their booth. "How does it look?"

Aunt Ruthie stepped back. "Lemme see, now." She cocked her head to the side, took two steps to the right, then stopped. "Right there." She pointed. "That bit is looped lower than the other."

Emory climbed down the step stool. "Okay, let me move—"

"Better?" A deep voice grabbed her full attention.

Dougal. Big and solid and smiling and more handsome than ever. All Emory could do was stare—and smile. The tug in her chest set off all sorts of warning bells but, right or wrong, she ignored them.

"Oh, Dougal, that is perfect," Aunt Ruthie said. "And you didn't need a step stool."

"Because he's a giant." Emory kept right on grinning at him—but resisted the urge to jump on him. The fact that he held an adorable toddler against his hip helped. "And who are you?"

"Hi." The little girl waved. She was all chubby-cuteness and dimples.

"Hi." Emory waved back, awestruck by the toddler. "You must be Tabby-cat."

The little girl grinned and buried her face in Dougal's chest.

"Tabitha, this is Emory." Dougal's gaze was warmer than the sun. "And Miss Ruth."

"Aren't you the most precious thing?" Aunt Ruthie gushed.

"How are you feeling?" Emory asked, looking to Dougal for an answer.

"She's feeling better. Henry got an ear infection now, so he's a grumpy *bear.*" He made a face at Tabitha, whose laughter was pure glee. "And Emilia's still all stuffy. Poor little critters." He bounced Tabitha. "I figured Tabby-cat could use some fresh air."

"What he means is we needed a break." Chelsea Barrett sauntered up, as sleek and model-like as ever.

"Everything's looking very festive." She inspected the courthouse lawn being transformed into a winter wonderland, then glanced at Dougal. "Wait, is this the place where you tripped and fell and cut your head?" She laughed.

Dougal, however, wasn't amused. If anything, he looked annoyed.

Emory shared the sentiment. She, too, found Chelsea annoying—but probably not for the same reason as Dougal.

"That sounds awful." Aunt Ruthie gave Chelsea a rather stern side-eye.

"Aw, he spooked easy back then." Chelsea wasn't the least bit remorseful.

"I was being chased." Dougal turned his attention back to Tabitha. "I was being chased by a wild monster. I'd have chewed my foot off to get away." The scared expression he made had Tabitha and Emory laughing.

Chelsea smacked him on the arm. "That's just mean."

Dougal ignored her pout.

Clearly, the two of them had some sort of inside joke—and it stung. Dougal had made it perfectly clear there was nothing romantic between him and Chelsea. Still, there was something between them. History. Memories. Nieces and a nephew and family. Dougal might not be interested, but she was fairly certain Chelsea was interested in him. Chelsea struck her as the sort of person who didn't give up easily.

"Need a hand with anything?" His gaze settled on her, steady and intent as ever.

Her chest tightened until her heart was aching. "I think we're good."

"We could use more lights." Aunt Ruthie pointed at the other booths. "We look a little chintzy in comparison."

"Or you could help hang more lights?" Emory shrugged, smiling at him.

"Come here, rug rat." Chelsea held her hands out for Tabitha. "Unca Doo needs to impress Emory for a minute."

Emory stared at the woman, shocked. What did that mean? Dougal had nothing to prove. He'd impressed her already—multiple times. She felt her cheeks go hot. Was their secret not so secret? Or was Chelsea hoping to stir things up?

Dougal shook his head, but he was grinning.

Even Aunt Ruthie was laughing. "I've got more lights in the car, Dougal." She waved for him to follow her.

Leaving her alone with Tabitha and Chelsea.

Chelsea bounced Tabitha. "He was talking about me, just then. The monster, chasing him." She pointed at herself. "I was on the hunt. And when I'm on the hunt, I'm relentless. Poor Dougal. I've never been one for subtlety, and he didn't know what to do with me." She paused, rolling her eyes. "He was backing away from me, tripped over one of those concrete parking block thingies and bashed his head." She laughed. "He was so embarrassed he had Buzz stitch him up. I felt so bad."

Emory sought out Dougal. She could imagine it all. Dougal wouldn't have appreciated a public display. He liked to keep his private affairs, private. If Chelsea had been interested in him, she should have picked up on that. *Hunting him?* Poor Dougal. He was hefting a large box from the trunk of Aunt Ruthie's car. From the looks of it, Aunt Ruthie was talking his ear off.

"He had zero interest." Chelsea went on. "Angus used to say he was too busy to go chasing after women or playing games. Which suits—he's on the serious side. You've probably noticed." She looked Emory in the eyes then. "You were married, weren't you?"

"I was. Sam died almost two years ago."

"Ohmygawd. That is awful, Emory." For the first time, Chelsea seemed sincerely sympathetic.

"It was." Emory nodded.

Chelsea seemed to puzzling something out. "You know Dougal is a great guy, don't you?"

"Unca Doo," Tabitha said, smiling up at Chelsea, then Emory. "Unca Doo, Unca Doo."

"Yes, yes, he's your favorite. I know." Chelsea sighed. "Anyway, Unca Doo is the real deal. All big and strong on the outside, but soft on the inside. You've seen him with his dogs? I mean, so sweet. He's just like that with the triplets." She paused. "He doesn't treat them like dogs… You know what I mean."

"I think so." She wasn't sure where Chelsea was going with this.

"He might act all cool and calm but, when it comes to you, he is *so* not. He's got it bad. During the storm, his mom and Angus argued with him about staying but no way, he wasn't listening. He announced he liked you and left. Announced it—to the whole family." She was watching Emory carefully. "He's, like, happy. He acts happy. Smiling and all that. Angus keeps giving him crap about it because it's weird. I don't know if you get how big a deal that is."

Every now and then, there'd be something about the way he'd look at her that made her wonder... She'd convinced herself she was reading into things. Attraction, definitely, and, maybe, affection, too.

"That is why I'm asking you to end whatever it is that's going on with you if you don't have feelings for him. And, yes, I know something is going on between you so don't even try to deny it." She smiled down at Tabitha, bouncing her. "Unca Doo is an in-it-forever kinda guy—which is why I gave up on him. I know he deserves a woman who'll give him the same. That's not me. Not yet, anyway." She shrugged. "If he's still single after I've sewn all my wild oats, who knows?"

Chelsea's words kicked up an instant flare of jealousy.

"And they're almost back so I've got to hurry and get this all out." Chelsea took a deep breath. "If you're in this for a long-haul scenario, great and congratulations. If you're looking for a hookup, look somewhere else." She held up a finger. "And, basically, you're an absolute idiot if you let him go."

"Unca Doo!" Tabitha clapped her hands the moment she saw her uncle.

"Back again." He set the box on the ground and took Tabitha. "Miss me?"

Tabitha giggled. "Go bye, home?"

"Not yet." He shook his head. "Let's hang all the pretty lights."

"Down?" Tabitha asked. "Down, peez?"

"All right." Dougal stooped and set her on her feet. "You good?"

Tabitha wobbled a bit, then nodded. She toddled to the box and pulled it open. "Pay?"

"I'm not sure there's anything to play with in there." Dougal stood, his gaze locking with Emory's. "You good?"

Emory nodded. *No.* She was... She didn't know. Reeling. Delighted. Horrified. So, so sad. Of course, Dougal was an in-it-forever kind of man. And still, she'd strung him along to get what *she* wanted. Further proof she had no right to this—to him.

Dougal's gaze bounced between her and Chelsea, the muscle in his jaw clenching tight.

Instead of letting things get increasingly awkward, Emory knelt beside Tabitha. "I bet we can unroll the lights for Unca Doo."

Tabitha nodded. "'Kay."

She and Tabitha sat on the grass, carefully laying all the ornaments and decorations on the lawn for inspection and possible use. Tabitha was perfect and adorable, and Emory was besotted with the little girl in a matter of minutes. While they unrolled lights, Dougal used the staple gun to secure the lights where Ruth pointed. Chelsea helped, too, making sure there were no holes and that everything was symmetrical.

And the whole time everyone else went about their business, Emory was still processing the shock of Chelsea's words.

He was happy because of her? He liked her? Well, liking wasn't the same as love... But she couldn't imagine Dougal announcing he loved someone? It was hard enough to imagine he'd told his family he liked her. But he had.

She swallowed. Chelsea was right; she should end

things with him. She'd never hurt Dougal—never on purpose.

He'd said he was good with things the way they were between them. She wanted to believe that because she wanted Dougal so much. But now that Chelsea had told her everything, how could she pretend there wasn't more at stake?

Her gaze wandered to Dougal and her heart stopped. He'd tipped his hat back on his head and was assessing his handiwork, and he was so handsome Emory couldn't breathe.

"Unca Doo." Tabitha pointed at him and smiled.

"That's him." She smiled back at the little girl as she watched Dougal approach.

"You girls talking about me?" He dropped onto the grass beside them.

Tabitha stood, grabbed his arm and climbed into his lap. "Mine." She patted him.

"Yes, ma'am." He dropped a kiss on top of her forehead.

Emory watched, the building pressure in her chest growing painful. It was all too much, all of it. The sweet, tenderness between Dougal and Tabitha. The excruciating ache of loss as thoughts of her own baby surfaced. And, now, the knowledge that she had to give Dougal up… It hurt to breathe and her pulse was irregular. The stinging in her eyes came out of nowhere. She was not going to cry. Not here, when she had an audience. She blinked, staring out over the booths and people to the street—and saw Lucas headed their way.

What the hell was wrong with Chelsea? Did she have some sort of grudge against him that he didn't know about? Or was she on some mission to make things with Emory more difficult than they needed to be? It was beginning to feel a lot like sabotage.

He could either sit here and let whatever Chelsea had said have time to take root. Or not.

"Want to take a walk?" he asked, glancing at Emory.

She shook her head, not bothering to look at him.

"Just around the square. With Tabby-cat?" He kept his voice low, for her ears only.

"Wok?" Tabitha perked up. "Go."

He glanced down to see Emory pointing at something. His gaze followed and... *Dammit*. Lucas. He wasn't going anywhere now.

He took a deep breath. "How about we sit here and enjoy the sun?"

She nodded.

"Morning, all." Lucas was all smiles.

Dougal had to give it to him. The man didn't shy away from eye contact. Dougal managed a nod. All things considered, he thought it was mighty generous of him.

"Lucas." Ruth's delight was sincere. "When did you get back?"

"Just now." He hugged her. "Complications kept me longer than I'd anticipated."

Dougal had to give it to him—he had the long-suffering thing down. Of course, if the bastard turned out to be dying, he'd feel like an ass for being so hard on the guy.

"Hello." Chelsea stepped forward, hand outstretched and smile in place.

Oh hell. Dougal recognized that smile. But, unlike him, Lucas was probably more than capable of handling someone like Chelsea Barrett. Not that he had any intention of letting any handling take place between them.

"Lucas Baumgarten." Lucas was blindsided. "And you are?"

"My sister-in-law," Dougal announced. "Chelsea Barrett."

"Am I, though?" Chelsea smile sparkled. "I'm Angus's sister-in-law. I don't know what that makes you, Dougal." She might be talking to him, but she only had eyes for Lucas.

"Very nice to meet you." Lucas was still holding her hand.

"Likewise." Chelsea didn't seem to be in any hurry to let go, either.

"Well, now that we all know each other... How about an early lunch?" Aunt Ruthie didn't seem too pleased about the two's instant love connection.

"We can't." Dougal held Tabitha close and stood. "It's almost Tabby-cat's nap time." He didn't want to leave, but with Chelsea in the mix, things would take on a whole new level of complicated.

"Is it?" Chelsea pouted.

"Yep. Don't want to risk her getting sick again." Dougal hugged his niece. "I'm sure Lucas can help you get this finished, Miss Ruth." He gave Lucas a hard smile.

"Of course." Lucas's smile was smooth. "Happy to."

"Well, boo." Chelsea sighed.

"Maybe I'll see you at the parade tonight?" Lucas stepped closer to her. "I'd love to buy you a cup of hot chocolate."

"I think I can squeeze you in." Chelsea's pout gave way to a brilliant smile.

Dougal shuddered and turned to Emory.

She must have been watching him because she was trying not to laugh. He wished she'd go on and do it. He loved it when she laughed.

"I'll see you later tonight," he murmured. He wanted to make sure Chelsea hadn't screwed anything up.

"I'll be here." She nodded at the booth. "Bye."

"Bye." Tabitha waved.

"Bye, sweetie." Emory stepped forward. "Thank you for helping with the ornaments."

"Tank too," Tabitha said back.

Emory was laughing then, a wistful smile on her face. It tore at his heart a little. Knowing what she'd lost. Yet, here she was, standing tall. He didn't know if he had that sort of strength in him. Maybe he would, for Emory.

"Let's go, then." Chelsea hooked arms with him. "Nap time waits for no man."

They were halfway back to his truck when Chelsea asked, "Who was *that*?"

"Lucas?" He sighed, searching for the best way to stop this before it got started. He didn't want to tell her about Rory, but he wasn't a fan of lying so he didn't see any other option. If he tried to warn her away from him, she'd want the bastard that much more. "He's a real charmer. He's got a line of women waiting for back child support. Maybe they'll get something when his unemployment check comes in. His wife works at the grocery store. I think she's expecting number three?" He was laying it on thick and he knew it. Probably, too thick.

"You're kidding?" She was horrified.

"I wish." He breathed a sigh of relief. "Went to high school with him. He was a piece of crap back then, too."

He loaded Tabitha into her car seat, double-checking the buckles before closing the crew cab door.

Once they were on the way home, he glanced Chelsea's way. "Should I be worried?"

"Even if I say no, you will." Chelsea shrugged. "You might not believe this, but I do care about you. Not in the 'I care because I want to have sex with you' sort of thing. Over that. Now, it's like, I actually really care. Don't make me get all in touch with my feels, Dougal."

He shook his head. "Sometimes the things you say scare me."

"Because I'm honest?" She sighed. "If more people were honest, life would be so much easier."

He didn't argue with that. He did feel a little guilty for telling a heap of lies about Lucas.

"When you were sitting with her, with Tabby, I could see it. You and Emory and a whole bunch of babies." She turned to face him. "It made me a little nauseous but, you know, I figured you'd think it was cool."

He laughed then.

As soon as they got back, he handed Tabby to Chelsea and went in search of Angus. He found him wrapping up some drills with Pepper, a horse almost ready for sale.

"Looking good." Dougal leaned against the pipe fence, his boot resting on the bottom post.

"Course she is." Angus patted the horse's neck. "I trained her, didn't I?"

He snorted. "We need to get our stories straight."

"What now?" He slid out of the saddle. "Jesse." Jesse, who'd been standing by to watch, jogged over. "You clean her up and give her a cool down." Angus handed him the reins.

"You got it." He tried not to be too excited, but Dougal knew better.

Jesse Dawson had been with them for a while now, but he'd started at the bottom. It'd only been the last couple of months they'd stepped up his responsibilities. So far, so good.

"Thanks for taking Tabby with you." Angus gave him a shove. "What excuse did you have for going into town this time?"

"Chelsea." They started walking from the corral to the barn.

"Right. If she didn't get out of Savannah's hair, my poor wife was going to explode." Angus sighed. "Not gonna lie, I'm ready for the holidays to be over so it's just our little family again."

Dougal nodded. "But we ran into Lucas and, man, Chelsea liked what she saw."

Angus hung his head. "Damn. This is bad."

"Maybe not. I told her…" He chuckled. "I told her he was behind on multiple child support payments, unemployed and his pregnant wife was working at the grocery store in town supporting them."

Angus went from staring to laughing. "You don't think one of those things was enough?"

"I didn't see the point in messing around." Dougal was laughing, too.

Angus ran a hand along the back of his neck. "How's it going with Emory?"

"I made the mistake of leaving her alone with Chelsea again."

Angus stopped in his tracks. "Dougal, come on, now."

He clapped his brother on the shoulder. "You gotta stop doing that."

"I know." He sighed. "This *is* my first rodeo, Angus. Give me a break."

"Can't. You're my brother. It's my job to give you all kinds of hell." Angus smiled. "What about Lucas? Do we know what's true? What he's after? I'm not going to lie—I don't like having the bastard underfoot."

"Yeah. I get it. Believe me."

"Right." Angus glanced at him. "Sorry. You're in a tough spot."

Dougal stared out over the lower pasture. It might be winter, but the rain had perked up the landscape and colored it a faint green. He took a deep breath. "I damn near punched him." He winced as he said it.

"Almost? Why didn't you?" Angus grabbed him. "And how am I just hearing about this?"

"Because I didn't do it so there wasn't much to tell." He ran a hand over his face. "It was close, though. He knew exactly what he was doing and smiled at me the whole damn time, too."

"I'd have punched him." Angus spat the words out. "No regrets."

Dougal chuckled. "I believe you. But whatever happens with Lucas, I'm not going to let him have the upper hand. That's why I'd rather keep Emory away from him." He swallowed, giving voice to his fear. "He might have walked in on us—seen something..." He broke off. "Now he knows she's important to me. And that worries me."

"Well...damn," Angus muttered. "You really didn't punch him?"

Dougal sighed. "Did you hear anything else I said?"

Angus chuckled. "Yeah. But that was the best part."

Dougal checked his phone, hoping he had a missed call from Maxine. Nothing. So he did something he rarely did. He texted Emory. Or, he tried. He wrote and deleted six versions before typing, Everything okay? and hitting send.

Making cookies. She sent a picture of herself holding a plate of perfectly iced cookies.

He smiled at the picture. See you tonight. He was smiling for the rest of the day.

Chapter Sixteen

Emory was humming along to the Christmas carols on the radio, dancing back and forth between the counter and the oven. She'd made dozens of cookies for that night, and the kitchen smelled like cinnamon, ginger and frosting. "Talk about being in a festive mood, eh?" She broke off a small piece of sugar cookie and gave it to Frosty.

He spun in a circle.

"One more." She waited for him to sit, then rewarded him. "You're such a good boy." She stooped and dropped a kiss on his head.

Frosty was all wriggles and wagging tail.

Lucas came into the kitchen, his arms loaded with bagged groceries. "I got everything on the list."

"Thank you." Emory watched as he unloaded the bags and put everything away.

"No problem." He stored the shopping bags. "It's nice to be helpful." He poured himself a cup of coffee and nodded at the cookies. "Looks like you've made enough for the whole town." He gave her one of his megawatt smiles. "Have enough for a sample?"

"Of course." Emory held out a plate. "I have some

oops cookies. They're not as pretty, but they taste just as good."

"Thanks." Lucas took a gingerbread man. "I'm going to gain ten pounds before the holidays are over." He winked at her.

"I'll take that as a compliment." There it was, that uneasy feeling he put in her stomach. She wanted to be wrong about Lucas—for her aunt's sake, if nothing else.

"Emory, I need your help finding something." Ruth came into the kitchen, a perplexed expression on her face.

"What are you looking for?" Emory asked, washing her hands at the sink. "Hold on. Don't want to get frosting everywhere."

"Oh, some paperwork." Ruth shook her head. "I thought Lawrence had it all in his filing cabinet in the workshop but…"

Emory tried not to react. "I've never gone in the workshop, Aunt Ruthie, but I'm happy to look if you'd like."

"No. Lucas and I have gone through it twice." She sat at the kitchen table. "He would have told me if he kept important papers someplace else."

Lucas sipped his coffee, totally at ease. "It's really okay, Ruth. This is my problem. I appreciate your offer but I'll figure it out."

Ruth's face was a deep shade of red and her breathing was erratic. "*We* will."

"Ruth?" Emory filled a glass with cold water. "Here, drink this." She pressed the glass into her aunt's hand. "What's got you so upset? Did something happen?"

"Oh…" Ruth glanced at Lucas. "You were baking and Lucas had gone to the store and you know me—I can't sit still. It's laundry day so I started stripping sheets. And, I know you told me not to, I wanted you to have a nice clean bed."

Emory glanced at Lucas, whose smile had gone a little brittle around the edges.

"The phone was ringing and I answered it. I do that, get so caught up in what I'm doing that I get distracted. Well, I was. Distracted. So I answer the phone and this man…" She was shaking. "He asked me who he was talking to and I asked him who he thought he was talking to. He said he was calling for you, Lucas. I said this was your phone but you were busy and asked if I could help. And he said he doubted it, unless I had one hundred and fifty thousand dollars sitting around to pay Lucas's debt."

Emory watched all the color drain from Lucas's face.

"I told him I was horrified about the callous treatment you were getting, Lucas. That, you being so sick, shouldn't be badgered like this—that it wasn't good for you. The man had the nerve to laugh. He laughed." Ruth fanned her face.

Emory held out the glass. "Have a sip, please."

Lucas was staring at the kitchen table, his jaw clenched tight.

Ruth took a sip. "The man said Lucas would get a lot sicker if he didn't pay his bill." She shook her head. "Why would he say that? It was almost a…threat. So I asked him how he could live with himself, preying on a young man fighting cancer." She took another sip of water.

Lucas had turned to stone. There wasn't even the shadow of his usual smile.

"He said your mail was getting returned so I gave him this address…"

Lucas jumped up then. "Oh…" He took a deep breath. "I'm so…so sorry." He swallowed, his gaze darting from the back door to the hall. "You shouldn't have…had to deal with that, Ruth." It took a minute for him to mask his terror.

It was enough to confirm Emory's worst fears. An icy foreboding settled on top of her chest.

"I told him to send the bill and I'd pay it. He said he'd already given several extensions and it was going to a collection agency—but he'd try to get another one. One last time, he said." Ruth grabbed his hand. "All we need to do is sell those cars and you'll have more than enough. Like you said, Lawrence wanted you to have them anyway. We just need the titles."

Emory took a deep breath. First things first. "Aunt Ruthie, you're worrying me. I'll go and find the titles if you'll go lie down. Just for a bit?"

"Oh, sugar, I'm fine." She was fanning herself again. "Just a little worked up, is all."

"Still, I'd feel better if you put your feet up and had a rest," she pleaded.

"You know what? I think I'll go take a bubble bath." She reached over to pat Emory's hand, then gave Lucas a smile. "It'll all work out just fine."

Emory stared at the empty doorway long after Ruth had left. She didn't know where to start. "Who did she really talk to? And why did you freak out when she said she'd given them this address?"

He gripped the back of the kitchen chair. "Do you know where the titles are?" His narrowed gaze was more than a little unnerving. "It's in everyone's best interest for me to have them—soon."

"The hospital will take car titles in trade?" The words were out before she'd thought them through.

He blew out a slow breath. "You don't know how serious this is."

"You're right. I don't." She stood, crossing her arms over her chest. "Just tell me my aunt isn't in danger. That's all that matters."

He pushed off the chair, his hands fisting at his sides, before he turned and slammed out the back door. Minutes later, she heard the creak of the workshop door.

She sank into her chair, trembling. What was she supposed to do? If she knew where the titles were, she'd hand them over and send Lucas on his way. But... Even then, there was no guarantee the money would go to the person her aunt had talked to.

Frosty trotted across the kitchen to her and pawed at her foot.

"It's okay." She scooped him up and held him close to her. "Let's make Aunt Ruthie some tea, shall we?" Her aunt had never been in a state like that—not once. She was full of sass but she never got ruffled. Today, she had been. She turned on the electric kettle, put a tea bag into a delicate china Christmas teacup and assembled a tea tray. Shortbread cookies were her aunt's favorite so she added them and two tangerines to the tray, then carried it down the hall. Her aunt's suite of rooms was the only one downstairs. Once upon a time, it would have been the main bedroom of the house so it was larger than the rest.

"Aunt Ruthie?" She knocked. "It's just me." Frosty barked. "And Frosty."

"In the bath, dear. Come on in."

She balanced the tray long enough to open the door. Frosty led the way, tail wagging.

Emory had always loved this room. It was very Aunt Ruthie, a feminine space. Lots of soft fabrics and delicate furniture—mostly in paler shades of white and yellow, Dolly Parton's favorite colors.

"Knock, knock." Emory paused at the bathroom door.

"Your eyes are safe. The bubbles are piled high." Ruth laughed.

It was a relief to see her aunt's complexion returned to normal. Her hairpieces rested on one of the wig heads filling the bookcase on the far wall, but she still wore a full face of makeup. Without the beehive hairdo, she seemed smaller and more delicate. Or maybe all that had just happened was coloring the way Emory saw things now.

She set the tea tray on the counter long enough to drag the round velvet pouf close to the claw-foot tub. "Here you go." She set the tea tray within her aunt's reach. "What else can I get you?"

Aunt Ruthie smiled. "This is pretty much perfect, Emory. Thank you for taking care of me." She took the teacup Emory offered. "Oh, now, I almost forgot. Colonel Jimenez will be here this afternoon. What time is it?"

"I can take care of that. You have a nice soak." She was relieved the older gentleman was coming. He was just the sort of happy distraction her aunt needed. "You should ask him to come to the parade tonight. I think he'd like that."

Aunt Ruthie's grin was full of mischief. "I think I will." She sipped her tea. "I'm assuming Dougal will be helping out at our booth?"

Emory shrugged. "I don't know about that, but we will probably see him."

"I just bet we will." She giggled and took another sip. "I forgot how restoring a soak in a nice, hot bath is."

"You enjoy it." Emory blew her a kiss. "We'll leave you be." She and Frosty closed the bedroom door behind them. "I think she's okay now." Frosty wagged his tail in agreement.

She stared out the window at the metal workshop out back. But were they okay, really? Aunt Ruthie was calm and didn't seem any the wiser but Emory knew—she *knew*—that nothing was as it seemed. Lucas hadn't said anything outright, but he'd said enough. She suspected all of it was a sham—the medical debt and his illness. It seemed awfully elaborate to go to such lengths, but she didn't have a lot of experience with real-life sociopaths.

Frosty pawed at her foot and did a little spin.

"All right." She smiled at him. "Let's go out front so you can do your business, then we'll check and make sure everything is ready for Colonel Jimenez."

And shortly after that, she'd see Dougal. She had so much to tell him. As much as she wanted to call him, she stopped herself. If she called, he might feel obligated to come here, and what good would that do? He couldn't do anything more than she was. He had a life and a job. He didn't need to drop everything because she'd had an unnerving conversation with Lucas.

Chelsea's words still lingered.

Emory had meant it when she said she wasn't his re-

sponsibility. She wasn't. And she didn't want to be...
Or did she?

"We can't call him," she told Frosty as she pulled
open the front door. She would see him soon enough.
Between the two of them, they'd figure something out.
And knowing that was enough to ease some of the tension twisting her insides this way and that.

Dougal was sweating. The Santa suit was thick—add
on the stuffed T-shirt that gave him his Santa belly and
it was downright miserable. He was in the courthouse
gazebo, sitting in a massive red-and-white chair, listening to another child's Christmas wish. Since he liked
kids, it wasn't too hard to laugh and smile and act like
Santa. If he'd been dealing with adults, he'd have been
more like Scrooge.

It wouldn't be bad if he wasn't so hot. *Angus owes me.*

Not that he'd collect. Angus was home with sick kids
and a nasty cough of his own. Savannah was the one
who had put her foot down. She had told Angus he was
not going to play Santa and get all the kids in Granite
Falls sick for Christmas—and that was that. But since
Angus had agreed to take a two-hour shift, he'd had to
find a replacement.

And that's why Dougal was sitting here, listening to
Cassie and Sterling Ford's son, Clancy, whisper how
he wanted a pony and two more dogs instead of helping Emory out like he'd planned. He'd texted her to explain, of course. She'd sent back a thumbs-up emoji. He
guessed that meant she was okay with it.

"And a penguin," Clancy added.

"I'll see what I can find in Santa's workshop," he said,

handing the boy a small candy cane. "You stay good, now. And Merry Christmas."

Clancy slid off his lap and ran for his parents. Dougal watched the family. It seemed like just about everyone in Granite Falls was settled and happy. He wasn't a man prone to jealousy but, now that he knew what he wanted, he'd rather have it sooner than later. If Emory found herself loving him, it'd be worth the wait.

"You're doing great." Skylar Mitchell was his elf assistant for the night. "Only five minutes left." She gave him a thumbs-up. "One, maybe two more kiddos and Kyle should be here." Kyle was Skylar's husband, the next Santa in the lineup.

"Santa, Santa." Franny Lafferty came running, dragging her younger sister along behind her. "Me and Biddy are here and we've been really good this year."

He grinned. "I know. Santa always knows. I'm proud of you girls."

Biddy, who was hiding behind her sister, smiled shyly.

"You want to sit?" He patted his lap. He knew parents liked a picture of their kid on Santa's lap, but he'd rather have a happy child standing than a screaming child forced onto his lap.

Biddy shook her head.

"No, thank you." Franny sighed. "Can we tell you our list standing up?"

He chuckled. "Of course."

The minute the girls had their candy canes, Skylar addressed the line. "Santa is taking a five-minute break to check on his reindeers, but he will be right back."

"You're up, Kyle," Dougal murmured, taking the rear steps down out of Santa's workshop and headed through the Christmas village booths and vendors so he could change in the courthouse. He smiled and nodded when kids got wide-eyed and gasped, "Santa!" He passed booths with handmade wreaths and mistletoe sprigs, knitted hats and scarves, candles and lip balm, and cookies and hot chocolate… He paused and backed up.

Yep, it was Emory. "Evening, Miss Swanson."

Her blue eyes widened. "Santa?" But then she looked closer and her smile was brighter than the Christmas lights framing the booth. "Look at you, *Santa*." She came out of the booth to give him a head-to-toe inspection. She leaned in to whisper, "Is this what they call a sexy Santa?"

He grinned, loving the sound of her laugh. "You got a minute?"

She nodded. "Barely. Aunt Ruthie is showing Colonel Jimenez around so I'm on my own here."

"This won't take long." He took her hand and led her back in the direction he'd come—stopping at the booth selling wreaths. A bunch of mistletoe, tied up in a red ribbon, hung from a hook suspended off the booth's roof. "Mistletoe." He pointed.

She laughed. "So, I see."

"You know what that means?" He stepped closer. He knew pulling Emory against him the way he wanted to wasn't very Santa-like behavior. To stop himself, he held his hands behind his back. "It's Christmas, after all."

She was still smiling when she stood on tiptoe for a featherlight kiss.

It was still enough to knock the air from his lungs.

"Is that Mrs. Claus?" a kid passing by asked.

"She doesn't have white hair," another kid said.

"Maybe she's his sister. My mom always makes me kiss my sister."

"Ooh, gross," the first kid responded.

That had he and Emory both laughing.

"You should probably go change," Emory whispered. "Wouldn't want the kids to worry that Santa kissed a woman that wasn't Mrs. Claus."

He frowned and stepped back. He hadn't thought of that. "That's not good." He straightened and took a look around him. "It's a big responsibility—keeping a child's faith in Santa Claus alive. I'll be back."

"I'll be waiting."

He liked the sound of that. With a nod, he headed for the courthouse.

"How was it?" Kyle stood, already in Santa attire, right inside the courthouse.

"Good. Fine." Dougal tugged off the hat and beard. "Just be careful who you kiss out there." He brushed past him into the office and bathroom that had opened specifically for the Santas to use that night.

The minute the padded shirt was off, his body temperature dropped a good fifteen degrees. He washed off his face and chest in the bathroom, got dressed and headed out. He'd almost reached the booths when he came face-to-face with Lucas.

"Peace." Lucas held up his hands, the cocky-as-hell smile on his face. "I'll be out of your hair soon enough, so how about you hold back on the punches."

"Fine." Dougal had no intention of ever laying a hand on the man, but he'd keep that to himself. "Leaving town?"

He nodded. "This Christmas seems to be full of miracles."

Dougal shook his head. "Am I supposed to know what that means?" More importantly, should he care?

"No." Lucas chuckled. "Not really. But I'm leaving here with everything I hoped for—and then some. I've got no plans of coming back, either. I figure you'd like hearing that."

He did like hearing that, but there was one question he wanted the answer to. "You're not coming back because you don't want to? Or because you're... Because of your health?"

Lucas shook his head. "You mean, because I'll be dead? It was pretty touch and go there, I'm not going to lie. But, if things work out, I might survive after all. Like I said, miracles happen." He paused, his grin hard. "Perfect example? You've got a girlfriend."

"It's impossible for you to tell the truth, isn't it?" Dougal's patience was gone now.

"You know, everyone has their own version of the truth, Dougal. My experience differs from yours or Ruth's or Emory's—making my truth unique to me."

"I mean *facts*. Like, you do or do not have cancer. You are or you aren't dying. You came here to make peace with your past mistakes, or you came here planning on scamming Ruth." He stared at the man, refusing to back down. "Those are the only truths I give a damn about."

Lucas shrugged. "Too bad you'll never know."

"You really are a selfish son of a bitch, aren't you?" It wasn't a new development. But for the man to stand here, not bothering to deny any of the accusations Dougal was laying at his feet, was infuriating. "Ruth Baumgarten is a decent woman. She—"

"Yeah, yeah. She's nice and bighearted and all that. She is. She is kind and giving and she has more money than she'll ever need. *My* dad made sure of that." He sighed. "I'm not holding a gun to anyone's head, Dougal. When a person chooses to do something, even if you don't like it or agree with it, it's still their choice. There's no crime in that."

He was wasting his breath. "Your father would be devastated to see how you turned out, Lucas. I don't think he ever gave up hoping you'd grow a conscience or become a decent human being."

"Oh no, you mention my father and suddenly I see all my sins and feel terrible and repentant about my life choices." Lucas snorted. "You live your life, I'll live mine."

"That's fine—until your life makes a mess of mine or the ones I love. That includes Emory. And Ruth. If that happens, we have a problem." Dougal ran a hand over his face. "Are we going to have any more problems?"

"You can't scare me, Dougal. Your threats are hollow compared to the people I'm used to dealing with." Lucas ran his fingers through his hair. "But, no, we aren't going to have any more problems." He clapped his hands together. "Is your sister-in-law around? I figured I'd spend my last night in Granite Falls with—"

"You're kidding, right?" He was done talking. He wasn't going to get any other information from the bastard. There wasn't anything left Dougal wanted to know, anyway. With a tip of the hat, he walked past Lucas and headed into the Christmas village.

All he wanted now was to spend time with Emory. He'd tell her about his run-in with Lucas and hope it put her mind at ease. After that, he could go back to trying to win Emory's heart. He was no better off now than he'd been two weeks ago. There was so much he wanted to say to her—which meant he had one option. Emory was going to get a love letter for Christmas. But would it be from her secret admirer? Or was it time for her secret admirer to be revealed?

Chapter Seventeen

The minute Emory saw Dougal working his way through the crowd to her, her heart picked up. She didn't fight it, not this time. It was futile. Her heart already knew what her brain refused to accept. She had feelings for Dougal McCarrick—overwhelming feelings.

"Hey." He was all smiles.

"I'm not going to lie, I kinda liked the beard." Santa Dougal. Scruffy Dougal. Propped-over-her-in-bed Dougal. Smiling Dougal… She liked every version of him.

He laughed.

I like laughing Dougal, too.

"What's that look?" His gaze, intense as ever, held hers.

"Nothing." *I think I'm in love with you.* She swallowed.

In typical Dougal fashion, he didn't push it. "Parade?" he asked.

"Sure." Most of the vendors had already closed. Once the parade was over, things shut down and everyone went home—it was the grand finale. At least that's what Aunt Ruthie had said. She popped the lid on the remaining container of cookies and turned off the strands of battery-operated lights. "Hope we can find a spot to see."

Dougal had a spot. Every year, the McCarricks, the Laffertys and the Mitchells would take lawn chairs up on the roof of Buzz's clinic—Granite Falls Veterinary Clinic and Animal Hospital. But this year, they were the only ones to show up.

"Since everyone started having kids, they stopped coming up here. Worried about safety and all." Dougal set up two folding chairs. "It's just you and me. Is that okay?"

Emory was more than happy with the arrangement.

The parade was adorable. From the high school rodeo club to the senior Jazzercise class, the string of holiday-bedecked cars, trucks and trailers kept on coming. They sang along to the Christmas carols the high school marching band played and shared the last of the cookies.

When it was all over, they lingered until the streets were empty and there was only the occasional strand of tinsel or paper streamer blowing down the street.

"Now what?" she asked, in no hurry to end their time together.

"I talked to Lucas."

She couldn't be more surprised. "When?"

"Tonight." He ran a hand over his face. "He said he's leaving tomorrow."

Tomorrow? "I don't think Ruth knows that." She was pretty certain her aunt would take his departure hard. "I talked to him, too... Well, sort of." And she told him everything that had happened that morning. When she was done talking, Dougal's jaw was clenched so tight she feared it would break.

"I don't trust him. And I don't like you and Ruth being..." He broke off and stood. "Let's go."

"Okay. Where?" She followed him, stowing her chair alongside his and taking the metal staircase down the side of the building to the sidewalk below. "Dougal?"

"I was thinking…" He stared down at her, the streetlamps casting shadows over his handsome face. Even so, she felt his gaze on her. "I'd like to stay close tonight. Maybe, stay with you—"

"Okay." She nodded. "Let's go."

They walked down Main Street. Her hand brushed his, but he didn't reach for her. By the time they'd reached the bed-and-breakfast, the air between them crackled. Every nerve was strung tight and quivering with anticipation. She led him around the main house and down the path to the carriage house. "Oh, wait… Towels." She opened the door for him. "I'll be right back. Make yourself at home."

"Hurry." His hands gripped her waist.

She nodded, shaking and breathless now. How she managed to make it into the bed-and-breakfast, find towels and back again without tripping or falling or waking the whole house, she didn't know. But she was grateful.

Finding Dougal shirtless was a pleasant surprise. "Towels." She clutched them to her, completely distracted. "I… Looks like you're getting ready…"

"With you, I'm always ready." The proof positive was straining against his jeans.

"Oh… Right…" She was having a hard time breathing.

"I thought we could take a shower." He nodded at the towels. "You went to all the trouble of getting towels and all."

She swallowed. "Right." This man had given her multiple orgasms and yet, finding him shirtless had her completely flustered. But he *was* shirtless. And gorgeous... Of course she was staring at him. There was the possibility she was drooling, too.

He crossed the room in two steps. "What's got you so tongue-tied?" he whispered.

The rasp in that whisper sent a shudder down her spine. "Well..." She rested a hand against his chest. "You're not wearing a shirt."

"Would you rather I was?" He was watching her, a slow smile forming. "I can put it back on."

Her gaze locked with his and any hesitation melted away. "No..." She shook her head. "No, I'm the one who's overdressed—"

He cut her off, sealing his lips to hers.

There was nothing like kissing Dougal. The taste of him, all hard angles and heat, wrapped around her. And when she melted into him, his grip tightened. The way she wanted him was unrelenting. One look. One touch. One whisper. That was it, she was a puddle of desire. That he seemed just as affected by her was exhilarating.

"You taste so good," he whispered against her mouth.

There was no resisting him. When he cupped her face and pulled her into him, she gave herself to him. She felt no restraint, no hesitation. She parted her lips and slid her fingers up and into his hair.

Showering with Dougal was an adventure.

He was equally adventurous in her bed.

But her favorite part of the night was when he was sound asleep and wrapped around her.

Since Sam's death, she'd convinced herself that she didn't need or want a man in her life. She'd failed so epically in her marriage, what made her think it would be better the second time around? There was no guarantee. Life wasn't a guarantee. But she had this chance with Dougal... Maybe.

Chelsea seemed to think Dougal cared about her, but he'd never said as much. In fact, he'd said he was happy with *this*. That this was good... There was no denying it was good. But could it be even better?

She buried her face against his chest and gave in to sleep.

When her alarm went off the next morning, Dougal was gone, and Frosty was standing on the bed next to her, tail wagging. "Well, good morning." She sat up, running a hand over her tangled hair. "Dougal?"

Silence. Had she really expected him to be here? If he had stayed, how was she going to explain his presence to her aunt? She showered, fed Frosty and headed to the main house. Colonel Jimenez was an early riser, and he'd be wanting breakfast.

Emory was pulling biscuits from the oven when Aunt Ruthie walked in.

"Good morning." Aunt Ruthie was sifting through the mail. "Are you making Anthony biscuits and gravy? You thoughtful girl."

"Anthony?" Emory flipped the bacon she was frying. "When did Colonel Jimenez become Anthony?"

"Do not get cheeky with me, missy." But she was blushing. "I swear I caught sight of a shadow leaving your place in the early hours of the morning. A cowboy-hat-wearing shadow."

Emory pretended to zip her lips.

"Look." Aunt Ruthie held up a familiar-looking envelope. "I was wondering what happened to him…" She handed it to Emory. "Don't burn the bacon."

Emory tucked the letter into her apron pocket and went back to cooking.

"Oh." Something about Aunt Ruthie's tone had Emory turning. Her aunt was sitting at the table, one hand pressed to her chest, the other holding a new letter.

"What is it?" She was at her aunt's side in an instant.

"A letter from Lucas." She waved the letter. "He's left. He's gone. He said he found the titles yesterday…" Ruth frowned. "He rented a trailer for the cars. He wanted to get that squared away so I wouldn't worry over him anymore. That he'll make sure those creditors don't come around or harass us." She sniffed. "Oh, and he's grateful for letting him be part of the family…" She shook her head. "That boy…"

"Are you okay?" Emory didn't give a fig about *that boy*.

"Fine. But he doesn't have the titles. I found them last night. I don't know why I hadn't thought of it, but they were in a box of things Lawrence had set aside for Lucas—in case Lucas did come home." She smoothed the note flat on the table. "Now what do you suppose he's going to do with two cars he can't sell?"

"He can sell them… I'm not sure it'll be legal, but I'm not sure he's worried about that, Aunt Ruthie."

"I know. I know. I'm a sucker for a lost cause." Ruth sighed. "Lawrence told me to watch out, that Lucas wasn't always honest. But, you know me, I wanted to give the boy a chance. I know it didn't all add up but I kept thinking, in time, he'd talk to me." She glanced at Emory. "Lawrence told me to decide whether or not to give that box to Lucas. I was going to. I brought it down with me. It's all wrapped up and under the Christmas tree." Aunt Ruthie put the letter on the table and patted her hair. "He's gone and made things harder than they need to be. Not to mention, sneaking off when the whole house is sleeping is just downright shady."

Emory had to smile at that. "Maybe something urgent came up?" Like evading whoever her aunt had spoken to on the phone... Would they still come here looking for Lucas? Or would he do the right thing? Was that what he meant when he'd written that he'd make sure those creditors don't come around or harass them?

Ruth took another deep breath and stood. "There's nothing to be done about it all, I suppose. He'll have to work it out on his own. Now, I'll take the coffee. I'm sure Anthony is waiting."

"Well, okay, then." She smiled at Frosty. Leave it to her aunt to roll with the punches. "That went a lot better than I expected." She stood. "I don't have time to sit around. The McCarrick holiday party is in three days and I have a ton to do." As long as there were minimal interruptions she could get it done. But, if there were interruptions, she hoped they were all named Dougal McCarrick. She'd happily make time for the man she was madly, deeply and irrevocably in love with.

"You're a terrible patient." Aunt Nola pressed her hand to Dougal's forehead. "Grumbling and snapping. Just drink your orange juice and hush up."

It was true. He didn't like being sick. He was used to being in control of his body. Coughing. Dozing off. Aching all over. It sucked. And there was nothing he could do about it. He'd been stuck in his place for two days, eating soup and sleeping. And while he'd exchanged texts with Emory, it wasn't the same. Not to mention he had a letter for her—a letter he'd put a whole lot of time and thought and heart into.

"What are you frowning over?" Aunt Nola was staring down at him.

He pointed at his mouth. "Am I supposed to answer? You told me to hush up."

"No. Don't answer me. I don't want to know." She put more soup in his refrigerator and headed for the door. "You get better. Tabitha's been asking about when you're going to read to her."

He smiled. He missed spending time with Tabby-cat, too. He knew he wasn't supposed to have favorites, but he connected with her most out of the triplets. They liked doing quiet things and staying out of the way. Plus she'd taken to Emory right away—just like Dougal.

"They're cute rug rats—even if they're the reason you're sick." Aunt Nola opened the door. "You've got food, water, medicine. You rest."

He'd rested enough. If he had to spend one more day cooped up, his mood was only going to get worse. As soon as she left, he'd saddle up Finn, go for a ride and no one would be the wiser. "Bye."

She rolled her eyes. "You're welcome."

"I'm sorry." He sighed. She'd done nothing but take care of him. She'd made sure he knew she wasn't happy about it, but she'd done it all the same. "Thank you, Aunt Nola."

She nodded. "That's better." And she left.

Dougal stood up—and instantly felt dizzy. "Hell." He used the back of the recliner to steady himself.

Willow was at his side, whimpering up at him.

"I'm okay." He patted her side. "You don't need to worry about me. I just need to go slow." It took him ten minutes to get cleaned up and into clean clothes. By then, he was worn out. He sank back into his recliner. "I just need a minute." Gertie jumped up and dropped her ball in his lap. He sighed and threw the ball. "One of us should get some exercise."

His phone started ringing. As soon as he saw Maxine's name scrolling across the screen, he answered. "Hello?"

"Max, here. I've got something for you." She cleared her throat. "Dammit. I'm getting another call—I gotta take this. Are you familiar with the Baumgarten Bed-and-Breakfast? We're headed there now. Be about thirty minutes."

They were headed to Ruth's place? Now? "I'll be waiting. Thanks, Max." He hung up and called Emory.

"Dougal?" There was a smile in her voice.

"Max called and she's got something." He coughed. "She didn't say why, but she's headed to the B and B. I'll be there soon."

"She is coming here?" She paused. "I'll give Aunt Ruthie a heads-up. Dougal, are you sure you're up for this? You sound awful."

"I don't feel all that great but I'm coming anyway." There was no way he'd let Ruth and Emory deal with this on their own. "I'll keep my distance, though. Maybe we could sit on the porch?"

"Okay. Be safe. And bring the girls—Frosty would love that."

"Yes, ma'am." He was smiling as he disconnected. "Let's go." He grabbed his hat and keys off the hook by the door and let the dogs lead the way.

"Dougal?" Angus peeked out of the office at the end of the barn. "Should you be up? Where are you going?"

"Into town." He held the door open so the dogs could jump in. "I'll explain later." He climbed into the truck and started the engine. With a little wave, he put the truck in gear and headed to town. He didn't speed—he wanted to, but he didn't. By the time he got there, there was an SUV with *Texas Rangers* on the doors, a local sheriff's car and an unmarked black sedan.

"Dougal." Emory stood on the front porch, wide-eyed with worry.

He jogged to the house. "What's going on?"

She headed straight for him, but he held up one hand to stop her.

"I don't want to get you sick." He sighed. "It's killing me not to hold you but…" And he'd just said that out loud. Talk about bad timing.

Emory went from surprised to resigned. "Lucas was arrested this morning. Now they're searching his room." She nodded at the flurry of activity taking place inside the big old house.

"How's Ruth?" He didn't see the older woman.

"She's taking it in stride. She's tough, that's for sure." Emory stepped closer to him. "You okay? You look—"

"Like death." Max came out of the house, smiling. "I'd shake your hand, but I don't want whatever you've got."

"Fair enough." He nodded. "What can you tell us?"

"Lucas Baumgarten hangs out with the wrong people— present company excluded, of course. We've got the FBI joining us today. Lucas might be a small fish in a big pond, but he's managed to get himself in a whole heap of trouble. As soon as we're done getting Mrs. Baumgarten's statement, I'll fill you in."

"I knew he was trouble but…" Emory shook her head, her arms wrapped around her waist.

Damn, but he wanted to comfort her.

Ruth came outside a few minutes later. She was surprisingly calm. An older gentleman came out and sat beside her in the porch swing. "Dougal. Land sakes, son, you look rough. Are you sick?"

Dougal nodded. "I'll stay over here."

"Dougal, this is Anthony Jimenez. Anthony, this is Dougal. He and Emory are…" Ruth's brows went up. "Well, I'm not sure how to answer that. I only know that he tends to show up whenever Emory or I need something."

"Nice to meet you." Anthony nodded. "Glad these two have someone looking out for them."

Max joined them shortly thereafter. What she had to say couldn't be easy for Ruth to hear. "For the better part of a decade, Lucas has been conning women out of money. He was either needing money to help his mother or he was terminally ill and didn't want to leave his debt for his mother."

"So, he's not sick?" Ruth sniffed. "That poor woman. I wonder if she has any idea what her son is up to."

"He's not sick. No, ma'am." Max went on. "But that's just part of it. Lucas has a gambling problem. And rotten luck. Sometime back, he took out a loan from a less-than-reputable operation to cover his losses. When he couldn't pay it back, they had him doing little side jobs for them." She leaned against the porch railing. "And because our boy's not so sharp, he thought it'd be a good idea to take a cut every once in a while—figured no one would notice. Until they did."

"How did you all catch him?" Dougal asked.

"You helped with that." Max shook her head. "If you hadn't called me, it would have taken a lot longer to put the pieces together." She smothered a yawn. "He met up with someone the FBI was tailing. Lucas must have said or done something his contact didn't like because they beat him up pretty bad. Anyway, between Lucas and the man he was meeting with, their phones, some items the other guy had on his person, he was arrested. He's got warrants in other states, too. Fraud. Theft. Drug smuggling."

"Are they looking for anything in particular?" Emory asked.

Max shook her head. "He was here so, you know, they want to make sure he didn't leave anything behind. From the looks of it, he did a clean sweep." She paused. "We'll get your cars back to you as soon as they're cleared from evidence."

"But it's over now?" Ruth asked, waiting for Max's nod. "Now we can relax. Just in time to enjoy Christmas."

Dougal glanced at Emory and thought over what he'd written in his last letter. He still had it, tucked into his back pocket. He could change his mind and rip it up or he could leave it in Ruth's mailbox before he left. He'd kept it simple and spoken from the heart. If she read it, she'd know exactly how he felt.

Dear Emory,
I'm too old for Santa but, if I could make a Christmas wish, I'd ask for you. A chance to love you. If you'll open your heart to me, I promise to love you with all that I am every day. You're the only gift I'll ever need or want. And, as long as I live, you'll never regret choosing to love me.
Your secret admirer,
Dougal

Later, when he was heading to his truck, he walked past the mailbox. It was too much. Emory had been up front about what she wanted from him—and it hadn't been his heart. So it didn't make sense for him to double back and put the envelope in the mailbox. But that's what he did. Now all he could do was hope for a miracle: that Emory could find a way to love him, too.

Chapter Eighteen

Emory slid her hand into the pocket of her apron. The letter was there, safe and sound. Dougal's letter. She'd kept it with her since she'd read it. And she'd read it at least a half a dozen times. She should have known. Dougal. It had always been Dougal. All the encouragement and praise, the words that painted pictures in her mind, and made her feel seen and worthy. Now, he'd made her feel so loved.

And tonight, after this party was over and she could give him the attention he deserved, she'd tell him how thankful she was that he'd chosen to love her.

"You look smart." Aunt Ruthie smoothed one of the red-and-green tablecloths into place.

"I'm going for professional." She winked. It had been a long time since she'd worn her little black dress and heels. It had been her go-to for catering events. And tonight was already quite an event. Nothing was going to fluster her.

Instead of being upset that Savannah's father had brought in extra help to serve food, she was grateful for the extra hands.

Instead of wondering why Chelsea Barrett was giving

her side-eye, she'd stay cordial and out of the woman's line of fire for the evening.

"Don't be nervous," Aunt Ruthie whispered, squeezing her hand. "Everyone seems to be enjoying themselves. And the food, of course."

"I'm not." Not about the party or her food. It was what was going to happen later, with Dougal, that had her nervous—in a good way.

"You're up to something." Aunt Ruthie grinned. "You look like the cat that ate the canary."

"I'm just choosing to live in the present, is all, Aunt Ruthie. Not the past." She gave her aunt a hug. "Thank you for setting me straight."

"You would've gotten here eventually, Emory. I just gave you a little push." Aunt Ruthie patted her back, then let her go. "How on earth could you resist that?"

She followed her aunt's gaze to the middle of the dance floor. And her heart tripped over itself. Dougal was holding Tabby-cat and dancing with her. She wasn't sure who was smiling bigger, the giant man or the precious toddler. Either way, it was quite a picture.

"Emory." Savannah grabbed her arm. "Let me introduce you to my parents." She led her to two very attractive middle-aged people. "My father and mother, Richard and Lana Barrett."

"You're the caterer?" Lana's took her hand. "Why on earth are you hiding yourself here? You're so talented. You should open your own place—Richard and I would be happy to help you with that."

Richard Barrett was much less enthusiastic. "Always looking to invest in good people."

"Chelsea and I told her the same thing." Savannah

smiled at her. "See, I told you. You really could make a name for yourself."

While Emory appreciated the praise, she knew what she wanted and where she belonged. "I'm quite content where I am, but I'm so happy to hear the food is good."

"Good? To be truthful, our cook is on the verge of retirement." Lana patted her husband's shoulder to gain his attention. "There's a lot of money in being a private chef."

Richard Barrett sighed. "Yes, there is." He turned to look at her, then. "We should have lunch tomorrow."

It had been a while since she'd had to deal with assertive men—and Richard Barrett was definitely assertive. "Oh, but—"

"Lunch would be nice." Savannah nodded. "As a thank you, if nothing else."

"Why does Emory have a panicked look on her face?" Chelsea stepped between Emory and her father. "Really, Dad, you need to take it down a notch. This is a party. Smile. Laugh. You know, party." She hooked arms with Emory. "You'll have to forgive him, Emory. He has a permanent case of jerk-itis."

Emory was too startled to say anything—or to resist Chelsea steering her across the room. But, as she was being steered across the room, her gaze happened to find Dougal. He was sipping punch, listening to whatever Angus was saying. But he was scanning the room, looking for— His eyes locked with hers.

She wondered what caused the furrow between his brows. And why he wasn't smiling at her.

"Take my advice, avoid my father. If he corners you, you'll wind up tied to some contract working for him.

Yeah, sure you'll get paid lots of money, but you'll be working for him. Believe me, there's not enough money in the world to make up for it."

Emory wasn't sure where this sudden bout of camaraderie was coming from. "You're not close?"

"He's fine. He's a lot better than he was, that's for sure. I guess Savannah almost cutting him out of her life knocked some sense into his cold, hard, shriveled heart." She shrugged. "Plus he dotes on the triplets."

She couldn't once remember using cold or hard or shriveled heart to describe either of her parents.

"I'll let you go now." Chelsea released her arm. "You owe me. Trust me, you really do." She gave Emory a narrow-eyed look. "So, what's the deal with Dougal. Since he keeps sending you long tortured looks, I'm guessing you haven't set him straight yet?"

"What are you talking about?" Talking with Chelsea was a lot like being trapped in a revolving door. Constant motion, things spinning past her and the inability to focus.

"Well, you're not playing detectives together anymore and, once the party wraps up, the two of you won't be seeing much of each other. He's here, doing ranchy things, and you're in town, doing cooky things. How would that work?"

"Did I do something to you to make you dislike me?" Emory stared the other woman in the eye.

"What makes you think I dislike you?" Chelsea stared right back.

"Every time we talk, you're warning me away from Dougal." She took a deep breath. "It's as if you feel the need to tell me, *every* time you see me, that Dougal and

I could never make it work. As if I don't know the odds are stacked against us." She waited for Chelsea to say something, but the other woman remained silent. "Or did I miss something?"

Chelsea's gaze narrowed again.

"Nothing?" Emory waited. "You usually have so much to say on this subject."

Chelsea's brows rose, but she only crossed her arms and stood there, gorgeous and aloof.

"We have so much to learn from one another. He loves his family and I love mine—that's common ground. I am damaged but he loves me anyway. And I love him." This was not the person she wanted to say these things to. "But a relationship is between two people. Those two people would be me and Dougal. There's no room for you, Chelsea. So I'm asking nicely, butt out."

Chelsea was smiling now. "That's what I wanted to hear."

"Pardon?" She was beyond confused now.

"Dougal deserves someone who's going to stand up for him and fight for their relationship. Congratulations— you just passed the test." She hugged Emory, tight. "We are going to have such fun."

The sound of a spoon tapping crystal had the room quieting.

"I just wanted to take a minute to welcome you. To-morrow is Christmas Eve, so I hope everyone's got their shopping done." Angus glanced at his wife. "Savannah wanted to bring everyone together, not only to celebrate the season, but to say how grateful we are to be part of such a supportive community. It's comforting to know that my kids will grow up under the watchful eyes of all of Granite Falls. It'll make their high school years a little less stressful for me, anyway."

There was a ripple of laughter.

Once the toast was over, the second round of appetizers should be served. After the band started playing, the desserts should come out. Emory had confirmed and reconfirmed with the staff Mr. Barrett had brought in, and there was nothing left to do.

She took in the happy faces and free-flowing conversation. This time of year should be all about friends and family. She saw Aunt Ruthie laughing along with Colonel Jimenez. Emory couldn't be sure, but she got the feeling the colonel might be extending his stay. Savannah and Angus were juggling the triplets, but there was no shortage of devotion when the couple looked into one another's eyes. It was warm and intimate—the way love should be. The way she knew it would be with Dougal.

She scanned the barn but saw no sign of her handsome cowboy poet. Surely he hadn't slipped out? There was so much to say and she was bursting to say it. She loved him. And she didn't feel like waiting to the end of the party to tell him.

But first, she had to find him. She set off in search of him with a smile on her face and on her heart.

Dougal stared out over the clear night sky. He needed a minute. More than that. He'd been standing out here long enough for the chill to sink into his bones—but he still wasn't ready to go back inside. Not if he was going to keep it together and talk to Emory. Not on paper, but face-to-face.

He'd hoped he'd hear something—that she'd have responded to him. But she hadn't and he dreaded what was to come. He knew it was a risk to reveal he'd written those letters. He knew it could backfire. But it had been worth it. Even if his heart wound up broken, she was worth it.

He sucked in a deep breath, willing the cold air to numb the tightness in his chest. He did it again. But it wasn't working.

"Dougal?" It was Emory. "Are you okay?" She came to stand beside him. "Are you feeling better? Your nose isn't as swollen." There was a smile in her voice.

"I'm fine." He glanced at her—and she looked oh so beautiful. "You...you should go inside. It's getting cold." He didn't want her to catch a chill.

"You've developed a habit of worrying about me, did you know that?" Her gaze searched his.

He nodded and went back to staring into the night sky. He loved her. Of course he was going to worry about her.

"I wanted to talk to you." She placed her hand on his arm and stepped close enough for her scent to surround him.

It was the sweetest torture. "Talk." He all but spit out the word, dread sinking in on him.

"Dougal." She tugged on his arm. "Will you please look at me? I'd rather not say this to the side of your face."

If she was going to end this, he couldn't look at her. If he did, he'd wind up begging her to stay. "It's fine." He didn't move, he couldn't. "There's not much to say, is there? You said from the get-go you were only interested in a physical relationship. I said I was fine with that. You didn't lie. I did. It's my own damn fault."

There was a long pause.

"Dougal... I'm sorry it's taken me so long to figure this out. I knew, all along, I think. But I kept hoping things would change. I thought I could talk myself out of feeling this way."

He faced her then. "You can't talk your way out of feeling something, Emory. You either feel them or you don't. It's simple." He wasn't mad about it. Only sad.

She stared at the middle of his chest, her voice wobbling. "It's not. You know...you know what happened. How I let my marriage disintegrate and my husband—"

"It was an accident, Emory." He resisted the urge to tilt her chin back so she had to look at him. It was probably for the best. Her blue eyes would bring him to his knees. "It wasn't your fault. You've got to stop punishing yourself so you can move on. No matter how rough things were at the end, I believe Sam would want you to move on."

"I know that, now. I held on to everything that happened with Sam to keep you at arm's length. I don't want to hurt like that again. I don't want to lose...everything." She took a deep breath. "But, like you said, you either feel something or you don't." She stared up at him, her blue eyes sparkling.

Dougal bit back a curse. It hurt. Dammit all, it hurt.

"What's wrong?" She frowned.

He pressed his eyes closed. "I'm waiting for you to tell me goodbye."

"Oh, Dougal," she whispered. "Please, please look at me. I don't know why you love me. I don't understand it. I've dumped everything on you, cried on you, tackled you at least twice and you're still here."

His eyes opened then. "I can't help that I love you. It just is."

She was smiling. "Even though I cry on you—like now?"

He tugged a handkerchief from his pocket and offered it to her. "Don't do that." Seeing her cry made it hurt that much worse.

"I love you." She swallowed. "So much. It scares me."

He froze.

"But the thought of not loving you scares me more. You've shown me—"

"Hold on." It was hard to breathe and his heart, his poor fool heart, was stitching itself together—hopeful. "You love me?"

"That's what I'm trying to say." She grabbed his hand in hers. "I've tried not to. I've tried to bottle up how I feel or ignore it or tell myself that you'll change your mind—"

"No, ma'am." He cradled her face. "That's never going to happen."

"I know. I know. Because I feel the same way about you."

"Whether we make sense or not, there's no one I want to walk through this life with." The pain was gone. In its place was wonder. And relief.

"Does that mean you'll be my New Year's Eve date this year? And all the ones that follow?" Her voice broke as she said, "You make me so happy. I'd let myself go hollow inside and you've filled me full of joy."

"Emory." He leaned forward to rest his forehead against hers. This was real. And it was damn near perfect. "I'm not gonna lie. I thought... My heart was shredded."

"Your heart is mine. I'll keep it safe." She covered his hands with hers. "I'm so sorry I fought this for so long."

"I'm not." He kissed her forehead. "Everything that happened brought us here. Right here. Right where I want to be."

She nodded. "Where I'm meant to be."

He slid his arms around her waist. "Since I'm not letting go of your hand for the rest of the night, everyone in Granite Falls is about to find out that you're mine." He dropped a kiss on the tip of her nose. "And I'm yours."

"I like the sound of that." She stood on tiptoe and leaned into him.

He pressed a featherlight kiss to her lips. "Will you dance with me?" As soon as she nodded, he hooked her arm through his and led her back into the barn. He'd walked out feeling like a broken man. But now she was on his arm, walking at his side, and he couldn't have been prouder.

The dance floor was crowded, but he didn't mind. It gave him a reason to hold her close. And even though the music was upbeat and quick, he held her in his arms so they were more swaying than dancing.

"Dougal," she whispered. "If you kiss me, I think everyone will get the message."

"If you want a kiss, all you have to do is ask." He couldn't stop grinning.

"Okay. Dougal, will you ki—"

Dougal kissed her long enough so that everyone saw it and sweet enough so that there was no mistaking the reason for it. "I love you," he murmured against her lips.

"And I love you." She smiled up at him. "My secret cowboy poet."

"You keep giving me plenty of inspiration." He smoothed her hair back. "There will be plenty of po-etry in your future."

"Is that a promise?" There was fire in her blue eyes, but the sheer force of her love was what shook him to his soul.

"Yes, ma'am." His voice was gruff and thick. "It's a promise. The first of many."

* * * * *